THE
ISLAND
OF
FORGETTING

JASMINE SEALY

THE BOROUGH PRESS

The Borough Press
an imprint of HarperCollins*Publishers* Ltd
1 London Bridge Street
London SE1 9GF

www.harpercollins.co.uk

HarperCollins*Publishers*
1st Floor, Watermarque Building, Ringsend Road
Dublin 4, Ireland

First published in Great Britain by HarperCollins*Publishers*

1

A catalogue record for this book is available from the British Library

HB ISBN: 978-0-00-853289-5
TPB ISBN: 978-0-00-853290-1

This novel is entirely a work of fiction.
The names, characters and incidents portrayed in it are
the work of the author's imagination. Any resemblance to
actual persons, living or dead, events or localities is
entirely coincidental.

Printed and bound in the UK using 100% Renewable Electricity by CPI Group (UK) Ltd

MIX
Paper from
responsible sources
FSC™ C007454

This book is produced from independently certified FSC™ paper
to ensure responsible forest management.

For more information visit: www.harpercollins.co.uk/green

THE
ISLAND
OF
FORGETTING

Jasmine Sealy is a British-born, Barbadian-Canadian writer based in Vancouver, BC. Her short fiction has been shortlisted for the Commonwealth Short Story Prize (2017) and included in Best Canadian Stories (2021). In 2020 she won the University of British Columbia/HarperCollins Fiction Prize for this novel.

FOR BIM

For there is nothing dearer to a man than his own country and his parents, and however splendid a home he may have in a foreign country, if it be far from father or mother, he does not care about it.

—Homer, *The Odyssey*

That the native does not like the tourist is not hard to explain. For every native of every place is a potential tourist, and every tourist is a native of somewhere.

—Jamaica Kincaid, *A Small Place*

CONTENTS

THE
ISLAND
OF
FORGETTING

PROLOGUE: IAPETUS (1962)

Most days, I don't exist. I've always been good at hiding, at finding the shadowy places where I can go to be forgotten. When I was a little boy, I could slither through burglar bars like a greased cat. Fold myself into cupboards, alone in the dark for hours, only the dust to play with. Anybody who grows up a target learns from young how to make themselves as small as possible. Though maybe that's bullshit. Just look at my brother. He took the most hits of all and it's as if he sucked them in like hot air, expanding. Now he's larger than life. A big man in a big house. And I'm the mongoose who lives in the gully, the rat in the cane field, the stray dog beneath the floorboards.

Cronus, my brother, tells me to forget. That's what I'm trying to do. And some days I can. Some days I feel like I done walk this whole island top to bottom. Walk until the sunburnt roads scald my bare feet and then keep walking till I can't feel even that. Walk past chattel houses painted pretty pastel, eaves dripping pride like icing on a cake. Walk past brick houses with swimming pools. Past schools and farms and churches. Walk through the centre of the island where you can't see an arm's length in front of you for all the cane. Snap off a piece of it and suck it dry.

In the villages, where folks know me, sometimes I can sweet-talk one of the shop women into giving me a rock cake to fill my stomach. Pass by the rum shop and beg a bottle off one of the boys, if they're feeling generous. Sip it as I walk through Bridgetown, past the careenage where the boats bob pretty on the green water. On the sidewalk, locals and tourists alike dressed fine for a day in town. I walk with my feet in the gutter, so as not to get in their way. Here, too, I disappear. I'm invisible in a different way. I'm a drunkard, just like my father was. Or worse, a madman. No one looks me in the eye too long. Schoolchildren laugh at me. Church ladies clutch their purses and cross the street when I pass. Keep walking.

Eventually, one way or another, I always reach the shore. It's harder to hide on the beach. Men like me stick out on the white sand like skid marks. Sun too bright. Hotels crawling with policemen who sweat in their starched uniforms. Can never stay on the beach too long. All those bare bodies, all that sun glaring off the sea like polished silver. The tourists eye me warily out the corner of their eyes as if I'm a black cloud blow-ing in to ruin their vacation. They don't want to see me, don't want to know that I exist. Have to get back to the hills. To the gullies and the springs and the fields. To the cool, dark earth where I can be alone. Alone, always alone. But never free.

"We're free, brother." That's what Cronus told me the day we buried our father in Westbury Cemetery. He held my hand even as our mother whispered for him to let it go, her nails digging deep into the skin of my wrists. Something about us standing together, hands clasped, must have scared her. Maybe she was a little afraid of what new power could emerge in the void my father left.

After all, she'd seen what Cronus was capable of. She'd willed it so, begged him to be a good boy and help her. They thought I was sleeping, but I saw it all. That night, my mother placed the cushion in his hands herself. Daddy was out cold, asleep in his own sick. He didn't even stir when Cronus held the pillow to his face. But no, no, no. Better not to remember, not to think. The memories crawl like red ants around my skull. Daddy, not dead, sleeping. Then, dead, his body stiff and bloating already.

Afterwards, Mummy held Daddy's head in her lap, wailing. Cronus crawled into bed beside me, his whole body shaking. The next day, they called the coroner. No one in the village was surprised. Daddy had nearly drowned from passing out drunk in a pothole full of rainwater just months earlier.

"Those poor boys," the neighbours said. "Left without a father." And that was the story, which became the truth. But still the memories, they bite and burn. Walk, walk, walk. Drink my rum. Try to forget.

You see, Daddy was dead, but he wasn't gone. I could hear him every night, pacing outside my bedroom door. I could smell him. Sawdust and smoke and rum breath. When I closed my eyes, he was there, burning red in the backs of my eyelids like when you stare up at the sun too long. Even a dead star keeps burning, years after it falls out of the sky. And for most of my childhood I felt my father around me, hot and angry, threatening revenge like a black hole. I wasn't the one who killed him, but I was the one he was after. I was the one who saw it happen and did nothing.

Cronus knew that I was going mad. He saw it before anyone else and tried to keep it quiet for as long as he could. Kept me bathed and fed and in school, most days. When Daddy died, Mummy said she never taking care of no man again, even we. So Cronus fried bakes for breakfast and boiled rice for dinner and tucked me in at night, his hand cool on my forehead. He held me all night when I cried, when I woke sweaty and screaming. He shushed me so that Mummy wouldn't come in with a belt and beat me quiet. He told me that everything was going to be okay. Daddy was dead, there was nothing to be afraid of.

I never could find a way to tell Cronus the truth. It wasn't just Daddy I was afraid of. It was him, my big brother. I was afraid of what he showed me was inside him on the night he killed our father. I saw it in his eyes as he stood over Daddy's still-warm body, the cushion fallen to his feet. So, no, Daddy was dead, but he wasn't gone. His violence lived in my brother, in my mother, and in me. He was there, at the bottom of every rum bottle, waiting for me. I felt him inside me, like a searing itch beneath my skin. Like I had taken the sun and swallowed it whole.

And so, most days, I hide. From my brother, Cronus, from my dead father, from my mother even though she is long dead now too. From myself.

There have been some clear days, over the years. Days when the burning inside me simmered to a tolerable smoulder. Days when I could visit my mother in the hospice, let her hold my hand, feel it dry and chalk-like against mine and be present with her, the voices leaving me be for a few minutes. I would listen to her stories, her mind looser as she neared the end. There were things she told me then that I wish I had always known.

Like how Daddy was never the same after the war. How he flew airplanes over Germany for the RAF but, come peacetime, couldn't find anyone in all of London willing to rent him a flat. How Daddy had come back to the island defeated, and how, at night, he would wake screaming, sure that the bombs were coming for us all. Maybe if I had known all this sooner, things would have been different. Maybe I could have found a way to save him, to save us all. But it's too late now. He is dead, and Mummy too.

On good days, I could visit my brother and his new wife, hold my nephew Z against my chest and feel the weightlessness of his tiny body in my arms. Days when I could bathe in the spring and feel clean. Feel like I didn't need to drink at all. Steal a fresh shirt from a clothesline and catch sight of myself in a shop window and see something like a whole man. It was on a day like this that I met her.

She was standing at the bus stop with the other schoolgirls. In her hair were a dozen clips that sent silver beams of sunlight bouncing across the street. The minibus came, music blaring, and the children got on. I turned to leave, to continue my walk, but when the bus pulled away, she remained. We stood watching each other through the traffic. And then she smiled and waved me over.

She had a round brown face dotted with pimples across her chin. Her chest was dusted with baby powder and she smelled fresh and dewy like clean sheets. "I know you," she said. "You brudda is live near me. In that big house up Nelson's Road. I hear you mad." She laughed, revealing a wide red mouth, a piece of blue chewing gum nestled between her cheek and molars. I shrugged. She laughed again. "You don't look mad," she said, stepping a little closer. "You look good."

Later, when she hiked her school skirt up over her hips for me, and I breathed into her powdered neck, I felt so present, so real, that I almost started to believe her. But days like that one never last. He always comes back, my father. He whispers in my ear and tells me that no one is safe. That he once held me trembling in his hands, a newborn like Z. That even he was capable of tenderness once. That things that begin precious and pure become poisoned. That there is a rot in our lineage, a stink that lingers over us all. I could see it in the flicker of my mother's eyelids while she slept in her hospice bed and I knew that she too was haunted. I could see it in Cronus when he held his son, see the doubt there, the fear. And I could see it in the girl the longer she spent with me, see the way I rubbed off on her like a mangy dog leaves its stench along a clean, white wall.

So I left her, too. Buried myself back in the shadows. It's been months now, or maybe years. My brother looks for me. Even in my hiding I hear things, I know he wants to find me, to help me, to bring me back. But it's too late now. I walk and walk, until the island falls away to sea and the salty air brings me something like forgetting.

Part One:
ATLAS (1979)

CHAPTER ONE

WE'RE HALFWAY THROUGH THE MOVIE, AND THE WHITE boys still haven't shown up. It's raining in that Caribbean way that can only be described as despotic, but I've got to keep my window rolled down so the speaker can hook onto the door. My right arm is drenched. The air smells like gasoline and fried chicken and humidity. I glance over at Pleione, resisting the urge to ask her for the fourth time if she's alright. She's got her feet up on my dash, her toenails painted a pretty blue. Her hair is tied up in a red bandana, the strands at her neck escaping. I reach over and tug one lightly. It's damp. She swats my hand away, grinning.

"Hot in here," I say, grinning back.

"Shut up and watch the movie," Pleione says. But she shifts a little closer to me, so I can reach for her again, should I feel like it. The air between us is delicate, the soft-woven web of fragile peace between two people trying desperately not to piss each other off. We've been at it all day and the ceasefire is shaky.

The trouble started this morning, when our A Level results came in the mail. I received all Ones, which was expected but still felt, to me, miraculous. I held the paper at the corners, not wanting to smudge any of the lettering, as if the truth of it could be so easily erased. All Ones meant I had fulfilled my side of a bargain, an agreement I'd made with my uncle Cronus. He'd promised me, once I got the grades, he would take care of the rest. All Ones meant Cambridge or Oxford or the London School of Economics. All Ones was an escape hatch, a magical portal to some other world. Pleione had placed a steadying hand on my knee. "You did it," she'd said. "I knew you would. Nerd."

"You did well," I said, taking her hand in mine. "A Two in maths. You thought you'd failed that."

Pleione laughed. "Miracles do happen."

"Those are good marks, P. You'll get into UWI for sure."

Pleione withdrew her hand. "Thanks for that."

"There's nothing wrong with UWI," I said. "It's a good school."

She turned to me, eyes narrowed. "It's a damn good school."

"Exactly," I said, sensing danger. Pleione agreeing with me was never a good sign.

She took a breath, and when she spoke again, her voice was strained with false levity. "You know, Atlas, I'm happy for you. I know you've wanted to get out of here ever since you were a child. I know how hard it's been for you, growing up in that house, without parents of your own. I guess I just didn't realize I was one of the things you wanted to be free of."

"I never said that, Pleione," I pleaded.

"I could come with you," she said, her voice so earnest I thought I might cry just looking at her. "There are other universities in England. Just because I didn't get Oxford grades doesn't mean . . ." She trailed off, turning away from me again.

"Even if you got into another school . . ."

She snapped her head around again.

"When you get in," I corrected myself, "how would you pay for it?"

"I don't know, Atlas. I don't know how I'd pay for it. I don't have a patron, like you."

"That's hardly fair. I worked my ass off."

"Yes, you did. And so did I. Even though I knew there wasn't a golden ticket at the end of it all." Her voice cracked like thin ice. I didn't know what she wanted from me. We were essentially saying the same thing, but somehow, this didn't make it any less of an argument.

"I'm not an idiot," she said, softer. "I know it will be hard. I've always known that. I guess I just thought we would try to make it work. Together."

"I want that," I said, unsure if it was true. "I just don't want you to sacrifice a sure thing."

"I thought you were a sure thing," she said.

Part of me does want her to come to England with me. But when I try to picture her anywhere other than on the island, the image is too surreal to conjure, like a wave trapped in a jar and kept on a shelf. I wonder if she would be happy there. Uncle Cronus tells me London is grey and cold and starless. What would become of Pleione in a place like that? I picture her dry and brittle like a pressed flower. The truth is, I don't want to be responsible for her. I want to have my own adventure, to answer to no one but myself for once.

But for now, I'm just happy Pleione is speaking to me. I wish I was in a better frame of mind to appreciate her warm and for-giving presence. But I'm distracted. Z's car is still parked three rows ahead of us, two to the left. From this angle, I can't see whether he's sitting in the car, or if May is with him. I wonder if I should go take a look, but I don't want him to know I'm here.

I try to relax and watch the movie. Chances are the Marshall boys won't show up at all. Chances are Z will dodge this bullet, like he's dodged all the ones that came before. I'll drive out of here, take Pleione home. Maybe we'll pull over at the beach for a little bit, just for an hour or two, because her mother wakes up at four a.m. every day to season chicken and soak peas for lunch, and the first thing she'll do is check Pleione's room to make sure she's in her bed, and not with me. But an hour or two is plenty of time.

This is what I'm thinking about when Pleione shifts in her seat, bringing her feet down off the dash to peer out the windshield. "Is that Z?" she asks, pointing to Z's car.

I shrug. "Could be."

Pleione whips her head around and squints at me. "You mean you didn't know he was here?" In the seconds it takes me to decide whether or not to lie, Pleione figures me out. She sucks her teeth. "So, this is why you brought me out tonight? This is why I finally get a real date? So you can spy on your cousin?"

"What you talkin' about real date?"

"Don't start," she says. The rain is thrashing now. I hook the speaker back on the stand and roll the window up. Neither of us is watching the movie anymore. "Cronus sent you?" she asks. She's mad, but something in her voice tells me she gets it. I nod. Pleione sighs. "Z still seeing that white girl?" I nod again. Pleione sits back and crosses her arms, like she's physically holding her thoughts inside her body. She plays with the gold cross around her neck, weaving it through her fingers.

"Go ahead and say it," I say.

Pleione doesn't answer. She's turned away from me, her face in silhouette.

"I know what you're thinking," I say, removing my glasses to rub the bridge of my nose. "I need to tell Cronus that babysitting Z isn't my responsibility."

"Atlas . . ." Pleione says.

"And trust me, I'm sick of it too . . ."

"Atlas!" Pleione says again. I glance up, putting my glasses back on. I follow her gaze to Z's car. Three white boys surround it, one of them hunched over to peer into the passenger window, the other two hanging back, near the tail lights. I can't make out their faces. The passenger door opens and a woman gets out—May. She's got one of the boys by the arm, trying to pull him away.

"Shit," says Pleione, glancing at me.

I keep my eyes on Z's car. May is still holding on to the guy, and even from their shadows I can tell she's having no success trying to convince him to leave. I roll the window down a crack. Voices rise and fall over the music of the film. A car horn sounds. Lights flash. Z gets out.

"Stay here," I say to Pleione. She stares back, eyes wide. I get out and I'm soaked in seconds. I weave over to Z, keeping low. When I glance at Pleione, she has slid into the driver's seat and fastened the seat belt. I nod at her, she nods back. I creep two rows down and crouch beside the car parked directly behind Z's. From my line of sight, I can see the back of Z's legs, most of May, and one of the Marshall boys. The other two are hidden, which is not ideal. Z and I could handle all three of them if the element of surprise were on our side. In an ideal world, it wouldn't go down that way. In an ideal world, Z would just apologize and let May leave with her people. One of the white boys is yelling, telling her to get in his car. Z says something in response, though he's talking too quietly for me to make out what it is.

Then, everything happens at once and Z's on the ground, two of the white boys on top of him. May is screaming. There's no point trying to be sneaky in my approach anymore. I pounce from where I'm crouched, tackling one of the boys to the ground. I hear my knee pop a second before I feel the pain shoot up my thigh into my groin. I power through it and manage to land two good hits before he gets his bearings and starts fighting back. I roll around on the gravel with him for a minute. I manage to hold him face down, my good knee on his neck. I lean in close. "I don't want to fight you, man," I say. The truth is I'm not sure I can take him on with my knee acting up, but I'm hoping he doesn't know that.

The guy's breathing heavy. The ground is wet, and mud and small stones stream into his nose and mouth and eyes. His face is red and puffy. "Get the fuck off me," he says, his voice high and desperate.

"You gonna be chill?" I ask, pushing onto his neck a little harder.

"Just get the fuck off me," he says again, but this time I hear the defeat in his voice. I stand up, and he crawls away on his hands and knees, panting.

I glance at Z. He has managed to push the other guy off and get to his feet, and now they're circling each other. May is still wailing. The rain has stopped, and the heat creeps back into the night. Steam rises off the car hoods. A few people have gotten out of their cars to watch the scuffle. I step away, let my hands drop to my sides, and wait. I hear a double horn tap. Pleione has pulled the car up and is easing slowly towards the exit.

"Z," I say, quiet like how I talk to Uncle Cronus's dog when she's in one of her moods, growling at every living thing that strolls by the fence. I've always had a way with wild animals, the ones that are a little bit broken. But Z's not hearing me. He's locked in on the white boy, up on his toes, weight bouncing from side to side. He may be a spoiled rich boy, my cousin, but he knows how to hold his own in a fight. May has quieted down now, sobbing into the arms of the third white boy, her head against his chest. "Z," I say again, "let's go."

Z looks up finally, not at me, but at May, who's gathered up in the other Marshall boy's arms like a load of wet laundry. Z stares at her for a minute, glances at me, and then spits onto the patch of gravel between him and the other white boy. I step forward and put a hand on his shoulder. He tenses for a moment and then relaxes, letting me steer him towards the car. We climb into the back seat and Pleione hits the gas before I've even closed the door. I reach forward and squeeze the back of her neck through the headrest. Z's twisted in the seat. He stares out the back windshield long after we've left the drive-in and turned onto the side street that leads to the highway.

"You worried they'll follow us?" I ask him. He looks over at me, confused for a second, and then turns and rubs his eyes.

"Nah," he says. "They got what they came for."

"Where am I going?" asks Pleione from the driver's seat. She's a good driver, slow and methodical, the seat pulled up tight against the steering wheel.

"Your place," I say, "we'll drop you off and head home."

"Drop me in The Gap," Z says, like we've been hired for the purpose. "I need a drink."

"We should go home, Z, your dad's worried."

Z laughs, rubbing his eyes again. He looks tired, though from what I couldn't say. He hasn't been to class in weeks. Uncle Cronus has pulled every string he can to keep him enrolled at UWI. His eyes are bloodshot and the skin around his nails is picked raw. He takes a big, long breath. "I need to go back for my car tonight anyway, after the second feature."

"Alright," I say. "We'll drop Pleione off and then I'll come with you."

Z laughs again. I catch Pleione's eye in the rear-view. She raises her eyebrows. Z seems off-kilter, like a man with nothing to lose. I nod at Pleione and she turns her eyes back to the road.

CHAPTER TWO

Z WANTS TO GO TO HIS USUAL SPOT, A SMALL RUM SHOP with a few plastic tables and chairs crowded onto the sidewalk out front. The bar draws a rough crowd, which Z likes. He greets a few of the regulars as we enter—men with red-rimmed eyes who don't look up from their dominoes as Z smacks shoulders and bumps knuckles like a man running for office. I wonder if he sees the contempt that clouds their faces as soon as he passes by. Z wants to fit in here almost as badly as he wants to be able to hold May's hand in public. Z believes he belongs everywhere— it's the thing I admire most about him and the reason my date with Pleione ended up with me icing my knee at a dive bar. I stretch out on one of the plastic chairs as best I can, and Z returns with a couple of beers. He sits down and gives me an appraising look, as if he's just noticed I'm there.

"How's the leg?" he asks, clinking his bottle against mine lightly.

I try bending and stretching it. I feel the pain somewhere between my toes and eyeballs. I shrug. "Let's just say I won't be bowling any fast ones for a while."

Z smiles, like he's enjoying himself. He probably is. He takes a swig of beer. "That's alright. You were always more of a Yorker man anyway." He drains his beer and gets up immediately to head back inside. I think about telling him to take it easy but there isn't much point. He returns with two shots of white rum in plastic cups. He takes a shot, picks up the second one, and holds it out to me. I shake my head. Z shrugs and fires that one back.

"What happened tonight, Z?" I ask, before I can stop myself.

Z grins. "We kicked some ecky-becky ass, that's what!" He yells this, smacking the table with an open palm. He looks around at the other men in the bar for acknowledgement, but they don't glance up from their games. Z disappears inside for another drink.

I think about Pleione, about our fight earlier. Pleione wants a big family, like her own. She wants to get married in the same church she was baptized in, the same church where her parents were wed. She's always trying to get me to come to church with her, to "become more involved in the community." These are the kinds of things that matter to Pleione. And I am going to marry her, I know that the same way I knew Z was going to pick a fight with those white boys tonight. I've always had a gut feeling for things, never really been one to be caught off guard. "Steady as a trade wind," so Pleione likes to say. So I know I will marry her. I want to marry her. But I have to make something of myself first. I need to get off the island, figure out who I am when I'm not busy being Cronus's nephew and Z's cousin.

"Remember when we used to sneak out to come here?" Z asks, plopping back down into the seat beside me.

"I wasn't sneaking out," I say, "you kidnapped me. I was nine years old."

"You loved it."

"You can't keep seeing her, Z. You know that, right?"

Z hasn't lost his grin yet. He crosses his arms on the table and leans in close to me. His breath smells antiseptic. When he speaks, it's loud enough for the whole bar to hear, his accent broader now for his target audience. "I keep telling she that," he says, "but she just can't help sheself at all! You know what they say. Once you go black!" Again, the other men ignore him. Z's smile falters only slightly. He keeps drinking.

As it gets later, the street grows busy with people. A woman sells barbequed pig tail on the sidewalk opposite, the smoke engulfing her so that all I can make out is the top of her hat, which she has, inexplicably, shrouded in several plastic bags. In a nearby bar a man sings karaoke. I don't recognize the tune, his voice warbling the words. Something about a woman in a blue dress, come to take him away. So many nights I've sat in bars like this one, this street as familiar to me as my living room. Some nights I can't imagine living anywhere else. Other nights I feel like I'm trapped in a fishbowl, and if I stretch my arms out too wide, I'll touch the sides and the whole illusion will come crumbling down.

Z giggles beside me. "You know what it is about May," he says, his words all tumbling out in one breath. "It's those pink nipples." He's laughing so hard he can hardly speak, his head hanging low over the table. "I mean, don't get me wrong, cousin," he continues, "Pleione . . ." He kisses the tips of his fingers. "That's a nice piece of high brown ass."

I ignore him, focusing my attention instead on the people passing by. I'll need to buy a coat for London, and boots.

"But she doesn't have those pink nipples like May, does she? Pleione's got those eggplant nipples. Like two fat bruises."

"How the fuck would you know, Z?"

"I'm just fucking with you, cousin," he says, and then dissolves into laughter again. After a minute he quiets down. He looks into the bottom of his cup, swirls around the dregs of rum that remain, and drains it. "Fuck it," he says, speaking into the table, "she was St. John white trash anyway. Let's go."

We leave The Gap and I drive us the quick five minutes back along the highway to the drive-in. Z is quiet in the passenger seat, his head out the window catching the breeze. I know he only does this to sober up, so he can drive his own car back, but still I wonder what he thinks about in the rushing silence of the wind. In our family, I'm known as the contemplative one. Z is the clown, the playboy. I know him better than anyone but still I wonder if there's something I've been missing all these years, some important piece of himself he's kept a secret. I wonder if he ever feels trapped here, like I do. If the island is a fishbowl, Z is the godlike child standing above us all, tapping on the glass.

The drive-in has emptied out when we arrive. I kill the lights and ease the car in slowly, in case the Marshall boys are still around, waiting to ambush us. "They won't be here," Z says, reading my mind. "They don't care enough about us to wait."

It's true. They're probably back in their homes by now, or at one of the bars their crowd goes to, the ones that might as well have Whites Only signs on the doors. Z's car is the last in the lot, the ground still littered with chips containers and plastic cups. I pull in beside it and kill the engine. "You cool?" I ask. Z nods. He turns to me like he might say something else. Then he taps the dashboard a few times and climbs out.

We drive back along the winding, narrow roads of the interior. There are no streetlights on this part of the island, and in the yellow beam of the headlights, the dark road unfurls before me like a thick black tongue. The road is lined with cane that at times presses so close I can hear it whipping against the side mirrors.

Behind me, Z revs his engine, his headlights near and blinding in my rear-view. He leans on the horn, flashing his lights. Asshole. I know what he wants. The road widens and he pulls up beside me. Through the passenger window I see him, sleeves rolled up, fists gripping the steering wheel. He looks over at me, his eyebrow raised in challenge, his teeth clenched in a hard, chain-link smile. I contemplate slowing down, letting him get ahead. Fuck it. I shift into gear and hit the gas. Z is seconds behind me, but seconds is all I need and I'm in front, the distance between us growing.

We crest a hill, no one on the road but us and the moonlight. Cane fields give way to sleeping farms. In the distance the ocean is indistinguishable from the sky, but I can smell it. Z has closed the gap and pulled up beside me again. We race sidelong for a while, until the road narrows to a bend, cut rock rising either side like the earth has been cleaved just to let us through. I gear down and ease onto the break. Z tries to squeeze by, his side mirror clipping the rock, sparks flying.

We fly through a village, chattel houses flush to the road, their windows trembling in our wake. A pack of stray dogs follows alongside for a second, howling. I fly through a roundabout, pulling the handbrake to make the turn, my wheels screeching. We're the same, Z and I, despite what I tell myself. Whatever anger lives in him, I have it too. All I can hope is to keep it a secret, to never let Pleione know just how near collapse I am. Z knows, he sees it, draws it out of me, and holds it up as if to say, *Look, this is who you are*. There's no escaping this, not by studying in some staid English institution, not by chasing some idea of myself as anything other than this, the poor cousin, the orphan. Z never brings up my past, my alcoholic father who died before I was born. My mother who abandoned me. But even though he never mentions it, he somehow never lets me forget it either. He doesn't want me to get out, to make anything more of myself. He wants me to stay here forever, to always be his foil, his saviour. Tonight, for once, I cannot let him win.

With the village behind us, the road is empty again. Long and open. My foot is flat on the gas. A mongoose darts across the road, its body silhouetted in the moonlight, green eyes shining. It freezes, then runs back the way it came. I should know better, but I slam on the brakes anyway, the car skidding sideways. Z clips my bumper, sending me into a spin. I turn into it, but the momentum is too much and the car goes sideways into the cane field. I hit the wall of green and come to a jerking stop, my hands still gripping the steering wheel. I take a few breaths, the saliva pooling under my tongue. I swallow back the vomit and try to open the door. The car has been eaten up by cane. It's pouring in through the windows, and when I pull the handle, it won't budge. I unclip my seat belt and crawl over to the passenger side, the car rocking as I move. I freeze, waiting to see if it will roll, but it seems steady, and I manage to pull myself through the passenger-side window and out onto the road.

I land on my stomach, breathing in the warm night. It's silent, but for the ticking of my engine as it cools. I don't see Z. I get to my feet, fighting panic, head swimming, and follow his tire tracks around the bend. My knee is screaming, and when I bring my hand to my forehead, my fingertips stain with blood. I round the nearest bend, and there's Z's car. It's upside down, wheels still spinning. I try to run, but my knee buckles. I try to yell his name, but my throat is dry. The road seems narrower somehow, as though the cane is still pressing in around me. "Z . . ." I manage to croak, before collapsing to hand and knee and vomiting onto the asphalt.

I feel a hand on my shoulder, the fingers compressing the skin once, quickly, and then pulling away. I spit twice more onto the road and get to my feet. Z is standing upright before me. His polo is barely wrinkled, and but for a single line of blood that trickles steadily out of his nose, he looks like he might have just stepped off a yacht. The intensity of my relief is fleeting, followed swiftly by rage. I land a punch seconds before I've fully committed to the decision to hit him. He steps back, hands flying to his nose, where the blood is now streaming in earnest.

"Atlas, what the fuck!" he says, the words garbled by all the blood. He brings a hand to his nose and pinches it, looking at me over the top of his fingers. I watch as his eyes flicker first with shock, then anger, then with quiet resolve. With two quick steps forward he has me by the collar of my shirt. "What is the matter with you?" he says, the words spitting bloody onto my face. I brush him off and push both hands into his chest.

"What the fuck's the matter with you, Z? You drove me off the goddamn road!"

The anger has mostly left my system and the fatigue is setting in. The road is silent still, the nearest house a dark and distant smudge on the horizon. If another car were to come around the bend too fast, it would smash into Z's before we could stop it. I start thinking about logistics. Where we might find the nearest phone.

I picture waking Uncle Cronus with a call at this hour, picture him lying immobile as the tinny rings echo through the house. His condition has worsened in the past few months, and now he can only get out of bed once or twice each day, with help from one of us, or Aunt Rhea, or a nurse. It will be Rhea who will answer and relay the message to him. I can see it clearly, Cronus, a faint impression of the man he once was, waiting impatiently as his wife twirls the phone cable around her finger, revelling in the power she holds over him now. I can see her too, in her nightgown, glancing over at Cronus, loving the drama of it all. I hate that this is what Z and I will put him through tonight. Z is hunched over at the waist, hands on his knees, his upper body shaking. I walk over and put a hand on his back.

"Shit," I say, looking from Z to his overturned car. "You okay?"

Z's back is trembling beneath my palm. He takes a few wheezing breaths and stands up straight, tears streaming down his face. He's laughing so hard, he can barely get any words out. "You drove like the devil tonight. You made me flip my car, you fucking madman," he manages between gasps. He throws his head back, the moonlight catching the blood-red of his teeth.

Over the whistle of the wind in the cane, and Z's laughter, I hear the sound of an engine. "Shut up a second," I say to Z, limping towards his overturned car. "Someone's coming."

I get in front of Z's car just as the headlights come into view. It's a flatbed truck, labouring along the road at a walking pace. I wave my arms to flag it down and the driver rolls to a stop a few feet in front of me. I step out of the glare of the head-lights, keeping my arms raised, and come around to the driver's side. He's a white man, old but alert, his eyes burning blue even in the thick dark of the morning. "Good evening, sir," I say, "really sorry about this but we've been in an accident and the road is blocked."

The driver doesn't say anything or react in any way to what I've said. He has one hand on the wheel, the other rests on his lap. I'd bet my life savings that there's a shotgun somewhere in the truck's cabin, within easy reach. I taste blood on my lips and can only imagine what I must look like. I drop my hands to my sides.

"You alone, boy?" the driver asks, his eyes not leaving mine. His accent is broad, the kind of white Bajan drawl you only hear in this part of the countryside.

"No sir," I say, "my cousin was driving the other car. Well, truth be told, we were racing and things got a little out of hand." I smile and shrug my shoulders.

The driver looks from me to the overturned car and back. "Whose car is that?"

"That's my cousin's car. Mine is just around the bend. It's . . . well . . . it's stuck in the cane field."

The driver again says nothing. He has yet to kill his engine and the truck rumbles in the night like a hungry animal. He raises his chin slightly and reaches his hand a little further into the darkness at his feet. "That your cousin?" he asks, looking over my shoulder. I turn. Z is approaching swiftly, making no effort to appear harmless.

"Good evening!" Z says as he approaches, grinning. He looks maniacal, the blood drying around his mouth like a clown's smile. "We sure are happy to see you!"

"Stay back now!" the driver says, his blue eyes darting between us. Z freezes. I take a step back and raise my hands again.

"Yes sir," I say, keeping my voice calm. "I know we must be quite the sight. We don't mean to frighten you. We just need to reach a telephone so we can call Z's father and have him send along his man with a tow." Beside me I can feel the heat emanating off Z's body, the alcohol sweating out of him, the smell heady and damning.

The driver too is sweating. Thin beads trickle down his sunburnt neck. He flexes his fingers on the steering wheel and then tightens his grip again. He's terrified, I realize. I feel no power at this thought. Instead, I'm warier than I was before. Nothing more dangerous than a scared white man with a gun at his feet.

"Where'd you get the car?" he asks.

"Pardon?" I ask, confused.

"That there Chevy Monte Carlo. Where'd you get it?"

"She's pretty, nuh?" Z says. "I was eyeing the Grand Prix but in the end this lady won me over."

"Not many '77s around. Someone will be out looking for it. You boys had best get out of here." Z and I exchange a glance. I shake my head slightly, a small, pleading gesture.

"It's a '76," Z says, stepping forward. "And it's mine."

The driver is clumsy in his panic, and by the time he's able to level the shotgun, we're already running. I dive into the cane fields, where it seems I'm destined to spend the rest of my night. Z has dropped low and crawled around the back of the man's truck and into the bush on the other side of the street. The driver swings his gun around wildly, pointing at the shadows. If he fires, it's unlikely he'll hit either of us, but that's not a game I'm looking to play tonight. I shrink further into the fields. A rat crawls over my foot and disappears between the green shoots. The driver brings his gun inside and reverses quickly into a messy three-point turn, driving back the way he came.

Z emerges first, leaping catlike into the middle of the road and screaming epithets at the shrinking tail lights. I follow him, dusting ants off my shirt. The night is still and quiet again. "Well, there goes our ride," I say.

Z reaches over and pulls a leaf out of my hair. "He'll call the police on us as soon as he gets home. All we have to do is wait."

We sit in the middle of the road, to better spot any other approaching cars, but it's deserted, and after fifteen minutes or so, Z's restless. He gets up and heads to his car, crawling on hand and knee into the rear window. He's torso deep when I hear a triumphant noise, and he reappears holding a full flask of white rum at eye level the way a pastor wields a Bible. He sits down beside me, takes a long swig, and passes me the bottle. I take a sip, the rum a cathartic burn in my throat.

"So, little cousin," Z says, "I hear congratulations are in order."

I look at him blankly for a second, and then I remember the A-Level results. This morning feels like a lifetime ago. "Thanks," I say, raising the bottle in a toast and taking another swig.

"So I guess this means you'll be leaving us soon."

"Guess so."

Z takes the bottle and downs half of it in one gulp.

"Did you ever think about it?" I ask, realizing how strange it is I've never thought to ask him this before.

"About leaving?" Z says, shaking his head. "No."

"Why not?"

Z gestures to the empty road, the cane swaying in the moonlight, the big sky, bright with stars. "This is home. All my friends are here."

As far as I know, Z doesn't have any real friends. He gets along with everyone, his schoolmates, the men on the block, even the white boys, when he isn't trying to date one of their sisters. In secondary school he was Games Captain and swam on the school team. Despite a general laziness when it came to academics, he was beloved by his teachers and could have been Head Boy had his poor attendance record not disqualified him. Now, at UWI, Z hangs around with a hard-drinking crowd, most of them the sons of politicians and doctors and actuaries. Members of the black upper-middle class who all seem to be rebelling against the gentility their parents exemplify. They wear their hair in big afros and smoke rolled cigarettes and sport leather jackets despite the heat. They have loud and animated arguments about Chaguaramas, and Manley versus Seaga, and the relative dangers of Soviet versus American influence in the region. Z skips class to smoke hash with them but I don't think he likes any of them that much. I'm not sure Z likes anyone. Except perhaps May, and even then, I suspect a big part of her appeal is that loving her just might get him killed.

"Besides," Z says, "they hate us over there." He takes another long drink of rum, the liquid spilling out his mouth and dripping stickily onto his chin. He lets out a giant belch. "Look at what they did to our grandfather," he goes on, his words slurring slightly. "Had him fight their war and then treated him like dirt. He came back penniless. And then when my father went for university, it wasn't any better."

Uncle Cronus doesn't talk much about his time in London, except to tell bawdy tales of his escapades with white women, which he exaggerates with every retelling to torment Aunt Rhea. He'd gone on scholarship to study law, but never finished his degree.

"That was over twenty years ago, Z."

Z laughs. "You think things are better now? There are Nazis marching in the streets again. Eric Clapton's going onstage talking about keeping Britain white." He spits on the ground beside him. "They hate us."

Z doesn't know anything about British politics. He's just repeating what he hears from his Marxist friends. But still, I don't know what he's talking about either. I'd only thought as far as getting out. I hadn't really considered what things would be like when I get there.

"But I get it," Z continues. "I get why you want to leave."

"Why do you think it is? Because of my parents?"

Z shakes his head. "No," he says, "because of mine."

"Cronus has been good to me," I say, automatically.

Z laughs and downs another giant swig of rum. "Okay," he says. He's really drunk now.

"What?" I ask, irritated. I feel like there's something he's not telling me, some inner-circle family secret I've been excluded from. Like when I was young and Aunt Rhea would send me on errands around dinnertime, so that by the time I came back, the family would have finished eating together. I would take my meals alone, in the kitchen. Cronus wouldn't stand for any overt cruelty, but she always found ways to put me in my place. Z knows, he saw it, but we've betrayed each other too many times for this to matter now. In a house where love and affection are doled out like candy, it's only natural we became competitors.

"You don't know the half of what he's done," Z says, really slurring now. He looks around for a second, dazed. "Fuck this," he says. "I'm walking." He rises clumsily to his feet, swaying slightly, and heads off down the road.

I sigh inwardly and then rise to follow him. I catch up, placing a hand on his shoulder. He spins around, swinging wildly like a man battling ghosts only he can see. I dodge the swings and hold on more firmly to his shoulder. "Christ, Z," I say, "you're wasted."

Z laughs, the laughs turning into hiccups and coughs, and then sobs. He collapses onto his knees. I try to catch him as he goes down, but he slips through my arms. He looks up at me, his eyes swimming red. "You don't know one shite," he says. He's barely conscious. His chin dips into his chest, an unbroken dribble of saliva dangling from the corner of his lip. "You don't know . . ." he continues to mumble. I can hardly make out the words.

"Z," I say, reaching for his face. He swats at me and misses. He moves and speaks as though he's underwater. I hold his face in my hand and lift it. People often mistake us for brothers, Z and I, but we look nothing alike, really. Z's skin shines red, the way the backs of your eyelids look when you close them to the sun, as if he were lit up from the inside. His eyes are hazel, pretty eyes, the girls call them. Whereas I am big, dark, round, and soft, my features all blurring together—"like a storm," Pleione likes to say, "the face of a rough sea at night"—Z is lean, fair, sharp and jagged.

"Come on, cousin," I say. I pull him up under his armpits, stumbling slightly, and then catch him. We stand there for a moment like this, swaying like slow dancers, Z's weight on my chest. His breathing is ragged. He's crying, mumbling into my neck.

"You don't know . . ."

"What don't I know, Z?"

"You don't know what he's done. What he's asked me to do. You don't know . . ."

I can't recall if Z and I have ever embraced before. We're standing like this when the flashing blue and red lights appear in the distance. Z is dead weight in my arms. I hold him for as long as I can, until the police arrive, approaching us warily in the dark. I let him fall, dropping to my own knees, and raise my hands above my head in surrender.

CHAPTER THREE

THE NEXT MORNING, I KNOCK ON Z'S DOOR AROUND nine. When he doesn't answer, I knock a few more times and then open the door and peek inside. All night I've been unable to sleep, getting up every few minutes to check on him. I'm not sure if I did the right thing, not taking him to the hospital. I pictured him choking on his own vomit, rolling over and suffocating himself on a pillow. But by four a.m., exhaustion overwhelmed me, and I slept through the rest of the night.

I sit on his bed now, watching him breathe for a minute. Z's room is big and messy. Half-full glasses of water, some with cigarette butts floating on the surface, are scattered about. His bed is in the middle of his room, a square island in a sea of books and magazines and clothes. Z sleeps with his whole body extended, arms spread across the breadth of the mattress. What does it say about a man who sleeps with his soft belly exposed? I wouldn't know. I sleep tight to one side of my bed, my body curled around itself. "As if you are your only precious thing," Pleione would say.

Z stirs. He opens his eyes and looks at me. He doesn't seem surprised to see me here. His mouth is white and dry, and when he opens it, his breath smells like all the wrong things in the world. "Water," he says, pressing his eyes shut again as if the effort of speaking is too much. I reach for one of the many glasses that dot the room, picking one that seems the least polluted. Z sits up on his elbows, grimacing again, and takes a sip.

"My throat hurts," he says.

"I might have scratched it. I had to make you vomit."

Z nods and takes another sip of water. He hands the glass to me and collapses back onto the bed. "Thanks," he says. I'm being dismissed.

I rise and open one of the curtains slightly. Z's room looks out onto the yard, his window framed by creeping bougain-villea. The gardener is weed-whacking the grass by the fence, a green cloud trailing his progress. On the street beyond, two women are arguing. Or it seems they are arguing. They might be laughing, it's hard to tell the difference.

"When are you going to learn, Z?" I ask, moving away from the window. "You ain't ever going to be one of them. Even if you marry one of their women. Shite. That'll just make them hate you more. They may even kill you for it."

Z doesn't answer. I wander over to his desk where, surprisingly, a thick textbook lies open. It's a university text on game theory, the pages so crammed with random letters and numbers as to be indecipherable to me. The pages are littered with leaves and so I think maybe Z is only using the book as a surface to roll his joints. But, no, there amidst the mess of the desk is his notebook, the same equations from the textbook repeated in Z's looping hand. He may not be going to class, but he seems to be doing the readings.

Cronus would be thrilled to know Z's keeping up with his coursework and Z wants his father's approval just as badly as I do. But he will never tell Cronus he's studying, and Cronus would feign disinterest even if he knew. This is the nature of Z and Cronus's relationship—an infinitely refracted spectrum of resentment, distrust, and love.

My relationship with my uncle is just as unhealthy, but much more straightforward. The psychology of it is obvious even to me, and I'm not exactly the most introspective person to ever live. My uncle took me in when no one else wanted me, and I've been paying back that debt ever since, with perfect attendance, perfect grades. My clawing need for my uncle's approval is compulsive, the object of Z's ridicule and Pleione's gentle concern. But at least I'm aware of it. Z and Cronus's dance is more complicated, an intricate back and forth.

I glance over at Z. He's rolled away from me, facing the wall. "We should go talk to him," I say, "face the music." I hate the way I sound, the coaxing voice, the fear that hums beneath every word.

To my surprise, Z sits up and puts his feet on the floor. He holds his head in his hands for a few seconds and then looks up at me. His face looks rubbed raw, like a seabed when the tide's out. "Yeah," he says. "Let's go."

Cronus's room is on the ground floor. He used to sleep with Aunt Rhea in a sprawling suite that takes up most of the third floor, but ever since he went on bedrest, Aunt Rhea decided it was best to move him downstairs. He spends his days now in what was once the library, a small and stifling room in the east end of the house. Z and I check the room first, but finding it empty, we go instead to the garden.

When we were boys, Z and I spent whole afternoons in the garden, throwing rocks to shake tamarinds loose from the trees and gorging on the tangy brown fruit until we couldn't feel our tongues. Rhea and Cronus were strict with us, but the long arm of their discipline extended only to the back porch, and once we were outside, they didn't seem to care much what we got up to. We made air guns using old PVC pipe and potatoes and used them to shoot rats. We stole the engines out of the lawnmowers and used them to turn our bicycles into electric scooters. When Cronus and Rhea were out of town, we took their car into the yard and did doughnuts until the earth was all dug out, looking like a meteor had hit. And then Z would bribe the gardeners to replant the grass and cover our tracks. We were constantly jumping off things and onto other things, testing the limits of not just our own mortality, but of the world around us. How hard we could smash into things before they would collapse. Z barrelled in first, bushwhacking his way past any obstacles, and I followed closely behind, sprinting through the clearings he left in his wake.

On the few occasions we did get caught, or when our antics got wild enough to merit punishment, we did a walk not unlike this one. Cronus liked to involve us in our flogging. First, we had to find him. I have so many memories of walking down hallways, just like now, the dread growing in my stomach like some choking vine. Cronus would then have us pick our flogging instrument. I would search for the greenest, most pliant stem of bamboo I could find, or a dry and rotting branch that would crumble on impact. But Z would do the opposite, standing insolently before Cronus, holding the thickest belt, the one with the big, brass buckle that drew blood in seconds.

Now, we find Cronus by the pool. He's in his wheelchair, alone, the pool sweeper across his lap. He rolls back and forth, dragging the net across the surface of the water. Z approaches first.

"Daddy," he says, "let the groundsmen deal with that."

Cronus doesn't say anything, only continues his circuit around the pool, a surreal vision with his IV wheeling alongside him. Though he's been sick for years now, I still struggle to reconcile this wasting figure with the Cronus of my childhood. He has shrunk to half his size, his head a tiny, round nut beneath his baseball cap, his brittle body all strung up with tubes and wires. The sun is blistering already, reflecting off the pool in a blinding glare.

Z sighs and plops down onto one of the pool chairs to wait. Cronus speaks then, not raising his voice, but enunciating each word clearly. "Did I say you could sit down, boy?" he says. Z rolls his eyes and stands up, joining me beneath the speckled shade of the frangipani tree.

"No," Cronus says, beckoning us closer, "stand here." He points to the poolside, where the sun blazes. He tosses the pool sweeper aside and heads for the house. We start to follow, but he stops, spinning around in his chair to face us. "Wait."

With that he leaves us in the sun. I look over at Z. The sweat is already gathering at his temples and his skin is greenish. The sun feels like a weighted presence. I feel it under my clothes, inside my chest, like I'm burning from the inside out. Fifteen minutes pass, but neither of us move and I know that neither of us will. Grown men or not, we will not defy him, not while he lives. To do so would be to admit to ourselves that everything is changing. I'm not scared of Cronus, not anymore, not really. That would be irrational, in his current state. But still the dread blooms, a creeping premonition that's been building for months now. A sense that my life is going through some sort of tectonic shift, and that though I can't feel it, at any given moment the earth will slip out beneath my feet.

Cronus is dying, and when he is gone, nothing will be the same. I wonder if Z feels it too, this seismic interruption. I wonder if he anticipates the weight of responsibility that he is about to inherit. This house, this family, the hotel—I try to picture them all carrying on without Cronus, but the image fails to conjure itself, or if it does, it is distorted, like the floating branches of an uprooted tree, reaching towards the sky. And I am fleeing it all, like a crow before a storm.

Beside me, Z is drenched in sweat, his eyes closed, swaying slightly. I'm amazed he's still on his feet. The door to the house opens then, and Colette, the housekeeper, emerges. She's holding two large glasses of ice water, and she approaches us quickly, glancing over her shoulder at the house.

"Here," she says, "drink these quick." I take the glass, and it nearly slips out of my hand. I raise it trembling to my lips and drink it down.

Z only shakes his head. Colette kisses her teeth and gestures again for him to take it. He ignores her.

"Christ, Z," I say, "what are you trying to prove?" But Z ignores me too, his eyelids fluttering as if he is dreaming on his feet.

"I aino why I even bothering with the two of wunna," Colette says, speaking low and fast. "Couple of eejits, upsetting your father so." She looks at Z again, concern clouding her features, and then she takes the empty glass out of my hand and hurries back inside the house.

A few more minutes pass, and then she reappears, gesturing for us to follow with an impatient flick of the wrist. I start towards the door, but Z doesn't follow. I turn back, tugging gently on his sleeve.

He opens his eyes, looks at me dazed for a second. "What were you doing at the drive-in last night?" he asks. His voice sounds like crumpled paper.

"What?" I say. "C'mon. This sun is murder." But neither of us move, Z looking at me more intently now.

"Cronus told you to come," Z says. It's not a question.

I sigh. "Yeah. He was worried about you. The Marshall boys . . ."

"Typical," Z says, cutting me off, "just like when we were kids. Trying to win points by taking his side, selling me out."

"Z," I say, "it wasn't like that. I wasn't trying to come between you and May. I was just looking out for you. We both were."

"One day," Z says, his voice soft, "you're going to want something so badly, it's going to eat you up inside. And when it gets taken from you, you're going to know, then, what this feels like." A beat passes, our sour breath mingling, the air still and hot. Z taps my chest once, lightly, then turns and walks quickly into the dark interior of the house. I follow behind. When I reach Cronus's room, Z is already seated beside him. The old man is awake, propped up on pillows, eyes alert. Z takes one of his hands in his and holds it.

I take a small step inside. "Uncle Cronus," I begin. But Cronus only raises a hand in response.

"I'll speak to you in a minute, Atlas," he says. He looks down at Z then, who sits beside him, head bowed. "Leave us for now. I need to speak to my son."

I feel a familiar pang. Then I nod and leave, closing the

door behind me. The house is dark and quiet. In the kitchen, Colette is listening to a call-in-radio program, the voices echoing back to me like lapping waves, unintelligible.

Cronus has told me bits and pieces of his childhood, mostly stories about him and my father, their adventures. In Cronus's stories, he and Iapetus faced grave perils—falls from high trees, near drownings, snake bites. They stood up to mighty antagonists, like teachers who twisted their ears and got in the way of their adventures, envious school bullies, and old crones who chased them from their gardens whenever they snuck in to steal golden apples. But these antagonists were always defeated, like villains in an Enid Blyton novel. And I'm left with a hollow feeling, like everything I know about my past is a fairy tale. That I come from nowhere.

In my early teens, I began, timidly, to ask Cronus for more details about my parents. He would reply either with one of those same adventure tales, or with a dismissive wave of his hand, as if he had better things to do than to indulge me. When pressed, he would dole out rare and cryptic bits of information. Like once, when I was about thirteen, and I came home drunk for the first time.

It wasn't my first time drinking alcohol. Z and I had been stealing from Cronus's stash for years, mixing hideous cocktails and forcing down tiny sips in secret, the thrill of doing something wrong more intoxicating than the liquor itself. But this was the first time I'd ever been drunk. In those years, Z's parents forced him to take me everywhere, an imposition he rebelled against by bringing me along and then abandoning me at the earliest opportunity.

That night, he'd been forced to bring me to a football game at the National Stadium. As soon as we parked, he disappeared with a girl, leaving me in the care of his friends, who decided it would be a laugh to see how many shots of Cointreau I could drink before passing out. The liquor was candy sweet and I drank half the bottle, then threw up. When Z finally reappeared, I was half asleep under his car, having crawled there like an animal looking for a cozy place to die. I remember his blurred face crouched down beside me, looking sorry, scared, and furious. He stood then, screaming at his friends, getting in their faces. It didn't matter that he was only one guy, that he was the one who had left me in the first place. In that moment, he was my big brother. I remember staring up at him as he towered over me, backlit by the bright lights of the football field, looking like one of my comic book heroes, like Conan the Barbarian fending off evil sorcerers. Even as I hugged the back wheel of Z's car, my face black with dirt, the alcohol heavy in my gut, I felt safe.

We drove home, and when we approached the house from the driveway, Z held me in his arms. Even in my drunken state I relished this. I was like a feral cat that had been reluctantly and begrudgingly offered shelter. I didn't know what it was to be touched in tenderness. I had never been held.

Cronus stood at the door to greet us and beckoned Z to follow him. Z placed me gently on the floor of the hallway outside Cronus's office and went inside, leaving the door slightly ajar. I lay my face against the parquet flooring and breathed in the dust and fought the urge to vomit again. A single beam of yellow light shone diagonal across the hallway, and I reached for it the way a plant turns its leaves to the sun. I crawled until I could see inside Cronus's office. Z was standing, hands braced against the edge of the desk, his pants around his ankles. Cronus paced behind him. I don't remember what Cronus was saying, but I remember the crack of leather on leather as he looped his belt around his hands and snapped it repeatedly. This was the worst part of a beating, the buildup. Cronus working himself into a rage, the anger building, as blinding and ephemeral as a plume of smoke.

With every snap of the belt, Z flinched. But otherwise he showed no emotion. I hugged my knees and prayed for it to be over. When the first strike landed, Z turned to look at me. I closed my eyes but reopened them quickly. I understood that to look away would be a betrayal. If I ever wanted my cousin's respect, something I lived for then and still crave today, I had to watch. I don't remember how long it lasted. Their bodies were silhouetted against the gauzy yellow light like figures in a shadow play. Z was taller than Cronus by then, sixteen, wiry and strong. We didn't know it yet but the cancer was already blossoming in Cronus's gut, and he tired quickly. He fell back, panting, and Z silently zipped up his pants and left the room. I watched his feet disappear down the hallway, my cheek still pressed against the floor as though I might be able to sink through it, down through the basement, into the dirt beneath the house.

Some time passed, and I was drifting in and out of sleep when Cronus came for me. He helped me up, and I walked into his office, a place I associated only with fear and punishment. He ordered me to sit on his chair, a brown leather wingback. My feet didn't reach the ground. The next year, I would grow six inches, my body lengthening like a piece of silly putty. With the new height would come a sense of, not quite belonging, but presence. I could no longer be ignored, my physicality demanded observation. I started playing basketball and cricket, and at parties, even when I skulked in corners, girls approached me with their hands outstretched, reaching up to place their tiny fingers on my shoulders, as if trying to measure me to scale. But then, in Cronus's office, I was a none thing, a collection of fine bones and skin and trembling doubt. I wanted only to be wanted and settled for being tolerated.

Cronus began to speak, and at first my own exhaustion and fear were so overpowering that I had trouble making out his words. But soon I realized he was speaking about my father, in a way I'd never heard him speak before. He told me that my father had been a weak man. That he was someone who had lived in the past, haunted by memories better forgotten. He said that he had loved my father and had tried to help him, but that there was something broken in Iapetus that was beyond repair, some essential piece missing. I remember this part especially well, because I pictured the piece like a spine, some bit of hardware without which a body would collapse. I pictured my father then, whom I had only ever seen in photographs, as a sack of lifeless skin. It's an image that still comes to me now sometimes, on dark nights.

Cronus spoke for some time, and I can't remember everything he said. I remember only fighting to keep my eyes open, to suck all this precious knowledge in and store it in a deep well inside myself that I could draw from later. Cronus's point was that my father hadn't always been this way, that he had once been a whole, solid kind of person, and that bit by bit he'd let parts of himself go and Cronus had witnessed this and been powerless to stop it. Seeing me, then, in my drunken state, was a reminder to him that I had this same weakness in me, and that if he was not careful, I might lose myself too. I might disappear.

Cronus didn't hit me that night, but when I finally crawled into bed, the beginnings of my first hangover already seeping into the edges of my vision, I felt as though I had been thrown against a wall. The fear I lived with every day hardened inside me, soldering itself onto the core of my being. I would always live with fear, but now, that fear had a face. It was my father, becoming like him, or unbecoming, erasing myself, like he did. I swore to myself that I would never do that to Cronus, never fail him in that way.

And I never have, until last night.

Now, I collapse into the overstuffed mahogany chair beside the phone and call Pleione. She picks up after a few rings. Her voice sounds far away.

"Hello," she says, like she already knows it's me.

"Hey," I say, breathing into the silence.

It occurs to me then that she has no idea what happened last night, after we dropped her off. I think about telling her, and then change my mind. On the other end of the line, Pleione's home buzzes with sound. I can hear food frying, the traffic of the street, her younger siblings playing wildly. I can picture her, the phone crooked between her head and shoulder while she busies herself with something. Peeling potatoes or hanging out washing or reading some dense book.

Her family lives not far from here, but sometimes it feels as though she's from another country. She knows the island better than I ever will. Not the history of it, the things you learn in books, but the daily pulse of it. The bus routes, the rising cost of milk, the best place to have a bicycle repaired. She knows the folklore and the myth. The right herbs to boil for teas to cure any ailment. How she knows these things I don't understand. She just seems to belong here in a way that I never have.

"Do you know anything about my parents?" I ask her, surprising myself. I know nothing about them besides what

Cronus told me. I've never thought to ask Pleione if she'd heard more from her neighbours, or the people in her church.

Pleione is quiet for a moment. "Hang on," she says. There's a rustling noise, the sound of a closing door, and then the din in the background quiets. "Where's this coming from?"

I sigh and lean my head against the back of the chair. All the furniture in the house is plush mahogany, upholstered with itchy velvet in plum and gold. The furniture seems to suck all the light out of the room, so the house feels like an opulent black hole.

"There were rumours," Pleione is saying, her voice careful. "About Iapetus. You know how Bajans can be. A good-looking fella like that, red skin, going off the rails the way he did. People talk."

I close my eyes and press the phone against my ear, feeling the electric heat of it buzz into my skull. I wait, knowing she'll keep talking if I stay quiet.

"And there was talk of a girl," she says. "Atlas, are you sure you want to hear all of this? I mean, it's just gossip. I don't know how true it is."

But even as she says it, I don't believe her. If she didn't think it was true, she wouldn't tell me. Pleione knows something about me, about my past, more than I know myself, and has kept it from me. I feel a sudden surge of anger, a burning that begins behind my neck and floods my chest. I swallow it down.

"Tell me," I say, trying to keep the hurt out of my voice.

"She was young. Very young. Maybe thirteen. Iapetus was older," she says, the words coming fast now. "But still a boy himself."

She told me what she knew. The love affair ought only to have lasted the length of Iapetus's fleeting moment of lucidity. But instead, the girl, my mother, followed him into darkness.

Her parents searched for her for months, the church collected money, the police put up flyers. She was found eventually, living in squalor. She was put into the juvenile correctional facility, locked up for the charge of "wandering," a criminal offence. Each time she was released into her parents' arms, her sobriety lasted only as long as it took her to find Iapetus. This went on until eventually even her own family wanted nothing more to do with her. The church ladies stopped praying. There was a pregnancy. A birth. Iapetus disappeared to somewhere even the girl couldn't find him. So she came to Cronus, demanding money, and was told she would receive it only on the condition that she hand over the baby, and never show her face again. The girl agreed. She'd given so much of herself away already. What was I, other than one more thing to be bargained with?

"So is she still alive? Where is she now?" I ask, and even I can hear the accusation in my voice. Pleione doesn't answer right away. I breathe heavily into the phone.

"Atlas," she says, "I don't know. How could I know?"

"You seem to know a lot." The anger is burning now, churning in my throat like bile. Pleione says nothing, and so the anger just continues to choke me, like acrid smoke trapped in my lungs. I exhale.

"I'm sorry," I say, "I'm sorry."

"What happened last night?"

I grip the receiver. The room has yellowed around the edges. I feel like I am going to throw up again. I reach around for the dustbin and hold it between my feet. I can smell my own sweat, an animal smell, like cut grass and saliva.

"Nothing," I say. "Everything's fine."

"Did something happen in The Gap? Did Z say something?" There's an edge of panic in her voice. I hear it, and another wave of nausea overpowers me. I let the phone slide from my hand and throw up into the garbage. I can still hear Pleione calling my name, her voice a distant echo.

CHAPTER FOUR

CRONUS IS DEAD. THE END WAS SLOW, PAINFUL, AND graceless. In the weeks before, the cancer reached his brain. Cronus's cries could be heard from all parts of the house, seeming to seep into the walls and spread like radio waves. He called out for his mother, the desperate mewling cries of a lost child. He often tried to escape and had to be monitored around the clock. One night, while I dozed fitfully beside him, I woke to find him slashing at the window netting with a pair of scissors. He spoke to himself, long, incoherent ramblings that seemed to drive him to despair. At first, I listened closely, in hopes of more crumbs of information about my parents, but soon I gave up. Whatever world my uncle had retreated to, it wasn't one whose language I understood.

His funeral was a grand event, with a few members of parliament and several prominent businessmen in attendance, all of them interchangeable, paunchy little men who dabbed at their foreheads with monogrammed handkerchiefs and glanced often at their watches. We gathered in St. Michael's Cathedral on an overcast afternoon, the sky plump and grey, the air still and breathless. Aunt Rhea sang "Amazing Grace," Z gave a eulogy. Throughout, a single pigeon cooed from the rafters, setting my teeth on edge. I sat in the back with a kind of numb detachment, Pleione at my side, her hand on my knee to stop it from shaking.

I've hardly seen Z since. His father's death ignited something in him. He rushes around in a constant state of business, attending meetings with estate lawyers and investors at the hotel and other men too, whose involvement in the family's affairs I'm not privy to.

It's been ten days since the funeral, and I'm in bed, shirtless, staring up at the ceiling fan, when he knocks at my door. I can't remember the last time Z was in my room, and I sit up, somewhat startled.

"It smells like someone died in here," he says, stepping inside. The irony seems to hit him and he smiles a small, tight smile. I glance around at the room. It really is a mess, my clothes scattered about in damp piles.

"Yeah," I say, "I need to do laundry." I rub at my face, trying to wake myself up. Z's wearing a white button-down shirt and khaki pants. He smells faintly of aftershave and rum.

"Get dressed," he says, and leaves before I have a chance to reply.

I find the least wrinkled shirt I can and pull it on with a pair of basketball shorts. I follow the sound of voices to Cronus's office, and there I find Z sitting behind the desk, Aunt Rhea standing at his side, and three suited men sitting across from them. They all look up when I walk in.

"Sorry," I say, turning to leave.

"Wait, Atlas," Z says. "Have a seat. This concerns you." I head to the window, propping myself up on the ledge, and stare at the floor.

"Would it have been so difficult to put on shoes?" Aunt Rhea asks. She directs her question to the room, as though one of the other men can offer some explanation for my behaviour.

I clear my throat. "Sorry," I say again, "I didn't realize—"

"Let's get on with it," Rhea says. The three men all begin to speak at once and Rhea sucks her teeth, throwing her hands up in annoyance.

"Martin," Z says, addressing one of the men.

Martin clears his throat. "As we were saying earlier, it's all fairly straightforward. As next of kin, Rhea will become the deed holder for this house and land, as well as the valuables within and any and all other assets, including his cars, clothing, art, and jewels. As for his majority shares in the hotel, Cronus requested that these be transferred directly to his son, a matter that I believe was previously discussed between the two of you."

Martin looks over at Z, who nods. Rhea brings a hand to his shoulder and squeezes it briefly. "Atlas," Martin says, rising awkwardly from the chair and stretching a suited arm out towards me. "Cronus requested that this be given to you directly."

I take the envelope, which is thin and brown and slightly sticky. "Thanks," I say, my voice small. I glance over at Z and Rhea, who are staring at me expectantly. I ignore them, tucking the envelope under my arm and looking back at the floor. The men all rise and say their goodbyes, leaving the three of us alone.

"Well," says Rhea. "Well." She lets out a small sob, and then, catching herself, turns away to face the wall. She stands for a few seconds like this, her shoulders hunched, her chin in her hand. Then she sucks in a large breath and straightens, like a fern frond unfurling. I make to leave, feeling suddenly like I'm not supposed to be here. It's a miraculous feeling, like finding a word that has been on the tip of my tongue. I don't belong here. And soon I won't have to. I make it a few steps towards the door when Z stops me.

"Hang on," he says, "I need to speak with you. He turns to his mother then, placing a hand on her arm. "Can you give us a moment, Mum?"

Rhea nods. She heads for the door, stopping beside me as she passes. Her lipstick is a garish purple and she looks like a painted corpse. "My husband was quite fond of you," she says. And somehow, it sounds like an accusation. I begin to stumble a reply, but she's already gone.

I turn to Z, who still sits at his father's desk, organizing papers. He looks up at me, and I know. Before he even says anything, I know what is going to happen. I am filled with the sense that I have lived this moment a thousand times before. That my life is a series of false choices, an illusion of free will, like so many branching rivers all leading to the same inevitable sea.

The next day, I spend the morning at the hotel, helping Z to organize the front office. It's around five when Pleione comes to meet me. She has painted her nails a pale pink, almost white. The colour matches the swirling floral pattern on her dress. Everything about her perfect prettiness is a mystery to me. How is her skin so soft? How does she get her hair to look so different each time I see her, sometimes snatched high into a bouffant, other times falling in soft tendrils at the nape of her neck? In a few years these mysteries will reveal themselves to me—hot combs and weaves, shea butter and talcum powder.

Whenever Pleione laughs, she throws her head back and exposes her whole neck, which is long and slender, and with her mouth wide she looks like a seagull angling to swallow a small fish. I've always wanted to tell her this. I think she's beautiful. But I know this is a strange thing to find beautiful. I'm stupid about women, but not stupid enough to think comparing one to a bird is a good idea. This is what I'm thinking about as we walk down the beach towards where it is less crowded. This girl who knows me better than anyone, but who still feels sometimes like a complete stranger. The sea is flat and withdrawn, the sun sagging like a ripe and heavy fruit. We sit at the water's edge.

"We could still go," Pleione says. Her hand is close to mine in the sand, our fingers not quite touching. Her legs are extended in front of her and with her heels she makes small circles in the sand, which are washed away every few seconds by the lapping waves. "Atlas," she says, "we can. You have your scholarship for the tuition. And I could work."

I nod, not answering. She looks at me and smiles. She has the whitest, straightest teeth I've ever seen. I can't see her eyes behind her big black sunglasses. I smile back.

"I have an aunt in Lewisham," she goes on. "We could stay with her until we find work. People do it all the time. Just pick up and go." She goes quiet for a minute. "We'd have to get married first, of course. My aunt is old-fashioned like that."

"Is that right? And what if we didn't live with your aunt?" I place my smallest finger on her smallest finger. Our hands look like starfish on the white sand.

"Where else would we live?"

"Oh, I don't know," I say, "in Soho maybe. In one of those artist communes."

Pleione laughs, a barking sound. "Sharing a bathroom? You wouldn't last a minute, rich boy."

We're silent again. It feels like there is a decision being made somehow, in the silence. "You wouldn't want that," I say finally. "That's not the life you signed up for." The truth is, I'm the one who's afraid. I want to see the world, but sometimes the thought of leaving the island fills me with a sick sense of dread. And to do it now, alone, without the support Cronus promised me. But I'm afraid to admit my ambivalence to Pleione. It's much easier to do this, to pin it all on her, my sacrifice.

Pleione looks at me the way she sometimes does, like I don't know a damn thing. Like I'm the sorriest soul she's ever met. "I want lots of things," she says. "I want to travel. I want to go to museums. I want to see snow." She brings a soft hand to my cheek. "But I want to be with you most of all. Whatever you decide, that's what we'll do."

Last night, after speaking with Z, I returned to my room. I opened the envelope from Cronus, still hopeful that it contained the magic key to my other future. Or at least, some explanation. "There's no money," Z had said, "not right now." The hotel was barely breaking even. "It will take all of us to make it work, Atlas," Z had said, "the whole family. We need you here."

In the envelope there was no cheque, no letter, no golden ticket. Only a single photograph, fuzzy at the edges, water-marked and limp in my hands. Two boys, stiff in starched shirts, one almost a foot taller than the other. The older boy had an arm around the younger, and neither boy was smiling though it seemed to me as if the younger was suppressing a smile, like he had just been told to be serious, for the photograph. My uncle

Cronus I recognized, and the younger boy I assumed to be my father, Iapetus. I stared at the photograph for a long time, until the sun set outside and I had to squint to make out their faces. But there were no answers to be found there. Those boys were strangers to me, their lives unknowable. It doesn't matter how I got here.

CHAPTER FIVE

TIME PASSES, THE YEARS COLLAPSING ONE AFTER THE other into the past like dominoes. I attend UWI, studying English Literature. I spend every evening and weekend at the hotel, helping Z. There is much to be done, the building in need of renovation. When Cronus first opened the hotel in the early '60s, it was one of only a handful of beachfront properties on that stretch of the south coast. Then the Hilton opened, and soon other big resorts began popping up. Despite the competition, Cronus's hotel thrived.

Nearby hotels served high tea and dressed their staff like sailors, in middy blouses and stiff caps, instructing them to smile at the guests, speak only when spoken to, and look only at the tourist women's feet. But Cronus was savvy and knew that times were changing. These new tourists weren't old British money anymore. They weren't looking for a staid, refined experience. They wanted to let loose, to get into a little bit of trouble. They wanted to feel like they were among friends.

So Cronus had his bartenders pour with a heavy hand and his waitresses dance their way to the tables in bikinis and grass skirts. The hotel hosted wild parties that Cronus would emcee himself, serenading the tourist women until they turned red and had to be dragged away by their husbands. He was the owner, but also the concierge, procuring whatever the guests required—from strip club recommendations to Cuban cigars. If you wanted to hunt green monkeys, you could ask Cronus. If you wanted to visit a rum shop and play dominoes with the locals, Cronus would take you there. If you wanted to find a local girl to keep you company during your trip, Cronus would supply her.

To turn a profit, the hotel relied on loyal guests who returned year after year. They liked that the staff knew their names, their favourite drinks, their preferred rooms. They liked that the place was just a little bit sordid, that the parties sometimes got a little out of hand, that there was an element of danger, a glimpse into the "real" Barbados, just enough to titillate them but from which they were always buffered.

But in his final years Cronus had let things slide. The hotel had gone from shabby chic to just shabby. The flamingo-pink exterior had faded to a sickly salmon. Now the showers don't drain, the septic tank leaks, the roof sags. The rooms have never been updated; even the linens are almost twenty years old. Once Z got ahold of the finances, he learned there was rampant theft by the staff; the bookkeeping was a mess. It takes us weeks just to sort through the chaos, to get a grasp of what needs to be done. Z and I do much of the repairs ourselves, working for hours in silence, our T-shirts tied around our heads, our hands growing calluses with the labour.

I am exhausted, but content. The work helps to heal the cavernous hole Cronus's death has left in our lives, and Z and I get along better than we ever have, united in purpose. Z consults me on most decisions, like a partner. When he talks about the future of the business, it is always in the first person plural. "We will turn this place around," he says.

I know he will want me to stay even when the work is done. But I am still determined to leave. I want to see the places I have only read about in novels. I want to breathe cold, unsalted air. I tell myself that I will do what I have to do to honour my uncle, to repay the debt I have lived with my whole life, and then, Pleione and I will break away on our own.

Maybe we won't go to England, after all. Why limit ourselves? We can go anywhere. Pleione keeps talking about Harlem, probably because she's been reading so much Langston Hughes. She has this idea in her head of buying a car and driving from New York to California. She says she wants to dip her big toe in the Pacific Ocean. She tells me the distance is almost four thousand kilometres. Barbados is thirty-two kilometres wide, east to west. Who could we become amongst all that wide open space? "We would get lost," Pleione says. "I've never been lost before."

Pleione and I are wed a week after graduation. The ceremony takes place at her small parish church, her extended family filling the pews. The women all wear loud pastel dresses in fabrics not made for the heat, thick wools and satins, their hats topped with fruit and feathers. Looking out over the sea of powdered strangers, sweating through my own suit, I spot Aunt Rhea in the back. She looks deeply uncomfortable, her purse on her lap, pulling herself to the far corner of the pew as though the gaucheness of Pleione's kin might be catching. Z is my best man, cool and collected beside me in his own much better fitting, suit.

My upper lip tastes of salt, and sweat drips into my eyes, blurring my vision, so that when Pleione begins her march up the aisle towards me, she appears not quite real, like if I were to blink, the whole scene might disappear. Then suddenly she is beside me, her gloved hand in mine, and I can feel the flutter of her pulse beneath her skin. She doesn't look at me. A single bead of sweat drips down her temple, running a streak through her foundation. When the minister directs us to exchange rings, I finally catch her eye, and there I see my own feelings mirrored—joy, fear, resignation. She winks at me, the corner of her mouth twitching. *Here we go*, she seems to say. Afterwards, in the photos from that day, you can almost spot the slight bulge under her dress, the way she brings her hand often to rest on her belly.

We move into a small, wooden house in the hilly centre of the island because it is all we can afford. Our friends think we're crazy for choosing to live so far from town, until they come to visit, and then they never want to leave. The silence is intoxicating, the only sound for miles the whistling of the wind through the cane arrows or the distant lumbering of a passing tractor.

Pleione and I take long walks through rolling pastures, hills of green sloping into the distance, the ocean a thin blue line on the horizon. We scramble on hand and knee down the steep walls of the gully. There, the air feels like a hot towel across the backs of our necks. Pleione points out the plants she knows only by the names she was taught as a child—bellyache bush and monkey hand and crab eye and cerasee. She tells me their uses, all the teas and brews she will make with them. She digs up one of each, spreading them out reverently on her open palm, fingering their feathered roots. At night when I take her fingers in my mouth, I can taste the earth.

We are giddy with the freedom of our space, dancing barefoot on the veranda, making languorous love on the creaking floorboards. This is the first time that Pleione has a room of her own, having shared a bed with two of her sisters for her entire life. For the first few days in the new house, she sleeps in until noon, making angels in the sheets, trying to stretch her fingertips to the furthest corners of the mattress as if to take up every inch of space she possibly can. I write more than I ever have, filling page after page in my notebook. Moving out on our own feels like adventure enough, and we go many months without discussing travel at all. Pleione takes a job at a primary school in the nearby village. I work at the hotel and I write. Our life is small and quiet and full, and we are happy.

But sometimes I wake at night and find I cannot breathe. The cottage becomes a coffin, the walls and ceiling so close I can feel them pressing in against my chest. Not just the cottage, but the whole world feels compressed as though it has been gathered up in the hands of some great god and squeezed into a ball like crumpled paper. I wake up flailing. One night I send an elbow into Pleione's expanding belly and she banishes me to the couch.

"Tell me what it feels like," she says, over a breakfast of fried bakes and jam.

"Like the world is shrinking," I say, "like the sky is pressing down on me."

"We can still go, Atlas," Pleione says gently, with a hand on her belly. "Before the baby comes. There's still time."

What happens to a dream deferred? It grows and grows until it becomes so large it's hard to imagine how you ever thought it attainable. A hulking mass in your peripheral vision, always just out of reach, like living in the shadow of a mountain.

I still talk confidently of leaving, tell Z he must hire a new manager soon so that I can start the transition. The training of my replacement will fall to me; Z doesn't take an interest in the day-to day-running of the hotel anymore. He claims he is doing the "big picture work" of shoring up investors and building a brand. He is considering a run for local office. "I won't be here much longer, Z," I tell him. But time keeps passing, the days piling up. Pleione is right, there's still time. There's simply too much of it. Too many next months and next years. My dreams drown in all that time like an overwatered plant.

Then our daughter is born. Pleione delivers at home, with her mother and sisters present, while I smoke cigarette after cigarette in the garden. When I am finally invited back inside, close to dawn, Pleione is sleeping. My mother-in-law hands my daughter to me, already washed and swaddled. Calypso weighs barely six pounds but my arms shake from the effort of holding her. I place a kiss on her forehead and she squirms, her face purple and livid, and lets out a scream that rivals those her mother made giving birth to her.

Calypso cries for two weeks straight. After a few days, we take her to the clinic, sure something must be terribly wrong, but the nurses laugh and send us home. One night, in a desperate attempt to calm her, Pleione strips the baby down to a diaper and carries her out into the garden, laying a blanket on the cool, damp grass. She lies beside Calypso, a hand on her heaving chest. The baby blinks twice at the night sky, takes one ragged breath, and falls asleep. I lie down beside them, looking up at the stars, dizzy from the sudden silence, near drunk on the promise of sleep.

"I didn't think it would be like this," Pleione says, her voice slurred in half sleep.

"What?"

"Motherhood."

I laugh and then swallow it, not wanting to wake the baby. "What do you mean?"

Pleione doesn't answer right away and I think she has fallen asleep. My sweat has dried in the night air and I curl into Calypso, her body a tiny furnace between us.

I am almost asleep when Pleione answers. "It feels like I've fallen into a black hole." She holds her hand up above her face, gesturing with her index and thumb like she's trying to pluck a star out of the night sky. "There is no air. No light. I've lost all sense of time. This is our life now. This timeless non-place. This void."

"You're just tired," I say, trying to make light of it. "Try to sleep." I think she's trying to tell me something, I can hear it in her voice, a warning, a plea. I want to ask her if she's okay. I want to tell her to keep talking, tell her that I am listening. But I can't keep my eyes open.

When I wake hours later to the rising sun, I am alone. From inside the house I can hear Calypso fussing, her cries soft and mewling. I find her alone in her bassinet, and when I pick her up, she smells freshly bathed. The house is spotless, the bed made, the floor mopped, the dishes still drip-drying in the rack. On the kitchen counter sits a bottle of formula with a note beside it that says simply, "4 oz. at 7 a.m." I look at the time, it's just past six.

Our car is still parked in the driveway, so wherever Pleione is, she went by foot or bus. I figure perhaps she has gone for a walk or down to the village shop. I feed Calypso and she falls asleep on the bottle, mercifully quiet in my arms. I hold her for the nap, not wanting to risk waking her by putting her down. Another hour passes and Calypso wakes, her face contorting. For a moment I am dumb with panic. Her crying intensifies, and I place her down in her bassinet, my breath catching. I make another bottle, spilling the powdered formula in my haste, and attempt to shove it into Calypso's mouth, but she won't take it. I try a pacifier next, then my own finger. Calypso screams through it all, the sound like a car alarm. I pick her up again, pacing back and forth with her in my arms, her body taut and furious.

I call Pleione's mother, keeping my questions vague, not wanting to alarm her, but she hasn't seen or heard from her. I then try Cynthia, Pleione's best friend, whose own son is only a few months older than Calypso. The phone rings and rings and I'm about to hang up when she answers, her voice low.

"Atlas?"

"Where is she, Cyn?"

"She just needs some time. Just a day or two to get her head right. This happens to women sometimes, after the baby comes. You have to give her some time."

"Is she there? I'm coming." Calypso lets out a wail and I jump. I'd forgotten she was there.

"She's not here, Atlas. I'm not telling you where she is."

Calypso's cries intensify. Anger swells in my chest like flood water. "She just left. Who does that? Leaves her baby alone like that?"

"Atlas. She didn't leave her alone. She left her with you." There's a rustling and Cynthia says something to someone in the background, but she must have covered the mouthpiece because I can't make it out. "You doing alright?" she asks finally, to me. "You want me come bring food?"

I hang up the phone without replying. I cradle Calypso in my arms. She has a soft halo of hair around the crown of her head and I bury my face into it. Her chest flutters like the breast of a small bird, her bones just as fine and brittle beneath her skin. "We'll be alright," I whisper, to her, to myself.

Pleione is gone for three days. She returns as suddenly as she left. I take Calypso for a sunrise drive to the coast to get her to sleep and when I get home Pleione is there, in the kitchen, frying plantains. She drops the slices into the oil, not flinching when it splatters up onto her forearms. I put Calypso in her bassinet and step carefully up behind Pleione, placing a palm flat between her shoulder blades. My hand nearly spans her upper back. She is vibrating slightly, and this close, I can see the tears that flow steadily down her cheeks like condensation on a glass.

"I missed you," I say.

She turns to me, burying her face in my chest. "I'm here now," she says. Calypso cries, and Pleione goes to her, and that is all we ever speak of it. Life goes on, in its way.

Anyone who doesn't know Pleione as I do wouldn't notice any change in her. But I see it, the gradual hardening, like a piece of skin scabbed over too many times. She had always been pious, but now she starts going to church more often, sometimes three times a week. I catch her sometimes, staring out of a window while washing the dishes or rocking Calypso to sleep, and in her eyes, I see something of the old Pleione, the one who wanted to see snow. But then the moment passes, and her features are once again clouded with grim resolve.

Business at the hotel picks up again, so when her maternity leave is over, Pleione decides not to go back to her job at the school, but to work at the hotel with me. "It makes sense," she says. "This way we don't have to find daycare for Calypso."

We get on with things. We make do. There is joy too, and love. Sunday naps with Calypso between us, the bedroom baking in sun, a cloud of sweet, drowsy happiness filling the room. First steps, first words. We try for another child. This could be our adventure, we think. But it never happens. We don't know why and don't bother trying to find out, because we think it will happen eventually, when the time is right. We're not in any rush. But soon, Calypso is out of diapers and enrolled in primary school, and it still hasn't happened. And then Calypso is sitting the eleven-plus exam, starting secondary school, and we can't imagine doing it all again, so we don't.

With Calypso getting older we decide we need to move back closer to town. It makes sense; the commute to the hotel is long and Pleione wants to be closer to her mother, who is too old to make the trek out to the country these days. So when Z offers us the caretaker cottage at the hotel, we accept. The cottage is even smaller than our country house, and being on the hotel grounds means we never stop working, are always available to the guests. There are no more parties, no more friends coming to visit. But we tell ourselves it's only temporary. A free place to live while we save for a home of our own.

Time, time, time. This is how it passes, a life made up of one practical decision after the other, a thousand small concessions. And then you don't often think about them anymore—all of those paths not taken, those lives unlived—but you carry them with you always. And there goes Pleione in her work skirt, a basket of towels or linens balanced on her head, her eyes squinting against the sun. So beautiful the way she weaves through space, swathed in pinks and greens like a hummingbird. I try to grab her hand as she passes by me, try to pull her in for a kiss, try to tell her to stop, just for a moment, put the load down and sit awhile with me by the shore, like we used to.

But, no, she tells me she can't, she has to keep moving, or else the basket will tip, and don't I have somewhere to be? Here, she tells me, take this, handing me a load of my own. And so we keep moving forward, never losing our balance, lest all those regrets go tumbling to the floor for all to see.

PART TWO:
CALYPSO (2001)

CHAPTER SIX

THE RAINS BEGIN IN MARCH. TOO SOON. THEY SWELL the gullies inland, carrying silt and sewage to the coast. The eddies swirl with greenish foam, the sand smells like dying things. The gutters are flooded, and when the tourists arrive in buses and taxis, they have to leap over thick brown puddles. I stand under the eaves of the hotel bar and watch the drops land like tiny grenades on the sand. The tourists gather their books and towels and run for cover.

We learned hurricane preparedness in school, were taught how to shutter windows and avoid power lines downed by falling palm fronds. In primary school they taught us a song: "June, too soon / July, stand by / August, a must / September, remember / October, all over." A tune for the seasons. But here we are in March and it's been raining for weeks. Half our bookings have been cancelled.

My mother says we're cursed. My mother blames every bad thing, even the weather, on my father's and my refusal to attend mass. "The girl is too idle," my mother says often. *The devil makes work of idle hands.* She's not wrong. I know I should be helping more with the hotel. I see how tired my parents are, how they fall into their bed each night, silent, facing the walls, too drained from a day of smiling at strangers to have anything left for each other.

But this will not be my life. I know I'm destined for something beyond this place. The rain may be bad for business, but how can I fault the sky for letting go when I too am thick and full to bursting with repressed energy? I want to run along the beach, get soaked to the bone. I like to lie on my back in the sea and feel the cold rain hit my face. But my mother forbids it. "Sea ants swarm when it rains. You will get bit," she says.

"Middle of the busy season," my father says, coming to stand beside me, his eyes scanning the horizon as if he can spot an end to the rain there, some invisible respite in the black clouds.

"We'll be alright," I say, my hand on his shoulder. My father is built like a boulder, broad backed, a wide flat face like a rock good for skimming. He never talks about it, but I sense the same restlessness in him that I feel in myself. Sometimes he will stop what he's doing in the middle of a task. Simply drop his tools and walk away, as if he's suddenly remembered somewhere else he's supposed to be. I never follow him when this happens, because I understand. Sometimes you just need to be anywhere other than where you are. Sometimes you need to walk away to remind yourself that you can. This is something my mother would never understand. I don't think she's ever run in the rain just to get wet. This difference is at the heart of every argument we've ever had.

But my father is different. When I was a child he would read to me at bedtime, usually English classics—Chaucer, Dickens, the Brontës, Austen. Stories of pale people in grey places. I would spend my free time roaming the beach, pretending I was a heroine in one of the novels, descending the candlelit stair of some great manor, roving the moors in a gown, my hems "six inches deep in mud" like Elizabeth Bennet's. Whenever I ask my father why he stayed in Barbados, why he didn't go visit these places from the stories he loves so much, he always says the same thing, "I'm where I need to be." I blame my mother. My ever-practical mother, her hands always full, tending to the business of her tiny universe without complaint.

When I was little, before we moved to the hotel, my parents and I lived in a village in the countryside, up in the hills in the centre of the island, nestled amongst the cane fields. My parents used to have parties every weekend, their friends all a collection of knees to my eyes. They would get drunk on rum and coke and spend Sunday afternoons playing dominoes and barbecuing pig tail on the front lawn, yelling about politics and art and movies. I was too young to know what they were talking about, but it all seemed so glamorous to me—my mother in big white sunglasses, a cigarette burning to nothing in her fingers, the orange ember a dot that danced around her face as she gesticulated. People always stopped to listen when she spoke, and even as a child, I knew this was a special kind of power. But all this changed when we moved onto the hotel grounds. Nowadays, most nights my parents fall asleep in front of the TV, exhausted. And my mother quit being interesting the same day she quit smoking. I will never be like her, content with such a menial life. And I will never be like my father, I will never fall in love with someone who makes my world smaller. No one is keeping me trapped here.

My mother appears now, clucking like a hen. She comes to stand beside my father and me, her eyes narrowed at the rain as if she can make it stop just by the sheer force of her disapproval. "They're calling for a tropical depression," she says. "We should make sure the generators have fuel." My father nods, but doesn't move, rapt by the rain.

"We could sing," I say. My mother glances at me, as if noticing me for the first time.

"What nonsense you chatting now, child?" she asks.

"We could sing a song to the clouds. Asking them to make the rain stop." My father smiles, but my mother's frown deepens.

"Stop being blasphemous," she says. She gives me that look, that one she's been giving me my whole life, like she's worried I'm going to burst into flames on the spot, my head contorting around my neck like a demon. I don't really believe I can control the weather, but it's fun to make my mother think I do.

My father likes to say my mother is a "bush Catholic." She says her Hail Marys and goes to confession, but that doesn't mean she doesn't still fear the obeah-man and brew bush tea when she's feeling sick. And ever since I was little, I've known she's sensed something was not quite right with me. Some fire that even a saltwater baptism couldn't kill. And there's times I feel it too, something dark flowering in my gut, wanting to burst free. My days are empty of intrigue but pregnant with possibility and I'm feverish with longing for all the things I have yet to experience. Maybe that's what my mother senses, this yearning. And maybe yearning is itself a kind of power, a kind of magic.

I catch my father's eye. "Rain, rain, go away. Come again another day," I sing, my voice low and gravelly like I'm casting a spell. I'm hoping to make my father laugh, but he's staring off into the rain again, his face clouded with worry.

My mother sucks her teeth. "Go and bring in the beach chairs," she says.

I drop into a low curtsy and scamper off before she can comment. I love the beach in the rain, free of tourists, the sea churning like it's trying to spit something out. I run until my lungs burn and my clothes are wet and plastered to my skin, then I collapse onto one of the same lounge chairs I've been tasked with bringing inside. I lay sprawled, my mouth open to the sky, catching the rain on my tongue. I'm bored. I think maybe I'll go to the hotel convenience store and steal a Coke and a chocolate bar. Or maybe I'll go down to the fisherman's wharf and see if my friend Matthew is around.

The beach is deserted, and the sea rises and rocks in the wind. I'm about to go inside when I hear the buzz of an approaching jet ski, whirring like a large insect. The jet ski gets closer and closer, the rider silhouetted against the grey sky. He rides right up onto the sand beside me and dismounts, shaking out his long blond hair with his fingertips. And as if on cue, the rain stops, the sun cuts jagged through the clouds like the tusks of an elephant. How can you not believe in magic in moments like this? The man draws nearer, and I feel a great swelling.

He is tall and fair, all shades of yellow like a sheaf of wheat, his wetsuit rolled down to his hips, his hair dripping wet. He stands above me now, his body blacking out the sun, which crowns his head like a halo. Neither of us says anything. I'm aware of how I must look, my dress sheer and flattened against my skin by the rain, my chest heaving. The sun shifts behind a cloud and the man's face becomes visible. He is older than I realized, my father's age almost. I prop myself up on my elbows, and for a long moment we simply stare at each other.

"Where did you come from?" I ask finally.

The man laughs, head back to the sky, as if he can't believe it, as if demanding an explanation from the gods. He looks down at me and shakes his head, laughs again. Then he sets off up the beach, towards the hotel. I watch him go. *Turn around*, I whisper to myself, willing it with my mind, *look back at me*. And right before he reaches the bar, he does, and I recognize that look. He looks at me the way men look at the shot of rum they know they'll regret in the morning, right before they down it anyway. I smile and give a little wave. The man disappears into the dark of the bar and I collapse onto the lounge chair. Now it's my turn to laugh. I'm definitely not bored anymore. The sky clears and the sun begins its slow descent into the horizon.

CHAPTER SEVEN

A FEW YEARS AGO, WE HOSTED A DELEGATION OF officials who were in the island for some environmental talks. Uncle Z was a member of parliament back then and had made the arrangements for the visitors to stay with us. We needed the business, the hotel wasn't doing well. Not that I knew much about these things then. I was a child still, though I was a force-ripe young thing, prancing about the hotel with my work skirt tied up around my thighs.

Men were already beginning to notice me, the local boys who brought fresh catch to sell and the minibus drivers who carted visitors to and from town. They watched me with the passive interest of animals who were well fed but always on the lookout for their next meal. I glared back at them, feeling safe in the shadow of the hotel. I was little more than a maid, my father only a caretaker, but I fancied myself the mistress of a mighty castle.

I watched the tourist women; bloated and red though they were, I thought they must all be boujie. Only boujie people could travel overseas and spend big money to sit on a beach and burn. I watched them, the way they laughed with their whole faces, their yellow teeth gaping. They wore bikinis with straps that etched into their skin, their backs raw and peeling. They drank constantly, hailing me over to order rum punch first thing in the morning, and by afternoon they were sleeping face down in their chairs, their fingers grasping at the sand as they dreamt. I wondered what white women dreamt about.

But mostly I thought about white men. About their flesh and how pink it was. White men both fascinated and revolted me. I wanted to know them, to slice them up the way the boys at school sometimes cut up toads and lizards, to see if they bled, if they were made of the same stuff as us.

The delegation arrived in a swarm of black suits, the men shrinking in the sun like raisins. They wore shiny brown shoes and carried matching briefcases. They mopped sweat from their brows, smiled at me when I served them lemonade, and said, "Lovely place. Such friendly people." They spent their days at meetings in town. When I asked my father what the meetings were about, he only shooed me away, telling me not to mind grown-people business. I suspected even then that he himself didn't know.

I worshipped my father, and I hated watching him serve the foreign men, the way his neck curved and bent as though his spine was folding under the weight of his heavy smiles and his "yes suhs, right away suhs." In the evening when the delegation returned from their talks, most of the men retreated to their rooms, calling every so often to ask if it was true that the a/c was really at maximum, and could it not possibly be made cooler?

Some would swim, waddling to the ocean in baggy shorts, their soft bodies trembling.

One man stood out amongst the rest. He took long walks on the beach each evening, roaming the shore, searching in the white foam, his suit pants rolled up to his knees. At first, I thought he was looking for shells, but one day, my curiosity drawing me near to him, I saw he was collecting pieces of bleached coral. He saw me watching and waved me over, placing a piece in my palm.

"They grow only one centimetre each year," he told me, closing my fist around it, "and they're dying so fast."

I looked down at the coral in my hand. I knew they were animals, had been taught that in school. But I didn't know they were dying; whenever I swam, I saw thousands of them, bright jungles beneath the sea. "Why are they dying?" I asked.

"It's too warm for them," he said. "When the water warms up, more seaweed grows. It gets too crowded. The seaweed poisons the coral."

I nodded. This made sense to me, in the tragic and dramatic way I thought of myself at that age: as a trapped and beautiful thing being choked by the weeds around me. The delegate was still holding my hand, his palms were rough, the skin around his nails calloused and peeling. Up close, I could tell he was a man who had dug through the dirt for something to eat. A farmer, or a fisherman, not like the other tourists, who looked like those deepwater fish I'd seen in a biology textbook once, the ones who never see the sun.

Over the next few days, I waited for the delegate to return each evening, shadowing him as he roamed the beach. I trailed him closely, finding excuses to speak to him. I brought him mounds of bleached coral, presented them the way a cat would a dead mouse to its owner. I offered him drinks. Towels. Sunscreen. I told him of all the best places I knew to study coral, of reefs where the fish were so thick you could part them with your open palm.

On the third day, he finally agreed to follow me to a sheltered cove that could only be accessed through a rough path at the back of the property. I felt like I had won a prize, as if he were a fancy car or a trip abroad, something I'd coveted but wasn't sure I knew how to handle. I needn't have worried; the delegate was slow and deliberate with me, and when it was over and I returned, sore and sand-burnt, to the small cottage I shared with my parents at the edge of the property, I felt as though I had learned to speak another language. The delegate opened something up in me, a dormant hunger I had always known was there but could never name. I was thirteen years old.

And by now, four years later, I've been with many more men, and some boys. Foreign exchange students who show up at the hotel for weeks after I end things, asking for me at reception, loitering on the beach with their friends, pretending not to care when I don't come to greet them. How quickly their desperation turns to anger. "Fuck that bitch," they say. "She's a slut anyway." Businessmen from places I've never heard of, with accents thick like molasses, who tell me they've never been with a black woman before, who cry when they leave, grown men reduced to blubbering boys, shoving parting gifts in my hands like dogs pissing on a tree stump to mark their territory.

There's nothing about the man on the jet ski that sets him apart from the hundreds of other white men who've been passing through this hotel since before I can remember. But I can't stop thinking about him. He reminds me of my first, the delegate with the rough hands. Something about the way he looked back at me over his shoulder, his stare like a dare or a challenge. He wants me, too. I saw it on his face that first day we met, when he found me lying in the rain, stupid and gaping like a beached whale. I wish I'd said something interesting. I didn't even get his name. In the guest log, he's registered under a corporation.

Almost a week passes, and I hardly see him at all. I resist the urge to ask my parents anything about him, but I watch him from afar. He does laps in the pool at dusk, when it's quiet. He has a small green tattoo on his right forearm, but I haven't gotten close enough to tell what it is. He drinks tea in the morning and beer in the afternoon. He smokes Benson & Hedges. Last night, dressed in a pale blue button-down and jeans, he asked the concierge for recommendations for a nightclub. I waited up until almost four a.m. to see if he would bring a girl back with him, but I didn't see him return. He wasn't at breakfast this morning.

Tonight, my parents and I are having dinner at my uncle Z's house, like we do once a month or so. Uncle Z still lives in the house where he and my father grew up. When I was little, I used to ask why it was that Uncle Z lived in this big house while we lived in the small cottage on the hotel grounds, but I learned over the years that there is no satisfying answer to that question, at least not coming from my parents. I always dread these dinners, the way my mother forces us to dress up, the way my father agrees with everything Z says, laughing at his disgusting jokes.

We park at the end of Z's driveway, behind an unfamiliar car. I groan. These dinners are bad enough without the added tedium of having to pretend to get along for a guest. My mother unbuckles her seat belt and peers over her shoulder at me, eyes narrowed. "Behave," she says. I give a mock salute and clamber out of the car. I wonder if Z still keeps his weed stashed in that same drawer in his office or if he moved it after I got busted for stealing some last time we came over.

We're greeted at the door with exaggerated enthusiasm by Aunt Hera, Z's wife. I roll my eyes at my father behind her back and stifle a laugh as he mouths, "Is that a kaftan?"

Hera is in hostess mode, clearly showing off for the guest, since normally she wouldn't bother to get up from the couch to greet us, preferring to lie there like a pharaoh while we each bend one by one to kiss her cheek. Z and Hera met while he was an MP and she was working as a cleaner in his office, but she still acts like we're the charity cases. I wonder if she knows her husband has slept with half the maids at the hotel. Old habits die hard, I guess.

Hera is a big woman, almost six feet tall and broad, and with her penchant for flowy garments and showy wigs, she tends to command a lot of space in a room. That's why it isn't until we are past the foyer and settled into the living room that I notice him. He is standing by the big bay window that looks onto the yard. It's dark out, so only his reflection is visible in the window, and this is what I notice first, his eyes mirrored on the windowpane, looking right at me.

I freeze, nearly dropping the bottle of wine we brought. My first instinct is to run. Something about his eyes, their reflection in the window, the way they found me before I was ready. Something about knowing that he was watching me, observing me, without my knowledge, the way a predator stalks its prey from behind tall grass. But I recover quickly and wink at him, not even bothering to check if my mother is watching. In the window his reflection smiles at me, sly amusement lighting up his features. At just this moment Hera calls out to him, and when he turns, his face is impassive.

"Odie," Hera says, "this is Z's cousin, Atlas. And his wife, Pleione." Odie. So that's his name. I wonder if it's short for something.

Odie steps away from the window to greet my parents. "We've met," he says, shaking my father's hand anyway.

"Oh, of course," Hera says, her voice in singsong. "At the hotel! Silly me. I hope they've been giving you the VIP treatment." She laughs, all gums and teeth.

Odie smiles tightly. "I've been very comfortable, thank you." He looks at me then. This is the closest I've been to him since that first time we met on the beach and the sensation is the same, like standing so close to a bonfire your skin starts to burn but still wishing you could get even closer, the cold wind at your back driving you into the flames.

Hera doesn't introduce us, and Odie doesn't ask, turning instead to my father to make polite conversation. I try to pay attention but my ears are ringing. Odie, I say to myself, rolling his name around my tongue like a mango pit, sucking the juice out. Odie, Odie, Odie.

Just then my uncle Z comes in. He always does this, preferring to wait until everyone is settled so he can make an entrance. He makes a big show of topping up everyone's drinks and then we head to the dining room. I wait for Odie to sit first and then choose a seat as far away from him as possible. It's all too much just to be in the same room with him. This isn't how this was supposed to go. I'm not ready for the casual intimacy of dinner, elbows bumping, knees grazing. I don't want him to see me eating up close, to hear the noises I make when I chew, to see me use a fucking napkin.

It's easier once we're all seated and the conversation flows. I sip the sweet red wine my parents brought and push my food around my plate. My twelve-year-old cousin, Junior, stares stupidly at my breasts from across the table, his mouth open, chicken fat glistening on his chin. I steal glances at Odie from time to time, but if he looks at me, I don't catch it.

Uncle Z is explaining how he and Odie met. He'd been contacted by a mutual acquaintance to help Odie's development company clear some construction equipment through customs. I don't really understand what Z does, but it always seems to involve finding loopholes and helping people avoid red tape. I think he might be a criminal but the kind of criminal who is friends with the prime minister and wins awards for service to his country.

"And so I mentioned our humble hotel," Z is saying, "and suggested perhaps Odie and some of the team would like to stay with us."

The hotel is something of a pet project of my uncle's. He owns the place but has no interest in running it. That thankless task falls to my father. My mother says that things were different when my great-uncle Cronus was alive; back then the hotel was the family's main source of income. But Z's got lots of other businesses now. I can't imagine him in his white polo shirt washing sheets or fixing a clogged toilet, the kind of work my father does every day. Sometimes he sends Junior to us for a bit of character building. The boy shows up, snotty and crying like an infant, and my father gives him an easy job, washing glasses or folding towels. Even those he can't manage. Slug-like, everything he touches ends up sticky. After a few hours he calls his mother to pick him up and she takes him for ice cream, praising him for his hard work. I would hate him, but he's too pathetic.

"What project are you working on, Odie?" my father asks. He sits beside me, eating his chicken in slow, deliberate bites. Everything my father does is slow and deliberate, as if he's a wild animal trying to conserve its energy during a drought.

"We bought the old Castle Hotel," Odie says. "We're demolishing it and building a five-star resort. First of its kind on the island."

My father stops chewing and puts his fork down. "That's a historic property," he says. "I'm surprised Town and Planning gave the go-ahead."

"It's a dump," says Z, before Odie can answer. "It's about time someone did something with it. And Odie's company does excellent work. They did that big resort in Montego Bay last year. The Sandals or Hilton or whatever it is."

"It's a lovely property you built in Jamaica," Hera says, turning to Odie. "The buffet is incredible. And the activities. Even a waterslide!"

Odie smiles and begins to reply but is interrupted by my mother, who asks, "You've been?"

Hera takes a big swig of her wine. "We were invited to the grand opening."

"Oh," my mother says, her voice small. She catches my father's eye and raises an eyebrow.

I wish they would all shut up for a second and let Odie speak. I want to hear what his voice sounds like. I want to hear him say my name, to hear what it sounds like in that strange accent of his, not quite English or American, but something in between, like the actors in those black-and-white movies my mother likes.

But they drone on and on about the project. I have a hazy idea of what they're talking about. On the call-in radio program

my father listens to devotedly every afternoon, I'd heard mention of a plan to build some new resort, bigger than anything
built on the island before. These kinds of foreign investments
always get the whole island talking. In the rum shops, the
church pews, and the minibuses. Everyone wants to know who
has been hired and who hasn't, whose pockets are being lined
and whose aren't. A few weeks ago, after school, Matthew,
whose older brother works construction, was talking about
how he'd heard they were bringing in all foreign workers for
the job. I'd ignored him, figured he was just spouting conspir-
acy theories as usual. But now that I know Odie is involved, I'm
going to have to start paying more attention to the news.

My father, who usually never has more than two words to
say at dinner, seems particularly riled up. "I'm just surprised
that they are allowing the building to be destroyed rather than
preserved. And to build a big all-inclusive resort."

"Don't start, Atlas," Z says. He wields his fork like a god
brandishing a tiny trident. "You'll offend our guest."

Odie laughs. "I'm not so easily offended," he says, and I
swear he's looking at me when he does.

My father presses on, in a rare challenge. "You know as
well as I do that those resorts aren't good for local business. The
tourists don't venture outside the compound."

"Look, Atlas," Z says. "We're a speck in the sea. The idea that
we can thrive without foreign investment is a fallacy. Our soil's
shot to shit. We've got beaches but so does every other island in
spitting distance. We have to compete with all-inclusive resorts
in Jamaica, Cuba, and Mexico that are half the price."

"Cronus used to say people come to Barbados because
they're looking for a local experience. Something they can't get
in those other places," my father says.

Z smiles, without showing his teeth. "My father used to say a lot of things."

"I think it's exciting," Hera says. "It's about time they built something a bit more exclusive. You know, I was down Paynes Bay the other day and you should have seen how ghetto it was. All kinds of people drinking and partying. The tourists looked so uncomfortable and I can't blame them!"

My father looks as if he's about to say something more and then changes his mind. I watch the fight go out of him all at once.

"We should build a waterslide at our hotel, Daddy," Junior says, and Z laughs.

"That's a good idea, Junior. You're thinking like a businessman," he says, reaching over to cup Junior around the back of his skull.

An awkward silence falls over the table. I think that perhaps Odie will try to fill it, to say something reassuring to my father or try to defend his work, but he just eats his chicken, appearing entirely unbothered.

"Enough shop talk," my uncle says, leaning back in his chair and pushing his empty plate away from him. "Calypso!"

I jump at the sound of my name, letting my knife fall, the sound like a gunshot. "Yes, Uncle," I say, keeping my face neutral.

"Odie tells me you made quite an impression on him at the hotel," Z says, his voice heavy with insinuation. My mother coughs. My father raises an eyebrow at me. I am suddenly aware of every muscle in my face.

"I only said that the service in general has been excellent," Odie says, smiling at my parents, who smile politely back. My mother looks down at her chicken like she's trying to figure out which bone would be the easiest to stab me with.

"Calypso is a good girl," my uncle says. "We'll be sad to lose her at the hotel next year. But she's destined for bigger things. How's school, Calypso? Still top of your class?"

I smile and take a sip of my wine. It's true, I am top of my class, but it's something I don't know how to talk about. Maybe if I put in more of an effort, I would feel less awkward about the compliment. But the truth is I figured out sometime in primary school that all I had to do to succeed at school was read and remember things, a skill that I was apparently born with. It's not something I work particularly hard at. At school, my high grades make me the target of disdain both from the other students, which you would expect, but also from my teachers, who seem to resent that I don't find them intimidating. Even my mother has grown tired of hearing about my academic achievements. "Good marks will only get you so far," she likes to say, "trust me on that."

"I'm doing okay," I say. Odie is staring openly at me now, the same amused smile from earlier playing on his lips.

"Don't be modest," Z says, turning to Odie. "She's going to be an island scholar, like her father."

The fact that my father won a Barbados Scholarship is something my uncle loves to mention at any opportunity. Z enjoys putting himself down, joking about his own mediocre school record, but somehow it always ends up making my father seem pitiable in comparison. Why my father, the smartest man I know, spends his every waking hour managing a hotel for next to nothing is another one of those questions I've given up asking.

Receiving all this attention and praise while Odie watches should feel good, but it doesn't. Instead, I feel like I'm being handled. Like I'm a circus animal being taught how to bounce a ball on its nose. Z has an end-game, he always does. Except, for once, it seems our goals might align.

After dinner, my mother and aunt disappear into the kitchen to wash up. Junior is coaxed into bed with the promise of a treat in the morning. I escape before my mother can force me to help with the washing-up, claiming I need to use the bathroom. Really, I just need a minute to myself. I don't think I've taken one full breath since I first caught sight of Odie's reflection in the window a couple of hours ago. I walk into the backyard, down the sloping hill, past the pool to the shadowy hedge. I smoke a cigarette and look up at the stars.

The sky is cloudless, the moon a thumbnail sliver. I don't know the names of any constellations. I can't even tell the stars from the satellites. At school last year, the girls all went mad for astrology, figuring out each other's birth charts at lunch hour. Then one of the mothers got wind and complained to the principal about her child being exposed to paganism, so the teachers shut it down. I never could believe in any of that stuff anyway. The same way I could never bring myself to pray properly. There's nothing the stars, or the heavens above, can tell me that I don't already know. My nerves calmed, I head back inside the house, dodging the kitchen and joining the men where they have gathered on the front veranda.

They are playing dominoes and drinking straight rum. I sidle up behind Odie, resting a hand on the back of his chair. "Can I join?" I ask, staring down at my uncle. He narrows his eyes at me and then shakes his head.

"On the next round. This game's almost over." I roll my eyes but don't argue, taking a seat at the table to wait.

They are smoking cigars, the smoke rising around their heads so that sitting there together, hunched over their dominoes, the three men look like gods perched high among the clouds. Though they were laughing and chatting when I walked in, they are silent now, and I'm sure it's because I'm here. I know that even if, or when, Odie and I get together, I will never disrupt the natural order of things. I can sit at the table but that doesn't matter. In many ways, Z, and even my father, will know Odie better than I ever will.

"Sing us a song, Cali," Z says. Then, to Odie, "She has a voice like warm butter."

"Is that so," Odie says, his teeth clenched around his cigar. He still hasn't looked at me. "Some music would be nice."

He says it just like that, as if I'm a jukebox waiting to be switched on. Anger flares in the back of my neck. I imagine taking a domino in my fist and smashing it into his skull. How hard would I have to hit him to draw blood? Would he look at me, then? And just as urgently, I want to kiss every inch of the sunburnt flesh of his forearms, the veins there thick like leeches.

"Not tonight, Uncle Z," I say. "I'm really tired." Pride wrestles with longing in my chest. I want Odie to see me, really see me, not like this, on Z's terms. I have to be more to him than this, more than a piece of exotic fruit for him to sample. Sweet and low hanging, like a fucking mango.

Z slams a domino down on the table, the noise making us all jump. My father quickly follows suit. Odie hesitates, scanning the board. Z holds his next domino above his head, ready to bear it down on the table. Odie hasn't even played yet, but Z is three moves ahead. He's already won. Odie raps his knuckles on the tabletop. Pass. Z's hand comes down like a lightning strike. The sound is like a whip on wet flesh.

Z looks at me with red-rimmed eyes. "Don't be rude, Calypso," he says, the warning clear in his voice. "Our guest would like to hear a song."

I look over at my father, who nods silently, so I push my chair back and stand. If I'm going to do this, I'm going to do it properly. I position myself directly in Odie's line of sight.

I'm terrified, though I've been waiting for this moment, a chance to hold Odie's attention in my hand, to toss it around like a game of jacks. The fear resounds in my chest, a deep and aching echo. I swallow it and begin to sing. I choose a song without thinking, an old calypso. "Brown Skin Girl" by Harry Belafonte. About a man who disappears on a sailboat, leaving his lover to care for their blue-eyed baby.

The superstitious might say I am an enchantress, that I sing a spell to keep him near me. Maybe I believe it too. I know I have a kind of magic in me, a power to make men do things they shouldn't. Maybe this is why I'm scared to sing, scared to use my powers, to set in motion the chain of events that I know will change everything.

When I finish, and open my eyes, Odie is looking at me at last, his blue eyes burning. The laughter has disappeared from his face, his mouth set now in a grim line. "Calypso," he says, and there it is, my name in his mouth like promise. "Sing it again."

CHAPTER EIGHT

ODIE AND Z HAVE BEEN SPENDING A LOT OF TIME together. The gossip among the hotel staff is that Odie has a taste for local rum and women, and Z is a reliable source of both. When I heard this, I'd been carrying a tray of empty glasses, and I let them fall in a shimmering cascade to my feet. But later, alone with my thoughts, I'd been calm. So what if Z takes him to every brothel on Bay Street? What we will have will eclipse everything. Whenever I am near him, I feel the effect of his presence at the centre of my being, around my navel, like being yanked back into the seat when a car accelerates too quickly. There is nothing like this feeling. It makes sense that it is called a crush. There is a pleasurable weightiness to my body, as if I'm carrying around a second skin. Like when I was a child and my father would bury me in a deep hole at the beach, that feeling of compression against my chest, the sand like a cold hug.

When his eyes are on me, I forget what it is to walk normally, all my actions are pantomimed like a child teetering around in her mother's stilettos. Kneeling on the terra-cotta tile beside the pool to change out the chlorine, I try not to slouch in case he's watching. Holding my hand to shade my eyes in a way I hope looks cinematic, I say to myself this is madness. You are mad. I'm disgusted with myself, at the lengths I will go to be noticed by him. I can feel the slow building of energy between us, like storm clouds gathering. That we are supposed to be together feels so inevitable to me, I can't imagine what Odie thinks he will accomplish by delaying it.

Tonight, I'm waiting in front of the the hotel for Matthew to pick me up. It's about ten p.m. and the air is hot and still, sure to rain. For once, I'm not thinking about Odie, but rather about a verse from a Derek Walcott poem we read in class today.

> *The fishermen rowing homeward in the dusk,*
> *Do not consider the stillness through which they move.*
> *So I since feelings drown, should no more ask*
> *For the safe twilight which your calm hands gave.*

I wanted to ask my father about it, but he was in a foul mood today when I got home from school. He's been cranky ever since we had dinner at Z's. I figure he's worried about the hotel Odie's company is building, about how it will affect our business. But there are a hundred hotels on this island, I don't see what one more will change. I suspect there's something else going on. He and my mother have been up late, huddled over paperwork in the dining room. I don't bother asking them about it, they wouldn't tell me anyway. They don't take me seriously enough to include me in those kinds of matters. Not that I care.

This damned hotel could burn to the ground tomorrow and I'd dance on the ashes.

I can hear the languid conversation of two guests on the balcony above me. Some of the newer hotels sit far back from the road, at the end of long, winding drives, guarded by men in booths. The tourists at those hotels want to feel secluded, apart. But our hotel predates this trend. It is a large, squat building that sits right on the busy road leading into town. It's a relic from a time when travellers wanted to lounge on their balconies and watch the locals bustle to and fro as if acting in a play for their amusement.

Now, we have to offer these street-facing rooms at a heavily discounted price compared to those on the seaside. And the guests complain about the noise of the traffic, the minibuses with their sing-song horns, the chattering schoolchildren who crowd at the bus stop every morning and afternoon, the music blaring from the neighbouring rum shop where the men sit squatted on upturned drink crates arguing about politics and women and everything under the sun. I'm not sure when it happened, when the tourists stopped being charmed by all that. I'm not sure which is worse: being a spectacle or being invisible. I walk around the side of the hotel where the staff entrance is located and where deliveries are made and light a cigarette.

Tonight, Matthew's taking me to a party at some white boy's house in Fort George Heights. Matthew's neither rich nor white, but he's always getting invited to these kinds of parties. He has a lot of friends and he finds it strange that I don't. He likes to tell me I just haven't met the right people yet, or that I need to be nicer to all people, generally. My friendlessness is a great tragedy to Matthew, who collects friends like Boy Scout badges.

There was a time, back in primary school, when I did have friends. Back when we used to spend our lunchtimes playing jacks and skipping marbles, before the boys started noticing me, and the girls noticed the boys noticing me. I didn't know any better, the boys chased me, and I didn't know I wasn't supposed to let them catch me. I didn't know that when they asked to see what my parts looked like, I wasn't supposed to show them. And I definitely wasn't supposed to demand to see theirs in return.

Where are these rules of girlhood written, as if in stone? And why is it some girls seem to know them all by heart, without ever being told? All as one, as if by some sort of secret consensus, the girls decided I was to be avoided at all costs. And the boys too would join in their gossiping, shunning me in public, only to corner me in empty hallways, or on my walk home from school, and declare their love in pathetic, breathy outbursts. By the time we got to secondary school, I'd decided to embrace the persona. They all thought I was up to no good anyway so I might as well live up to the hype. So now I roll my school uniform up under my belt, so the skirt falls high above the knee. I flirt with the minibus drivers, sit on their laps and let them call me baby. I may not have any friends, but I figure I'm better off without. I'm getting out of here anyway. I'm sick to death of this tiny rock, filled with small-minded people.

Matthew says I should make more of an effort to make friends with the girls at school. He says they're not all bad. "They just think you're uppity, that you look down on them," he says. And he's not wrong. I find their conversations asinine. What so and so wore to church the week before, whose father was caught running around behind whose mother's back, who got what mark on what test. Could they be any duller? Next year, I'm going to ace my CAPE exams and get a scholarship to go to university overseas. I'm going to study music. My parents don't know about this part of the plan. My father thinks I want to go to law school. But I'm going to be a singer. And the same girls who chat behind my back will be stuck behind a desk somewhere, bank tellers in low heels, married to the very same boys who pant after me now. Pathetic, malicious busybodies, the lot of them.

All except for Matthew, the only person on this stupid island who doesn't make me want to drown myself from sheer boredom. But he doesn't count. We've been friends since we both could walk. His mother, Cynthia, is our senior housekeeper and my mother's oldest friend. She knew my mother back before she found the Lord and became the insufferable nag she is now. Cynthia says my mother used to be wild, always the last to leave the dancehall. She says the boys couldn't get enough of her, that my father had to beat her other suitors away with a stick. I can't picture it.

Cynthia tells me these stories because she thinks it will bring me and my mother closer together, but the effect is the opposite. I wonder, where is this version of my mother and why don't I get to have her? That's what working in this place does to you, it robs you of your light. That's why I'm getting out of here as soon as possible.

Tonight, I'm wearing a denim skirt and a little blue top that ties around my back and falls in a triangle to my navel. I'm overdressed. I'll probably spend most of the night sitting on a sofa, making small talk with girls I don't like while Matthew plays FIFA. I'm suddenly very tired at the thought, but it's too late to call Matthew to cancel, he's already on his way.

"So, this is your secret smoking spot," says a voice from the shadows. Suddenly Odie is nearer to me than he has ever been, materializing at my side, seemingly out of nowhere. He smells of chemicals and his hair is damp. He must have just finished his nightly swim.

"It's no secret. My parents know I smoke." I'm struck by how childish this sounds, like a four-year-old claiming to be, in fact, four and a half.

Odie laughs. "How liberal of them."

I shrug. "Not really. They just don't care about . . ."

"About what?" Odie says, stepping closer to me. "About you?" He takes the cigarette from between my fingers, stealing a drag. Not far from where we stand, the door to the kitchen opens, a rectangle of yellow light carved into the darkness. One of the porters appears, lugging two garbage bags. He whistles a tune, heading away from us, and disappears around a bend. The air smells like stale grease. At our feet, the ground is littered with cigarette butts and broken glass. My mouth keeps filling with saliva, and I swallow it down again and again.

"No. I suppose they do care about me, just not about what I do. If that makes sense?"

Odie laughs again. "Not really, but I know what you mean. How old are you?"

"Seventeen," I say, and Odie whistles, taking a step away from me, his hands up in mock surrender. I laugh and lean against the wall. "How old are you?"

Odie leans on the wall beside me. Our arms aren't touching, but almost. "Old enough to know better."

I laugh. "Is that a line?"

"No," he says, suddenly serious. We've turned to face each other now, still leaning the sides of our bodies against the wall.

"I've seen you watching me." He says it softly, not shyly but with a kind of quiet curiosity as if he's reporting on the behaviour of a peculiar insect he's found in his garden.

I lift my chin. "Okay. So?"

He takes a step forward. Up close, his face is lined and sunburnt, freckles and white spots crowding his forehead, his eyes bright blue and rimmed with short lashes that are so blond they shine white in the darkness. "Do you know why I'm here?" he asks.

"On the island?" I ask, embarrassed. I don't know much about his hotel project and I don't want to appear uninformed.

"I was speaking more specifically. Why I'm here right now, smoking in a service alley in the dark."

"Oh . . ." I say, unsure of where this is going. "No. I don't know."

He's very still, hardly blinking. I'm finding it very hard not to look away, to find some release from this tension, the energy between us pulled taut to snapping.

"Because I saw you. From the bar. I saw you walk by and I followed you. I had to follow you." He drags a single finger along the inside of my thigh, stopping just below the hem of my skirt. I'm so wet, I wonder if he can smell it.

I'm suddenly very aware of his body, of the realness of it, the dry pieces of peeling skin on his lips, the wayward hairs of his beard growing too high on his cheekbones. Rather than lessen my attraction, these flaws compound it. In abstract, Odie was a crush. But now he's within my reach like a piece of overripe fruit lying plump and sweet in the dirt and I want to peel him apart and taste his insides.

Just the warm pulse of his finger against my skin is enough to tell me that being with him will be different than anything

I've experienced before. I grip his elbow. He grazes a knuckle against my clit and I emit a sound like a chair scraping against tile. My scream echoes across the property. Odie pushes me against the wall and clamps a hand over my mouth. With his other hand he slides two fingers inside my underwear. I can hear the light melodic sounds of people drinking in the bar. Any minute, a hotel worker might emerge beside us, heading home for the night. An animal digs through the trash some- where nearby. Bats swoop low, diving into the palm trees. Odie's mouth is on my neck.

I struggle away from him but his grip is firm. I am sick. We are depraved. I bite his hand but he doesn't let go, his whole body pinning me now. The flesh of his stomach is soft and rounded. Even in this moment I know there's something wrong with me for wanting him. And that this wrongness is the thing I crave most of all. Over his shoulder I see the sweep of headlights turning into the alley. Odie moves his fin- gers inside me and I clench my thighs tight around his hand and come in jerking sobs. I hold on to his shoulders, my face pressed against his chest. We stand like this for a moment, my body limp and shaking, until the white glare of the headlights has washed over us. I yank my skirt down and step out of the shadows, just as Matthew pulls up beside us. "Get rid of them," Odie says, and walks away.

The car is full of people, piled one on top of the other in the back seat. A dancehall song blares over the sound of the exhaust pipe, which Matthew has rigged so that it always emits a low growl. I walk around to the driver's side and lean my elbows onto the window frame. The car smells of fruity body spray and weed. I greet everyone, most of whom I know from school. In the passenger seats sits LeDonna. We've been in class together since First Form and she can't stand me. Matthew lowers the volume on the stereo.

"Who was that?" Matthew says, peering out of the windshield to where Odie has disappeared.

"Just a guest," I say.

"This really is a full-service hotel," says LeDonna, and everyone laughs.

Matthew frowns, twisting in his seat to look at me. He lowers his voice. "Are you okay?"

"Yeah, of course," I say, laughing. "You know the guests always get a little handsy when they're drunk." I roll my eyes. When I look at Matthew, I'm not sure if he's buying it. I'm still a little out of breath. "Actually, I'm really sorry, but I should probably go make sure he's okay."

"Are you serious?" Matthew says. "Cali?"

"It's my job. If something happens to him while he's stumbling around drunk, he could sue the hotel."

LeDonna reaches over and gives Matthew's thigh a light squeeze. "Matty," she says. "We're going to be late."

Matthew ignores her. He's looking at me, eyes pleading. From the back seat his friends start to moan about the holdup. "Will you tell your parents about it?" Matthew asks.

He's so beautiful, Matthew. Close-cropped hair, high cheekbones, eyelashes that curl in on themselves like the barrel of a wave. He could have any girl he wants. I just want to be rid of him as quickly as possible.

"Of course," I say. "Go on, go have fun." I step back away from the car and give everyone in the back a small wave.

"Cali," Matthew says again, "come with us."

The car erupts in a chorus, cajoling me to get in. Only LeDonna is silent, staring sullenly out the window.

"Have a good night," I say, and turn away. When I look back the car is still there. I wave again and watch as Matthew slowly reverses out the alley and onto the street.

I head back inside through the kitchen, where the staff are closing down for the night. Out in the bar, the DJ is leading the tourists in a conga line that loops around the high-top tables and out onto the pool deck. The bar is busy. A rowdy group of English women have taken over half the tables and are trying to convince Marcus, one of our bartenders, to join them in a round of shots. They reach for his body like they own it, tugging on the corners of his uniform and running their hands up and down his arms.

I pick up a tray and clear a few glasses as I weave through the bar. After a few minutes it's clear that Odie isn't there. I head out onto the beach. I spot a lone figure wading in the shallows and I go out to meet him. We stand apart, not speaking, the waves lapping at our shins. It is raining now, the drops landing like cold bites on my skin. The sea is black and writhing, like a thousand ants. "This place," Odie says, his voice subdued, "is making me forget who I am."

"When I was little my mother used to read to me from this book of Caribbean folk tales," I say. "My favourites were always Mama Dlo and Papa Bois."

"Cali . . ." Odie says.

"They were lovers," I say, not sure where I'm going but sure, somehow, that if I keep talking, he will stay and listen. "Mama Dlo was a creature of the sea. Her hair looked like it was made of a hundred eels and her tongue was forked. And her husband, Papa Bois, was king of the forest, half man, half deer. When I first saw you, riding onto the beach on that jet ski,

I thought you looked like you could be their son. Something birthed from land and sea, just for me."

He turns to me now, and in the darkness, I cannot see his face. He shakes his head, as if waking himself up from a too-long nap. "I come from a real place, Cali, not a fairy tale. I didn't just appear. I have a life there. A wife, and children. That's my home."

I step closer and lean my head against his shoulder. I feel like a washcloth wrung dry. "I'm so tired," I say.

Odie brushes his lips across my forehead lightly, and then pulls away. "You can come up," he says, "but you can't stay the night." He turns then to head back up to the beach towards the hotel, not looking back to see if I will follow. I stare out to the sea for a moment longer. I imagine all the fishermen rowing homeward. They're probably in their beds by now, safe in calm hands. My pride flickers for a moment like a burnt-out light bulb before it dies completely. I turn and follow Odie inside.

CHAPTER NINE

ODIE CHECKS OUT OF THE HOTEL AND RENTS A BUNGALOW in a wealthy neighbourhood nearby. He never gives a reason why, but I like to think it's so that we can spend our time together without worrying about the prying eyes of the hotel staff, or my parents.

On the nights we spend together, Odie picks me up when he finishes work. Sometimes we drive around for a while. We go where no one will recognize us, sometimes to the northern-most tip of the island. Here, the hotels disappear, and the land is rugged, steep cliffs giving way to the violent Atlantic. We walk above the Animal Flower Cave, so named for the sea anemones that live within it. They are hunters, the animal flowers, that sting and paralyze passing fish. Predators disguised as prey. We walk the cliffs until the sun sets, holding on to each other, the ocean spray raking at our skin like sandpaper. One day these rocks will crumble, the cave collapsing in on itself, but for now they hold.

Most often we spend the night at Odie's house, the blinds drawn. He is often silent and moody after work. We don't talk about the hotel project. I leave him alone while he makes phone calls or stands hunched over blueprints. I swim in the lap pool in the backyard, doze or read in the hammock on his veranda, watch all the foreign channels on his giant TV, eat the food his housekeeper cooks for him. I'm never bored, and sometimes I even forget that Odie is there and I'm startled, and a little disappointed, when he does appear. I wonder if this is what vacations feel like. Solitude, I realize now, is the ultimate luxury. All my life I've sought it, running from my parents, carving out secret hideaways in the hotel where I could go to disappear. "What mischief have you been up to?" my mother would ask when she inevitably found me. But I wasn't up to anything. The joy was just in being alone, in having no one to answer to, in being under no one's scrutiny.

I wonder if Odie's wife misses him when he's away, or if she enjoys the time alone. I think about Odie's wife often. I know nothing about her, have never even seen a photograph, but she appears to me some nights in my half sleep, sitting quietly at the end of Odie's bed, watching us. She doesn't seem angry in these apparitions, only wary. Every now and then Odie receives a call from her while I am over. He always takes the phone into the bedroom and closes the door.

Sometimes after these calls, he is even more quiet than usual, sullen and withdrawn. Other times he finds me wherever I am in the house and wrenches the clothes from my body, pushes my face into the arm of the couch or the rough tile of the pool deck, and takes me quickly and desperately from behind. "Does that turn you on," I ask him, after one of these times, "punishing me?" I had scratched my cheek against the plaster wall of the hallway and Odie lapped at the small trail of blood with his tongue. But it was Odie who seemed the more deflated afterwards, curling up on the floor like a beaten dog, as if he was the one being punished.

Sometimes a whole week will go by and I won't hear from Odie at all. We will make plans for him to pick me up and he won't show. On these nights I call him over and over, hanging up before his voicemail picks up. Each time I swear I won't call again, but a few minutes later I am unable to stop myself. It's as if I'm no longer in control of my body. It would be one thing if I were simply going mad, but it's another to be aware of it happening and unable to stop it. I hate what I'm becoming, what he's making me.

On the nights we do spend together, I never sleep over. Odie says he doesn't want my parents to miss me, but I suspect he just doesn't want to wake up beside me. There is something unforgiving about dawn, the inevitability of it. If we never wake together, then it's like I'm not real, like what we're doing is just a dream.

It's Saturday, and tonight Odie's company is throwing a fancy party for some investors who are visiting from Canada. I lie on his bed, watching him dress. He struggles with his tie, and I beckon him to me, sitting across his lap to tie it myself.

"Where'd you learn to do that?" Odie asks. He has shaved his beard, and his bare chin is weak and pockmarked. I hope he grows it back soon. "Did you tie your father's ties for him when you were a little girl?" He cups my behind as he says this, shifting my weight onto his groin. Odie likes to bring up my father, to tease me. This is the game we play, volleying our age difference back and forth between us like a ball we can't let drop. Making a joke of it so we never have to really address it.

"What use would my father have for a tie?" I ask, smoothing his collar flat. "I wear a tie to school. It's part of my uniform."

"Mmm," Odie says. "I'd like to see you in your uniform." I give his face a little slap and shimmy back onto the bed. He's in a good mood tonight, playful. Things at the construction site must be going well. He finishes dressing, adding cufflinks, smoothing his hair into a low ponytail.

I lie back onto the pillows, watching him. "I look better in a dress," I say. Odie doesn't respond. I throw a pillow at the back of his head. He freezes, the pillow falls to his feet, but he doesn't pick it up. He glances over his shoulder at me, his eyes two thin blue lines. I glare back.

"Don't start, Calypso," he says, turning away. I toss and turn on the bed for a bit. I feel restless, irritable. There is a hot, itchy feeling in my gut.

"What would you do," I say, "if I showed up tonight?" Odie stiffens but doesn't respond. I know I have his attention though. I stand and walk over to him, snaking my arms around his waist. I breathe in the fresh scent of his shirt, already dampening with sweat. Odie sweats constantly, his skin always red and glistening as though his body is allergic to the island heat. "What if I went right up onstage in a tight red dress and sang a song in front of everyone?"

Odie takes my hands in his and untangles himself from my embrace. "Stop it," he says, still holding me by the wrists.

I step towards him, pressing my hips into his. "Would that make you angry?" I say, into his neck. Odie exhales, his grip tightening. I feel his erection growing against me. I lick at his earlobe, holding it between my teeth.

"Enough," Odie says, tossing me back onto the bed like a wet towel. I land awkwardly, my feet still on the floor. I look up at him, waiting, but he doesn't join me. He looks instead at his watch. "Let's go," he says. "I'll drop you home on the way."

"Can I stay here?"

Odie sighs again. "I don't need this, Cali. Not tonight." He turns off the light on his way out of the room, leaving me alone in the dark.

He is silent as he drives me home, and so am I. I look out the window, at the cloudy purple sky, no stars in sight. Odie stops around the corner from the hotel, our usual pickup and drop-off spot, and I've hardly closed the car door before he's driven away. I stand on the roadside for a minute, until his tail lights disappear.

At home, I pace up and down my room, pulling clothes out of my closet at random. I'm shaking with rage. Who does he think he is? I live here, this is my island. No one tells me where I can and can't go. At the back of the closet I find last year's Christmas dress, a chiffon red-and-gold thing my mother picked out. I pull it on, it's a little tight around my stomach and thighs, but it still fits. I find a red lipstick that's the same shade as the dress and put it on blindly. Gold hoops, gold heels. I don't bother with my hair, don't even glance at my reflection.

When I enter the living room, my mother is eating dinner on the couch watching the seven o'clock news and doesn't notice me. Part of me is glad, the other part wants to dance naked in front of the TV, yank the plate out of her hands, and smash it at her feet. "Look at me," I want to scream, "look at what he's done to me."

A few years ago, my mother and I went to New Jersey for the wedding of an old school friend of hers. We stayed in

that friend's basement in Hoboken, took the train into the city
for the day. I wanted to go to Times Square, but my mother
insisted we bypass it entirely. We spent the whole day at the
Met, my mother always a few paces ahead, listening intently
to her audio guide, taking notes in a small journal she kept in
her purse.

After hours of following my mother from piece to piece,
not really taking anything in, I stopped suddenly, my attention captured by a large painting of a young girl. The subject
sat reclined with her arms folded behind her head, her body
turned to face some unseen window. Her skin was yellow as if
bathed in sunlight and the white of her cotton underwear was
visible between tanned thighs. A cat lapped at a saucer of milk
on the floor beside her.

I knew, without being told, that there was something wrong
about the painting. And when my mother came to stand beside
me, I thought she would comment on the perverseness of it.
Instead she stood quietly next to me for what felt like a long time.

"What do you think she's thinking about?" my mother
asked, finally.

The question threw me. It hadn't occurred to me that I
was allowed to have an opinion about such things. But I knew
immediately what I thought the answer was. Sex. She was
thinking about sex, about all the sex she hadn't had yet, all the
sex she would have one day. How many afternoons had I spent
in bed, the sun shining through my window in just the same
way, exploring my body with my own hand? But I couldn't say
that aloud. I was sure there was something wrong with me for
thinking that way.

At school, the teachers told us to let down our hems and pull
up our socks, lest we distract the boys with our skin. The boys,

we were told, were weak and easily tempted. But I was the one who was driven to distraction most days, my thighs quivering beneath my desk. At lunch, the boys shared stashes of playing cards with naked women on them, traded beer calendars and lewd magazines. I wanted to be included in their conversations, to put words to the great aching want I felt every minute of every day. In class, we read books like *Green Days by the River* and *Catcher in the Rye*. The boys in these books were obsessed with sex, with how to attain it. I was also obsessed with sex but the girls in the books didn't seem to have much interest in it at all. They existed only as objects of the boys' desires. These girls seemed not wholly real to me, the boys chasing them around the way a dog snaps its jaws at a patch of sunlight.

So when my mother asked me about the girl in the painting, I didn't answer. We stood for a few minutes, and then moved on. After the trip, we settled back into our usual patterns of bickering and mutual distrust, the distance between us only becoming vaster as the years went on. But I think about that day from time to time and I always wonder what would have happened if I had answered honestly. Would things be different now? Would I have finally gotten to see this other Pleione, the woman from my vaguest memories, in the white sunglasses, cigarette smoke escaping from red lips?

I've been with guests before, something my parents know about and tacitly ignore. But this time is different. This thing with Odie feels like I'm dancing on the sharp edge of a blade. The balance of power see-saws between us and I can feel it slipping away from me. I imagine telling my mother about Odie, about the raw immensity of my feelings for him. What would it be like to share that with her? Would she understand how it feels to want something so badly? What would it be like to spit all this wanting out at my mother's feet the way a cat gifts a mauled bird to its owner? Would she feel disgust, or would she understand, recognize something of her own feral self in me?

I watch my mother for a moment more, her face slack and exhausted in the blue light of the TV. "Mum," I say, but she either doesn't hear or ignores me. So I head for the door, stopping at the kitchen to say good night to my father, who is rinsing his plate at the sink. He stands hunched slightly to the left, favouring his good knee.

He is so big the dishes look like toys in his hands. His body seems to expand to fill any space he's in. When I was little, and we were still living in our old house in the country, my father used to measure my height in pencil along the wall of the hallway. He would measure himself on the wall, too, adding a few extra inches each time, so that I would think he was still growing, like me. One day, his pencil mark reached the ceiling and I burst into tears. I was scared he wouldn't fit in the house anymore, and he would have to leave us. Then we moved out of that house and into the even smaller cottage of the hotel, where he has to stoop to cross the threshold, where it looks as though the walls are closing in on him, as if he's wearing the whole universe on his back.

"Daddy," I say, stopping in the dark of the hallway.

"Hm?" he says, not looking up from the dishes.

"I'm going out to meet some friends, okay?" He doesn't reply. The plate in his hand is clean but he runs it under the faucet again and again. I go over to him, placing a hand on his forearm. "Dad?"

He looks up then, his eyes absent behind his glasses. He's been like this lately, even more distant than usual. Working longer hours than ever before. He smiles at me now. "You look nice," he says. "Is Matthew picking you up?"

I nod. Up close, I see he's in need of a shave. His beard is all white now. His hair too, though he keeps that cut low, almost bald. "I don't have to go," I say. "I could stay in. We could play a game of Scrabble. I need my revenge for last time."

My father smiles again, and I already know what he'll say. "Not tonight. Too tired." He turns back to the sink, staring down at the plate like he can't remember what he was doing with it. I reach over and turn off the tap. We stand there for a moment. I don't know what I'm waiting for. Maybe for the strength to tell him that sometimes I feel so out of control of my body and my thoughts that I begin to wonder if my body and my thoughts are even mine, if I'm even a real person or just a piece of loose litter getting carried along in a strong wind. The strength to admit to him that I lost my balance at some point and now life feels like I'm just falling down one endless staircase. Maybe I'm just waiting for him to ask if I'm okay.

"Don't stay out too late," my father says finally. "I need your help with a big check-in early tomorrow."

Odie's party is at a nearby restaurant, and I decide I'll walk along the beach to get there. It's not really safe to be on the beach alone at night, but I'm not afraid. I feel like a piece of meat picked down to the bone. The marrow all sucked out. There's not enough of me left to be harmed. I walk along the shore, the night sea warm and lapping against my toes, my high heels dangling in one hand. In the bottom of my purse I find half a joint leftover from the last time I hung out with Matthew. I smoke it as I walk.

Light spills out of the beachfront hotels, some small, family-owned like ours. A little worn down, painted in gaudy pinks and lime greens. Others are newer, painted white. The beach chairs of these more upscale hotels are brown wood with beige cushions instead of the peeling blue plastic of the cheaper hotels. But really, when you strip away the trimmings, it's all the same. I pass hotel after hotel, the beach bars playing the same palatable reggae or steel pan music. The guests, faces greasy from fish cakes, drunk on cheap rum, collapsing off bar stools, or else sheltering in their rooms, the a/c blasting, their skin red and peeling and sticky with the aloe creams they lather on to treat the burns.

I can't stand the smell of them, sunscreen and sweat and liquor. In the morning, they will shuffle down to the buffet in their slippers and robes. They never dress properly, the tourists, even for a night out. I wonder if this is the appeal of the island for them, the return to some barbarous state where they can wander bare-chested, feast in the moonlight, and sleep all day in the sun. Savages, all of them. For years I've served them their drinks and made their beds and nodded and smiled through it all. When I am older, I promise myself, I will never smile another fake smile again.

The beach curves inland, the sand narrowing to a thin and rocky path, and I have to lift my dress and wade through the water in order to pass. I hold my purse and shoes high above my head and keep going. By the time the beach widens again, becoming sandy once more, I am drenched. After a few more minutes, I arrive at the restaurant where Odie's event is being held. They've taken over part of the beach for the party, set up tables and a tent, the whole thing lit up with torches and fairy lights. I find a half-drunk glass of wine on a table and pick it up, just to have something to hold on to.

From here I can see inside the restaurant, where some people are sitting in large groups, the remnants of dinner still littering the tables. Other people dance in a small clearing, and a local band is playing a medley of old calypsos. The crowd is mostly white and foreign, but there's local money here too. The Bajan women are dressed just a little better, in the latest fashions they've had their seamstresses copy from British fashion magazines, their hair set and nails painted with more care than the white women, who slouch in simple sheath dresses, their hair lank, faces bare. Real money, I've learned from watching tourists come and go over the years, is quiet. I look down at my sodden dress, caked in sand and seaweed, the lace ragged and plastered to my skin. I am both over and underdressed—like wedding cake served at a dinner party.

I fish around my purse for my cigarettes, but the packet is sodden. I try to salvage one, but it's too wet to light. There are other smokers milling about, and it doesn't take long for one of them to approach me. Men seem unable to resist rescuing a woman from a cigarette that fails to light. It's like they've all seen the same movie. This man is old, in his seventies probably, but with that youthful glow that rich white men who sail always seem to have. The man proffers a cigarette and I accept it and light it, blowing the smoke over my shoulder and out towards the shadows of the beach.

"You look like you're having a far more interesting night than the rest of us," says the man, gesturing to my dress.

I smile. "I went for a walk on the shore and got caught by a rogue wave. So embarrassing," I say, sounding not the least bit embarrassed. I hold the man's gaze and count the seconds until his eyes fall again to my chest. I barely make it to three.

"I can't blame you. These parties are so dull I often think drowning might be preferable." He laughs hard at his own

joke, the sound like a dog choking on a bone. I smoke my cigarette and wait for him to speak again. Most white men, I've
found, have never met a silence they can't fill. Odie's not like
this, though, and that's one of the things I find the most attrac-
tive about him.

A waiter nears, holding a bottle of wine. The man beck-
ons him over to refill his own glass. The wine I was holding
was white, but this bottle is red, so I down mine. It is warm
and slimy with someone else's spit. I take a big gulp of the red
wine to wash it down. The torchlights cast the party in strange
shadows that I keep mistaking for people. The man, who stands
closer to me now, is bathed in an orange light that makes his eyes
appear solid black, like little vacuums. A cool wind blows in off
the ocean and I shiver. The man steps closer, so that his arm is
pressed up against my own. It's a practised gesture, innocent at
a glance, but close enough that I cannot mistake his intentions.

"Are you here alone?" he asks.

"No," I reply, not offering any further explanation. I peer
over his shoulder, searching for Odie in the throng. I don't
expect him to claim me in front of everyone, to make intro-
ductions, to spin me around the dance floor. I just want him to
see me, to know that I am here. Just a look would be enough,
one glance through the crowd. Something to remind him that I
exist, outside of the little cave we have carved out for ourselves.
That although I obey the rules he has established, I have not
been tamed. I could burn his whole little world down if I felt
like it. And tonight, maybe I do.

"It has changed a lot, since the last time I was here," the
man is saying, gesturing with his cigarette to the shore, the sea
crashing invisible in the darkness. "Some would call it development. But I'm not so sure. Hotels along every stretch of shore.

Movie theatres. Supermarkets," he says. "It used to be the only traffic jams were the ones caused by donkey carts." His laughter dissolves into a fit of coughing. He pulls out a handkerchief from his blazer pocket and hacks into it.

I fight the urge to roll my eyes. This isn't the first time I've heard something like this. Tourists are always lamenting the loss of the "authentic island experience." Like we should all be living in huts and bathing in streams for their entertainment. The man is still talking but I've stopped listening. Perhaps I ought to go inside, look for Odie there. I wouldn't need to make a scene, just a quick walk-through.

The man is still droning on. "Though of course you're too young to remember Jackie Opel. The old Coconut Creek Club. Had some good times there. Harry's Nitery. The girls used to walk out onstage stark naked." I nod politely. Then I put out my cigarette and take a step towards the restaurant.

"Listen," the man says, grabbing my arm, "I know you say you're accounted for this evening. But I can be very generous, if you're willing to consider another offer." He curls his hand, wet and clammy like a sea snake, around my arm. A bit of spit has dribbled onto his chin. I try to pull away, but his grip is firm.

"Thanks for the cigarette," I say, "have a nice night." Again, I try to wrench my wrist from his grasp, but I cannot. I remember I thought he was a sailor when he approached me, and it is that I think of now, that his fingers are knots that seem to tighten the more I struggle. So, I still, not fighting him. He takes this as a good sign, pulling me closer to him, his face only inches from mine. I glance around to see if anyone is watching, but we're in the shadows at the edge of the party. The other smokers pay us no attention.

"Don't be like that," he says. "We're all friends here. Who do you belong to? Is it Jack Thomson? He's a buddy of mine. He won't mind sharing." He reaches up and under my dress with his ropy fingers, raking at the skin of my thigh. Without thinking, I take the glass of red wine I'm holding in my free hand and bring it crashing down onto the top of his head.

I had only meant to throw the wine on him, or to slap him, but somehow both of those things had happened at once. The man lets go of me, stumbling backwards, bringing his hands to his face. Broken glass juts out of his cheeks, collects like tiny crystals in his ears and along his eyelashes. He lets out a soft mewling cry. It would be better if he roared in anger, or hit me back, but instead he curls in on himself, holding his face, making that awful noise.

The others on the beach approach. I'm still holding the stem of the wineglass in my fist and I let it fall to the sand. Someone calls for a towel, and ice. Someone else suggests we ring an ambulance. I stumble backwards, towards the restaurant. I think I need to run, back up the beach the way I came. I don't care if the tide is all the way in now. I will swim home if I have to.

But this crowd won't let me get away. Someone points at me and I am surrounded, strange hands grasping at my shoulders, my dress. "It was an accident," I say. "I was just trying to make him stop."

"The police have been called," someone says, "hold her there." More people are appearing now, from inside the restaurant. They stare at the man, their friend, on his knees now, his face stained with wine and blood. And they stare at me, their faces all blurred together in the shadows. Isn't this what I wanted? To be seen? A figure pushes his way to the front of the crowd, emerging like a buoy through the waves. He approaches me, and then stops short, staring. Odie. I reach for him but those holding me think I'm trying to run and yank me back. Odie disappears back into the crowd. A few minutes pass, my head swims. I let my captors hold my weight. What difference does it make now if I collapse in front of them all? If I fall all the way apart?

Odie reappears, this time with Z in tow. My uncle draws near, not looking at me, addressing the other guests. "I will deal with her," he says. "She works at my hotel." The crowd murmurs. For some reason, this seems to satisfy them. I've been explained. I'm one of the staff, gone astray. They've had maids who've stolen from them. Gardeners who stared too long at their daughters. They look at Z with sympathy. Good help, hard to find. My captors release me to my uncle, who doesn't touch me, still doesn't look at me. He walks towards the restaurant, and I follow. We pass quickly through the dance floor, where some guests still sway, oblivious, and out into the parking lot. He gestures to his car. "Wait here," he says.

"Uncle Z . . ." I begin. But he only holds up a hand in response, shaking his head. He goes inside. I look at my reflection in the car window. I look like a piece of jetsam. Like a secret someone tried to drown that got washed back up on the shore for all to see. Uncle Z emerges from the restaurant, followed closely by Hera, who marches straight to the passenger side, gets in, and slams the door, without glancing at me. "I have never, in my life, been so ashamed," she says finally. She sounds as though she wants to cry.

On the short drive back to the hotel, no one speaks. Z pulls into the main entrance but doesn't kill the engine. I wait for instruction. Surely, he will come inside with me, ask for an explanation. We sit in silence, Hera's perfume a heavy cloud.

When Z finally speaks, his voice is so quiet I hardly hear him. "After everything I've done for your family. Everything I do . . ." He trails off.

"I'm sorry," I say, "that man. He was trying to—"

"Get out," Z says, his eyes catching mine in the rear-view. My uncle has eyes that always seem a slightly different colour whenever I see him. Sometimes green, sometimes light brown. Right now, they shine yellow, like caution tape.

When I enter the cottage, my parents are watching TV. It has only been a couple of hours. My father looks over, and smiles. "I know I said to be home early, but nine p.m. is a little sad," he says.

I smile back. Then I go over and sit beside him, propped on the arm of the couch. "What are we watching?" I ask, but my mother shushes us both before he can respond. My father raises an eyebrow at me. In a few minutes, my uncle will get home, and our phone will ring. But for now, I can sit with my parents in peace, watching TV, and pretend that everything is okay. I hold my breath, and wait for the tide to rush in.

CHAPTER TEN

"'She's gone, I am abused, and my relief must be to loathe her,'" mumbles Othello, from where he sits slouched in the second row, his head in his hand, the words directed down at his desk. "'Oh, curse of marriage that we can call these delicate creatures ours and not their appetites.'"

"Stop there, Demarcus," says Mrs. Cossey, our English teacher. Demarcus closes his book, sitting back in his chair, visibly relieved. He lifts the collar of his school uniform and wipes the sweat from his upper lip. The air is still and humid, the classroom cocooned in mid-morning heat. It's the last period before lunch and even Mrs. Cossey, usually a fanatic for the Bard, directs our reading while sitting languidly behind her desk, fanning her face with her own well-worn copy.

"Come now," she says. "How about we try that again, this time with a little more energy?" She rests her book down, scanning the room for signs of life. Her eyes catch mine and I look away, but too slowly. "Calypso!" she says. "Begin again from the top of Othello's soliloquy."

I open my own book. I haven't been following along, and it takes a moment to find the right page. Just this effort is almost more than I can take. It's Monday and I haven't slept since Friday. I hadn't wanted to come to school today, but my parents wouldn't hear of me staying home. I clear my throat, the sound like a match being struck, and mumble my way through the verse. I only make it a few lines before Mrs. Cossey interrupts again.

"Once more from the top, Calypso. And sit up straight, please," she says. I look up at her, and then down at the book. The words crawl like ants across the page. My eyes are watering but I resist the urge to wipe away the tears. I'm not crying. I've never cried at school, never given them the satisfaction, and I'm not about to start today. Mrs. Cossey raps her knuckles on her desk impatiently. Someone behind me says something I don't hear, and a few people laugh.

Word has gotten out about what happened at the party on Friday. Inevitable, really. In Barbados, someone's aunt or second cousin or neighbour is always somewhere, watching. If my classmates thought I was trouble before, attacking a white man has cemented my reputation as downright unstable. I'm probably not helping things, showing up today with bloodshot eyes, my braids frizzy and unravelling. I stare at the lines of text, willing them to keep still. But I can't focus. My stomach is hot and roiling like a pot of boiling water. I open my mouth to speak but no sound comes out. I worry if I open my mouth again, I'll throw up all over my desk. I can feel the eyes of the class on me, waiting to see if I fall apart.

Miraculously, the bell rings for lunch and we wait to be dismissed. In American films, the bell rings, and the students all make a mad dash for the door. But in Barbados, as the teachers are fond of reminding us, "the bell doesn't dismiss us, they do." Mrs. Cossey repeats her instructions for our homework and takes her time packing her things. We all rise as she exits the room, as is custom. I sway, holding on to the edge of the desk for support. I plan to spend my lunch hour at my desk, asleep. But Mrs. Cossey stops at the door, beckoning to me. "Calypso," she says, "my office." The girls giggle, or else mumble knowingly under their breath. I ignore them and follow Mrs. Cossey out of the classroom and into the sunlit quad.

Mrs. Cossey's office is on the ground floor of one of the old limestone buildings, looking out onto the belfry and the grassy field beyond. Shadows flutter through the half-shuttered shades. Children running to the canteen, running to the playground, girls running from boys, boys running from each other. As if overnight, I have become an observer of the world of children. All of the running, jumping, skipping now seems so alien to me, like circus acts.

I haven't seen or heard from Odie since Friday. He doesn't answer the phone when I call, and my parents wouldn't let me out of their sight all weekend. That night, after he dropped me off, Z phoned my parents as soon as he got home. After the call my father left the cottage and hadn't returned by morning. I didn't sleep. Instead I spent the night at the kitchen table, waiting for him to return. At dawn, my mother joined me. She didn't ask for an explanation, just made her usual breakfast of tea and fruit salad and ate it in silence. I felt sick. The kitchen was too bright, every noise, from the humming of the refrigerator to the sound of my mother's spoon against her mug, set my teeth on edge. I dug my fingernails into the tabletop and tried to breathe, but I couldn't seem to rid myself of this feeling. I couldn't name it either. It felt like being smothered from the inside out. Like my own body was collapsing in on itself, all my insides compressed into a dense ball.

"Mum," I said, "I don't know what to do. I thought I had it all under control but it's slipping away from me." My mother reached across the table and grabbed my arm so tight it almost hurt. I thought maybe she was trying to tell me something, but as it always is with us, the moment passed like a missed bus, fading around the bend, leaving me stranded and alone. "You just need to pray on it," she said finally.

Eventually, my father had no choice but to come home. "Whatever it is you thought you were doing," he said, "it's over now." No parties, no boys. School, home, repeat. I didn't argue. I'm lucky to have gotten off so easy. Uncle Z either convinced the man from the party not to press charges or worked his connections to have them dropped. The gossip at school doesn't bother me, it's nothing new. And soon they will grow bored of me and move onto the next scandal.

Mrs. Cossey sinks heavily into her desk chair, fixing me with a long stare over her tortoiseshell frames. She is a slight woman, with a head of dyed-blond Sisterlocks that she wears piled high on her head like a plate of spaghetti. I like Mrs. Cossey, she has always seemed like the most reasonable of all the teachers. Last year, she came to the defense of a group of Fifth Form boys who'd been threatened with suspension for refusing to cut their hair when it grew longer than the regulation length of half an inch. In this place, where it seems every adult is in search of something to correct about our appearance—the length of our skirts, the height of our socks, the shine of our shoes—she is one of the only ones who seems to care more about what we're learning, rather than how we look doing it.

"So," she says, as though resuming a conversation from which we'd taken a brief pause, "what are we going to do about your situation?"

For a strange moment I think she's talking about Odie. It isn't impossible that she could know, but teachers don't make a habit of calling students into their offices to discuss their love lives. "My situation?" I ask. "Is this about the reading?"

"What?" asks Mrs. Cossey, then she waves her hand as though shooing away a mosquito. "No, no," she says, "not about that. I don't care about that. I want to talk about your future. You received some of the highest CXC marks in the island, potentially top ten in the region."

I nod, unsure where this is going. Mrs. Cossey speaks with an odd inflection, pausing for long periods. She takes one such pause now, scratching at her nose and continuing to stare at me. I wait out the silence.

"And," she continues finally, "I suspect you are quite capable of being a national scholar, or, at the very least, of winning an exhibition, which would partially fund your studies. There are always private scholarships that could make up the difference." She digs around in her desk drawer, and for a brief moment, I have the ludicrous thought that she is going to write me a cheque. Instead she pulls out a packet of tissues from which she extracts one and blows into it. "Pardon me," she says, "it's cane season. The arrows in the wind, you know, terrible for my allergies." She gestures with her hand at the invisible cane pollen swarming around us.

I still don't reply. Sweat drips down the backs of my knees. I'm itchy all over.

Mrs. Cossey sighs again. "Have you given any thought to what you might like to study? You could stay here, of course, and attend Cave Hill. Law, perhaps? Or what about Jamaica? Mona has a very reputable B.Ed. program. But if you won a scholarship, well, you could go anywhere. England, Canada..."

Before Odie, I thought I would try for a scholarship, like my father. But I wouldn't squander it like him. I would use it to get out of here, set myself up somewhere in a big city, spend my days being admired in coffee shops and my nights being admired on a stage. When I imagined going away for school, I didn't picture listening to old white men speak in grand lecture halls or having lunch with new friends in a cafeteria or whatever it is that people do at university. Instead, I pictured myself alone, truly alone for the first time. Four walls and a door that locks, no one to answer to but myself.

I wanted to be a woman who lived in a cool blue room. Who sat in windowsills wearing nothing but a white vest and underwear, watching a grey wet world go by. I wanted to smoke cigarettes and eat only toast and always be a little bit cold. In my dreams, the city outside was always dark and unwelcoming. Not a soft and pretty place with balconies and cafés. Not a dazzling neon hub either. A kind of drab and orderly city. I imagined this would be somewhere like Glasgow, or Copenhagen. Though I don't know why. I had never been to any of those places. Never even seen a photo. But I could picture the room clearly, and even the little square of imaginary street I could see through my imaginary window: crowds of people, only the tops of their umbrellas visible, swirling by like small black manta rays through a stormy sea.

But this was all before Odie rode up onto the beach on that jet ski. Whenever I try to envision any life except for one with him in it, my body rejects the image, as if it is warding off a virus. I don't say any of this to Mrs. Cossey. Outside, the lunchtime noise grows louder, swelling to the desperate din that signals break is almost over.

"Of course," Mrs. Cossey says, "none of this will matter if you continue to sleep your way through Sixth Form." She smiles tightly, showing no teeth.

"I'm sorry," I say, wanting the meeting to be over, wanting only to be home, in the hotel, where Odie can find me.

"I'm sorry, too," Mrs. Cossey says, still smiling the small smile. Then she sneezes, three loud, angry sneezes in a row. "Good lord," she says, reaching again for the tissues, "this harvest might just kill me." She rolls her desk chair over to the wall-to-wall bookshelf and, without getting up, pulls a small volume from a low shelf. "Here," she says, "I want you to read this. You don't have to give it back to me. That's yours to keep."

I take the book from her hand and place it in my lap without looking at the cover. The bell rings and the floor shakes with the footfalls of hundreds of students, racing back to class. My stomach somersaults and I bring my hand to it, pressing into the flesh.

Mrs. Cossey glances down to where I knead my belly, then up at my face, something flashing in her eyes. "Go ahead to class, Calypso," she says, dismissing me.

When I arrive back to the classroom, it is empty, except for one girl, Nadine. She sits alone at her desk, reading. She glances up when I come in.

"Where is everyone?" I ask.

"PE," Nadine says.

"Oh," I say, hovering by the door for a moment, before plopping into my own chair. I put the book Mrs. Cossey gave me in my desk, shoved to the back among the mess of pencil shavings and scrap paper. Nadine regards me warily. She is possibly the only girl in class less liked than I am. The other girls pick on her without mercy, stealing her lunch, writing disgusting things about her in the bathroom stalls. "Aren't you going?" she asks.

"What?" I stare out of the window to the quad. I wonder if I could sneak past the guards, leave school now, go to Odie's and wait for him there. I'm not supposed to go to his house during the daytime, he's made that very clear. But I need to see him.

"To PE," Nadine says. "It started fifteen minutes ago."

It takes me a minute to remember what she's talking about. "Oh . . . no. I think I'll just skip it. Wait, why are you in here?"

Nadine sits back in her chair and closes her book. "I have a written excuse," she says, her voice haughty and defensive. "I just got laser eye surgery."

I hadn't noticed she was no longer sporting her signature wire-framed glasses with the thick lenses that had always made her eyes appear twice as large. This was one of the many things the other students made fun of her about. But if Nadine thinks losing her glasses will win her any points in class, she's mistaken. Laser eye surgery is expensive. She probably flew overseas for the treatment. This is exactly the kind of thing that makes the other students hate her so much. There are other wealthy students in our year but none who garner as much animosity as Nadine. She had a sleepover for her birthday party in First Form and the girls who attended dined out on stories about it for weeks afterward, each time the tales growing more and more ridiculous. She doesn't only have her own bedroom, but an entire floor of the house to herself. Her bathroom is made entirely of gold. She has three maids who wait on her hand and foot.

I don't believe half the things the girls in school gossip about, but even I have to admit, Nadine is weird. She wears her school skirts far below her knees, when everyone knows the fashion is to hem them as high above regulation length as you can get away with. She listens to strange foreign music on her Discman alone after school and always has a written excuse from her mother to get out of any physical activity. She once brought sushi to school for lunch, cementing her status as the class freak.

She regards me now, eyes narrowed, her hands steepled beneath her chin. "You look like shit today," she says.

"Thanks, Nadine," I reply. A teacher wanders by the window and I slink further into my seat, not wanting to be caught skipping. The last thing I need is more heat from my parents right now.

"The girls were talking about you at lunch. They were saying you got arrested for prostitution and spent the weekend in jail."

"Mhm," I say, leaning my head onto my hands. I'm so tired. Maybe I could sleep here in this empty classroom, just for a few minutes. Nadine is eating her way steadily through a pack of cheese crackers. She offers me one and I take it, letting it dissolve into a paste on my tongue before swallowing.

"I told them that doesn't make any sense. Prostitution isn't even technically illegal. Only solicitation. But they didn't understand the nuance." She pops a cracker in her mouth. When she speaks again, her teeth are caked in orange cheese. My stomach lurches. "You know what they call you, right?" I look up at her, to see if she's being mean, but her voice is light, conversational.

I nod. "Yeah. Rachel Pringle. They could use some new material."

Nadine nods, pensive. "You know, Rachel Pringle was pretty badass. Legend has it she once kicked Prince William Henry out of her brothel because he was being drunk and disorderly, wrecking the furniture and stuff. And then she sent a bill to the English Crown for damages."

"Really? That's actually pretty cool." This is the longest conversation Nadine and I have ever had, despite being in the same class since we were eleven. We've always competed for the top marks, her edging me out in French and geography, me beating her in history and English. We ought to have been allies, really, joined together by the tyranny of the other girls. But that's not the way these things go. Though maybe that could change, maybe things could be different. Maybe I wouldn't have to be alone. This thought rises unbidden, and I immediately suppress it. I'm not alone, I remind myself. I have Odie.

The bell rings. In a few minutes, the rest of the students will return to class. We have one more period until school is over, but I'm not sure I can make it that long. I need to get out of here. I take my water bottle out from my backpack and force down a few sips. The rim of the bottle smells stale, the water warm and salty. I pour a few drops into my hands and use it to wet my cheeks. Then I bring my hand to my chest, searching for a heartbeat, but I can't seem to find one. I feel an aching hollowness within me where my heart should be. I press harder into my rib cage, searching.

"Are you okay?" Nadine asks. "Cali?"

"Yeah," I say, "it's just the heat." I stand, swaying slightly, and gather my things. "Listen, if Dr. Cumberbatch asks for me, tell him I've gone to the sick bay, okay?"

I don't wait for Nadine to reply. Instead I walk quickly out of class, down the spiral staircase and across the quad towards the basketball courts. I get to the small, fetid stream that borders the school, known to students as the Dippy. When we were in First Form, we used to compete to see who could jump over the Dippy, and if you fell in, you were forced to spend the rest of the day reeking of sewage. I take the river at a running jump now, and just clear it, stumbling slightly in the muck. I cross the big playing field, slipping off my school tie and shoving it in my pocket, so no one who sees me walking in town will know which school I'm from.

I'm about halfway across the field, almost to the hole in the chain-link fence through which I can escape and blend into the crowds of Bridgetown, when I hear a yell. I look back and spot one of the school guards approaching, his arms raised above his head, waving. I take off at a run, and don't look back.

I don't remember the last time I ran like this, and I welcome the ache in my muscles, the breathlessness that crowds out all my thoughts. People are rarely seen running in town, and so the other pedestrians stare at me as I pass. How long will it take my mother to hear? "That mad girl from the hotel went pelting down the road in she school uniform!" I run harder. Outside a small corner store the men holler at me as I pass, but I hardly hear them. A car honks behind me and I move out of the way. As it passes, a child's face stares at me through the back windshield. The sun shifts and I realize it's my face, flickering ghostlike in the tinted glass.

I run until the narrow, potholed streets give way to wide, paved roads. Here, the houses are further apart, their yards fenced in. A few more bends and there it is, the squat one-storey house with its low pink wall. Odie's rental car isn't parked in the drive. I glance around and then scale the gate. I have to hike my skirt up to my hips to clear the spikes.

I sneak around to the back of the house, hoping Odie has left the back door unlocked. And that's when I see her. Odie's housekeeper, hanging out washing. She appears and disappears behind billowing sheets. I turn back, but it's too late, she's spotted me. I try to run but I'm winded and slow and she catches up with me easily, grabbing me by the collar of my school shirt.

"Come here you thieving so and so!" she screams, wrenching me towards her. I try to struggle out of her grasp, but she's too strong. She lands a slap across my face. "You come here to rob the body place. And in you school uniform! The audacity of these young people, hear!"

She goes on like this for a while, as if recapping the story for some invisible audience. "I catch she trying to rob the people place! Middle of the day. These young people have no broughtupsy at all at all."

By now I've stopped fighting. I let her talk herself out. When finally she pauses for a breath I say, "I'm not a thief. I'm here to see Odie. He's expecting me."

"Oh, he's expecting you!" the housekeeper says, looking around at the empty garden as if for someone to commiserate with. She looks to be in her early forties, thin and wiry but strong, her hair pulled into a severe bun at the top of her head. Her eyes narrow. She lets my shirt go. "Lord help me," she says. "How old you is?"

I raise my chin. "I'm not here to be questioned by you. I'm a guest of your employer."

She sucks her teeth then. And turns back to her washing. "Go on then," she says, dismissing me. "You may wait in the kitchen. But don't go dirtying up the place! I now finish mop."

I can still hear her mumbling as I head inside, stopping to undo my shoes and leave them on the mat. My legs are filthy, the hem of my school skirt caked with dirt. Blood oozes from a dozen small nicks along my shins. I head straight to the sink and hunch over the tap and cup my hands to drink, the water spilling down my shirt and onto the floor. I drink until my stomach bloats and I can't swallow another drop. Then I splash my face and wash my hands with dish soap. I take a paper towel and clean up the mess I've made. Then I sit at the table to wait.

A few minutes pass and the housekeeper comes in, holding a basket of clean linens. She's humming a tune under her breath. I recognize the hymn, though it's been a few years since my mother was able to cajole me into a church.

"Well you might as well help me fold, as you here," she says, beckoning me to my feet. She takes a sheet out of the basket and thrusts one end into my hands. We take a few steps apart, folding the sheet lengthwise, then we take a step closer, folding as we go. When we're only a few inches apart, she sighs, placing the sheet on the table and jutting out her hand. "My name is Ms. Clarke," she says, putting great emphasis on the zee sound of her title.

I hesitate, and then take her hand. "Calypso," I say.

She gives my hand a brief squeeze and then nods efficiently, as if relieved to be done with polite formalities. "And what part it is you go school, Calypso?" she asks. "If you don't mind my asking." She says the last part with more than a hint of sarcasm, which I ignore.

"Harrison College," I say, trying and failing to sound indifferent. As much as I like to think myself above Barbados's outdated school ranking system, I still feel a frisson of pride for attending one of the best schools on the island.

For her part, Ms. Clarke seems unimpressed. "I could never understand why it is them had to go and make all the secondary schools coed. Harrison College used to produce plenty of fine young men. I don't see how them can expect young boys to thrive with all uh these"—she pauses here, her eyes flicking up to meet mine briefly—"distractions."

"Oh, I agree," I reply. "Every day I think about how I'm jeopardizing the futures of my male classmates. The guilt overwhelms me."

To my surprise, Ms. Clarke lets out a loud, bellowing laugh. The sound is improbable coming from her tiny frame. Like a teakettle that belches instead of whistles. "You is a force-ripe young thing, nuh?" she says, still smiling. I don't reply. "Harrison College . . . ," she goes on, "my daughter did put that down as her first choice for the Common Entrance. But she did only pass for St. Michael's."

"St. Michael's is a really good school," I say. "I actually wanted to go there, because that's where most of my primary school friends went. But when I passed for Harrison College, my parents insisted I go there instead." I don't know why I'm telling her all of this.

"Rightly so," says Ms. Clarke.

"How old is your daughter now?" I ask.

"My eldest is nearing thirteen. I got two more. The middle child getting ready to sit Common Entrance next year. And the youngest only now turn six."

"All girls?"

"Yes," Ms. Clarke says, smiling. "The Lord bless me with three beautiful girls. I did often wish for a son. But truth be told, I don't know what I would do if I had got one. I didn't have nothing but sisters myself."

"I'm an only child," I say, as if confessing to some fatal flaw. I reach into the basket and pull out a towel. I roll it up into a tight cylinder, like we do at the hotel.

Ms. Clarke shakes her head and takes the towel from my hands. "Not so," she says, "he fussy like that. Got to be square, and flat." She refolds the towel, taking extra care to line up the corners.

"Do you know when he will be back?" I ask.

Ms. Clarke frowns. "I don't presume to know his comings and goings," she says, her voice absent of warmth again. The disapproval emanates from her body like a strong perfume. I don't mind it.

"Smart girl like you," she continues, "you planning and go university?"

I shrug, thinking of my earlier conversation with Mrs. Cossey. "Maybe. If I get the marks."

Ms. Clarke nods in approval. "I can do all through him who gives me strength," she says.

"Amen," I say, and Ms. Clarke's frown deepens.

"You know," she says, "there are other girls, many of them just as smart as you, just as pretty, who never going to have the kinds of opportunities you do."

I try to interrupt, to assure her she's mistaken about me. But she only holds a hand up, cutting me off.

"My eldest, Lucille," she says, "she does love to swim. Lord help me I ain't know where she got it from because I can't stand to even get my head wet. But she's be in the water every chance she get. You should have see she at sports day last term. Caw blen, my girl cut through that water like it did air. She win gold medal in breaststroke and freestyle. She only get silver in the butterfly, and oh she did vex. She don't like to be nothing but the best, my Lucille. The coach tell me she could make the

national team, if she train good. But you know them does prac-
tise after school every day at three o'clock, and Lucille have
to pick up her little sisters when they finish school. She have to
bring them home and cook them something to eat. Because I
can't do it, you see? I don't finish here until near six o'clock."

"I have a job," I say. "I work at a hotel."

"There are certain kinds of girls," Ms. Clarke says, raising
her voice slightly. The laundry is all folded now, but she still
peers down at her hands, as if they are busy at work. "Who take
up with an older man. And though I would never allow it for
my own child, I understand it. You see? When I see these girls
coming to and fro at all hours, I just say a little prayer because I
know them just trying to find a way."

"What girls?" I ask.

"But a smart girl like you. You should be at home of an evening, doing your homework. Not running around with a man
like that. It's not right."

"Ms. Clarke," I say, reaching for her hand. She lets me take
it. "What other girls? There are other girls? Staying here?"

Ms. Clarke squeezes my hand gently and smiles. "Calypso.
What a funny name. You parents had to know you would be
wayward with a name so."

A door slams and Ms. Clarke jumps, standing quickly and
gathering the folded linens in her arms.

Odie enters like an eclipse. He's dressed in a blue button-
down, khakis, and workboots that are caked in muddy sand. If
he's surprised to see me, he hides it well. He sets his briefcase
down on an empty chair and pours himself a glass of water. I
am perfectly still. Ms. Clarke stutters out a greeting and disappears into another room. Odie drains his glass and fills it again.
His boots have left a horrible mess on the clean tile. The back

of his neck is burnt red, his shirt is dark blue around the base of his spine where the sweat pools.

I hold my breath, waiting. In the time we've been together, I've taken Odie soft and limp in my mouth like raw fish. I've heard him whisper my name like it answered every question he ever needed answering. And still, looking at him, I feel like I'm folding in on myself, into smaller and smaller pieces, until I'm as flat and square as one of his towels. I'm not supposed to be here. Odie made that clear, never during the daytime, only when he calls me. This arrangement is as much for my benefit, Odie said, as his own. My reputation is at stake here, as much as his, he said.

Odie finishes his second glass, but still doesn't turn. I cannot gauge his mood, cannot anticipate what he will do, and this fills me with a sick kind of excitement. It's been years since someone struck me. The last time was in primary school when I was caught in the bathroom with a boy. I hardly remember him now, Dario or Mario or something. I had convinced him to show me his penis, in exchange for two silver dollars. He hadn't even unbuttoned his pants yet when a cleaner came in, hollering the place down.

I was the only one who got flogged, the teachers knew me well enough by then to deduce who had instigated the whole thing. It was Mr. Worrel who beat me, the deputy headmaster. He was an impossibly tall man, at least to my eyes at that age, towering over me like a streetlight, his big eyes glittering behind his round glasses. He'd talked to me for a long time before the beating, as I stood with my tunic hiked around my waist, my bloomers at my knees. I was wearing white cotton underwear with a small pink bow. That I remember. I kept my eyes down while he talked, looking only at that satin bow.

His lecture was long and winding, his voice growing more distraught. He had great regret for what he was called to do, he'd said. But felt he had no choice. The beating itself was brief, and not very painful. It seemed to take more out of Mr. Worrel, who collapsed onto his chair afterwards, his body rigid, like a felled tree. I remember he didn't speak, only waved one hand to dismiss me. I looked at him prone in his chair as I fixed my clothes. He was so stiff I thought that if I were to just tap him lightly on the side of his head, he would crumble beneath my fingertip, like shattered glass.

Odie looks a bit like that now, all the muscles in his back bunched beneath his shirt like knotted bark. I wonder if he will hit me. I wonder what I would do if he did. Sometimes, I find Odie nauseating. He's always sweaty. It seeps through the pores of his skull so his hair lies thin and flat across his scalp, the pink flesh poking through. After sex he reeks like turned milk. But what does it say about me, then, that I turn to him in these moments, my head buried in his neck, breathing him in? When he rises from bed to pee, his bones creak like the bedsprings themselves. I watch him sometimes, bathed in the harsh white light of the bathroom, neck bent, penis in hand, his long pale back exposed. He looks like an old man then, and I'm filled with a tender affection for him that threatens to give way to disgust. Other times, like now, he fills me with lust so intense it feels like fear. If he asked me to, I would lick his muddy footprints off the tile. He still hasn't turned around.

I had planned to apologize for Friday night. To explain, to beg forgiveness. But instead I sit ramrod straight in my chair. "Do you bring other girls here?" I ask.

Odie turns, finally, leaning against the fridge. His arms dangle at his sides, but there's nothing casual about the pose. I uncross my legs. His eyes flicker down, then back up. He takes two steps forward, so he's standing above me. I open my legs wider. He sinks to the floor between my knees and lays his head against my thigh. I run my fingers through the damp hair that falls onto his forehead. He kisses the inside of my leg and looks up at me, his eyes soft and sorry. I feel a frisson of disappointment, and them am instantly ashamed of myself. Like when I was a child and was always a little bit sad when a hurricane passed the island by, without wreaking any havoc.

He runs a hand along the back of my calf. "You're filthy," he says.

"I know," I say. "I ran here."

Odie nods, like this makes all the sense in the world. "It's happened a few times," he says, mouthing the words into my legs. "When I was drinking. It meant nothing." He kisses my leg again, and then again, pushing my skirt higher as he goes. He reaches for my underwear with both hands. I lift myself off the chair slightly and let him pull them down to my ankles. "Can you forgive me?"

I open my legs wider in response. Odie looks up at me like a dog waiting for scraps. But somehow it feels as though I'm the one on my knees.

Odie breathes deep. When he exhales, I feel it in my chest.

CHAPTER ELEVEN

About three weeks later, I'm standing at the main entrance to the hotel, once again waiting for Matthew to pick me up. As expected, my parents have been consumed by the duties of the hotel, too busy to keep tabs on me. I'm counting on this today. Matthew arrives, with his dad's fishing boat hooked to a trailer behind the car. I get into the passenger seat, the leather hot beneath my thighs. Outside the sun glints off every surface—the road, the hood of the car, even the silver-green leaves of the palm trees. I pull my shades down from my hair. I can tell from the way Matthew is gripping the steering wheel that I'm in for a lecture. I blow a fat pink bubble with my gum and let it pop against my lips, waiting.

"I don't know about this, Cal," Matthew says, finally. I sigh, more out of relief than exasperation. The sooner I can get on with the business of talking him around to my plan, the faster we can be out of here. I bring a hand to his knee. The flesh there is dry and warm, his coarse hairs rising to attention beneath my touch. I'll never tire of this, the way my hands can create a physical reaction in a man this way. When we were in primary school, back when I had friends, the girls in my class would play at being witches, holding our fingers beneath each other's flat bodies in an attempt to make them levitate. I feel a similar thrill when I touch Matthew now, even the slightest brush of my skin against his is enough to cause a reaction. Better than a magic trick. Matthew looks down at my hand for a second, and then lightly cups his own around it, like a child trapping a butterfly.

We're supposed to be in school today, but I've heard a rumour that they are demolishing the old hotel on the site where Odie's new one is to be built. Though I can't explain why, I feel like I have to see it. Maybe it's because every day I feel like I'm imploding from the inside and I think it might be a relief to see this feeling manifested. The original hotel has been around since before I was born, and though it's been empty for years, left to fall into disrepair, it still has a kind of old-world glamour to it. My father told me that when he was young it was one of the most fashionable resorts on the island. And now Odie is going to flatten it to make room for something newer, bigger, and flashier.

The construction site is under lockdown, entry forbidden. Odie's company has bought up all the wooden chattel houses in the surrounding neighbourhood, and they too are now cordoned off and will be razed later, with bulldozers. It will be next to impossible to witness the demolition from land.

"We're not doing anything illegal," I say, though I'm not entirely sure this is true. "I just want to see it, we don't have to get close."

"The sea can get really rough out this side," Matthew says.

"But you've taken the boat out here before, right? With your dad?"

"Yeah, a few times, but—"

"So what are you worried about then?" I pop my bubble gum again and grin. Matthew rolls his eyes at me. Then he laughs and starts the engine. He shakes his head slightly but doesn't say anything else.

We take the highway, the traffic stop-and-go. Just past the airport, Matthew exits at a roundabout. We'll be taking side roads the rest of the way. The air is cooler here, the road lined with tall grass, and I lean my head against the window frame and let the wind rush against my face. Matthew lights his cigarette and the car fills with smoke. I breathe in the heady smell. I like him most when he's driving; he handles the car with a confidence he never shows with me. He's so handsome, even in profile, his face like a royal bust on a copper coin. For a moment I consider telling Matthew to forget about the plan, to just keep driving. We could head up the coast to Bathsheba, spend the day at the beach getting stoned and swimming in the sheltered reef pools there. I haven't been in years. I could let him kiss me if he tried to, let myself be loved by someone good for once. But before I can say anything, Matthew turns off this road, heading a way I don't recognize.

"Where are we going?" I ask, feeling stupid. This was my idea but I don't have any real plan.

"Secret spot," Matthew says, winking. He's getting into the adventure, like I knew he would. "There's a hidden bay that the dealers use as a drug drop. Boats come in from Jamaica and Saint Vincent in the middle of the night and dock there."

"Have you been exploring alternative career options or something?" I ask. Matthew always seems to know things about the island that I don't. He can navigate his way through even the remotest villages, and he's always bumping into people he knows. He seems to have a thousand cousins. He's rooted here in a way that I'm not. He reminds me of my mother in this way.

"It's the closest place I can think of that's safe to launch the boat. We'll still have to motor a bit to get in front of the hotel though. Hopefully it's not too choppy."

We take the narrow, winding road through a village. The homes here are mostly chattel houses, some with permanent brick extensions built onto the back. Matthew slows to walking speed. A group of boys are playing road tennis, a single plank of plywood stretching the breadth of the road. They lift it out of our way, staring into the car as we pass. The closer we get to the coast, the fewer houses we see. The paved road gives way to gravel, and then dirt, until it abruptly ends. In front of us is a rocky plain, dotted with crabgrass and sea grape. I can't see the sea but I can hear it rumbling, the sound seems to be coming from beneath us.

"The bay is just there," Matthew says. "We'll need to reverse down." He drives in a wide arc so the car is now facing the other way, and then he puts it in reverse, twisting around in his seat. He's frowning, angling his neck to see past the boat trailer.

"You okay?" I ask.

He nods. "Yeah, my dad usually handles this part." We inch slowly backwards, rolling slightly downhill. The ground is craterous beneath us, and I have to brace my hands on the dash to keep from bouncing out of my seat. The boat trailer whines and creaks. We begin to pick up speed as the gradient steepens, the weight of the boat pulling us quickly backwards.

"Matthew . . ." I say.

He gears down, his foot flat on the brake. Sweat beads on his forehead. "It's okay," he says. "I got it." He yanks the hand-brake and the car lurches to a stop. I glance in the side mirror. The sea glistens just behind us. Matthew gets out and I follow, stepping onto sand. The cove is empty but for a single Blackbelly sheep tethered to a spindly tree. There's an abandoned net and an overturned bucket on the small crescent of sand. The sea is so close, crashing up against the rocks on either side of us.

"Damn," Matthew says. "It's rougher than I thought. I should have checked the tides."

"It'll be okay," I say. Now that we're here, I'm determined to see it through.

Matthew hesitates but doesn't argue, unhooking the fishing boat from the trailer and wading it out into the shallows. The waves smack against the bow, and Matthew struggles to keep it steady. He tries to climb on, but a big wave sends the boat sideways, washing it back up onto the sand. Matthew tries again, but this time the boat nearly capsizes. He hauls it back onto shore.

"Sorry, Cali," he says, panting. "It's just too rough. Maybe we can try to drive closer to the hotel. There might be somewhere we can park with a view."

I glance out at the sea. Close to shore, the waves tower over our heads, a constant barrage. But maybe twenty feet further out, the sea looks calmer, the swells rising and falling like the chest of a sleeping giant. No whitecaps, none of that swirling foam in which it is easy to lose all sense of space and time.

I strip down and dive in before Matthew has a chance to stop me. I think I hear him scream my name before I submerge. I can't see anything, the sand churning in the break. I stay deep, close to the sand, and pull a few long strokes before coming up for air. I mistime my ascent and a wave snaps my head back, sending me under and back towards the shore.

I dive again, looking up at the surface from below, watching the waves ebb and flow, leaving their feathery tails above me. This time I stay down as long as I can, until my lungs throb, and by the time I come up for air, I'm beyond the break. The swells are bigger than I thought, and the current threatens to carry me further east, parallel to the shore, away from the cove, where I risk being smashed against the cliff face. I swallow fear and swim out a bit further, keeping an eye on Matthew, making sure I stay level with him.

From here I have a good view of the shoreline. The perspective is unsettling. It feels strange to see the edges of the island rising up from the ocean, a literal rock in the middle of a vast sea. This place, the only one I've ever known, seems suddenly so finite to me, so contained. I have the strangest thought, like I could just keep swimming, out to the horizon, leaving it behind me, no more significant than a grain of salt cast over my shoulder to thwart the devil. Matthew is waving his arms, his body a collection of black lines in the distance.

The construction site is clearly visible from this vantage point. I can see where a small crowd of invited guests has gathered to watch the demolition from a safe distance. The hotel looks unremarkable from here, smaller than I remember it. The walls are a dirty white, the crumbling turrets a poor imitation of a real castle. It might have been a magnificent place once, but now it looks like a child's old dollhouse, neglected and abandoned. My father says there has been some pushback from local preservation groups who want the original structure restored, rather than demolished and replaced. They're here today too, holding a small protest just outside the police cordon, too far away to witness the demolition.

I tread water for another ten minutes or so, until my legs feel like anchors beneath me. Then, just as I'm about to give in, a siren blares, followed moments later by what sounds like fireworks, multiple bombs going off in quick succession. There's a pause and then a new sound, like the earth itself is cleaving open, and the hotel begins to crumble inwards. I try not to blink, not to miss anything, but it's over quickly. The building disappears into a cloud of smoke. The crowd cheers. The relief I thought I would feel doesn't come.

Until now, the construction project had felt abstract, its only significance in my life the hours Odie spent working on it, away from me. But watching that demolition has shown me more about Odie than he has ever revealed himself. Imagine coming to a place you've never been before and crushing one of its landmarks into dust. How small this island must seem to him, nothing more than a rocky patch of earth on which he can make his fortune. What could I possibly mean to a man who spends his life travelling from place to place, forever altering their landscapes in his wake?

I look back to the bay where Matthew is little more than a dot on the sand, and I am suddenly aware of how far I've gone. Fear seizes my arms and legs and I have to fight to stay afloat. I swim to shore in a panic, as if I'm being chased; with each breath the shore seems no closer. I reach the whitewater at last and I'm washed into shore by the tumbling waves. Matthew wades in, half carrying me onto the sand. "Jesus Christ," he's saying. His hands are warm. I collapse onto the sand and he kneels beside me. "Jesus fucking Christ," he keeps saying.

I lie back, catching my breath. My heart slows and my breathing quiets, until I can no longer hear it over the crashing of the waves. In the distance, more sirens sound.

"Do you hear that?" Matthew asks.

I nod. "Sirens? Are they doing another explosion?"

"I don't think so. Those sound like ambulance sirens."

The sirens get louder as they approach us, and then die suddenly.

"That sounds like they've gone to the construction site," Matthew says. "Maybe someone got hurt."

"That's not possible. He . . . they wouldn't let that happen," I say, sounding more confident than I feel. Just a few nights ago, Odie and I were having sex on his couch, the seven o'clock news playing on mute in the background. I was on top, and when he came, his body flailed beneath mine like a beached fish. "You're going to fucking kill me," he'd said, his face red, body slick with sweat. And I'd believed myself capable of it, then. I felt powerful, like I had a hold over him that could not be broken. But now I'm not so sure. Now I think Odie could send this whole island crumbling into the sea, sail away, and never look back.

"We should go," Matthew says, helping me to my feet.

We drive back the way we came, stopping at a rum shop for Guinness and fish cakes, which we eat pulled over on the side of the road, parked facing the beach. Matthew is quiet, and every few seconds he glances at me, takes a big breath, and exhales.

"Spit it out," I say finally.

"What?" Matthew asks, his mouth full of fish cake.

"Whatever it is you want to say, just say it."

Matthew chews and swallows. He stares out the windshield. Just a fifteen-minute drive away, back where we were, the sea was chaotic and rough, but here it twinkles a serene blue in the afternoon sun. "That was fucking scary," he says. He balls up his tinfoil and drops it at his feet.

"I'm sorry," I say, reaching for his knee. This time he doesn't hold my hand, but stares down at it, as though it's a problem that requires solving. He looks at me, leaning closer, his body twisted awkwardly over the handbrake. He presses his forehead into mine. "I thought I lost you," he says, breathing into my mouth. He smells like fish and beer. I resist the urge to pull away, instead bringing my hand to his shoulder, holding him at bay.

"Matthew," I say, "stop."

Matthew inches further forward, nestling into my neck. I don't fight him. We've been here before, a few times, and I know I just have to wait it out.

"I want you so badly," he says. I stifle a groan of impatience. He seems so young to me now, like a boy repeating a line he heard in a movie. He takes my hand in his and guides it up his shorts, towards his erection.

I yank my hand away as if scalded, lurching back from him so fast I nearly smack my head into the passenger window. Matthew shifts back into his own seat, not looking at me. I cross my arms and wait for the apology I know is coming. Matthew pouts for a while, his chest heaving.

"You know I'd never do anything to hurt you, right?" he says finally.

"I know," I say, "it's okay."

"But sometimes," he goes on, speaking as if to himself, "it feels like that's what you want."

"What do you mean?"

Matthew sighs. "I think you want someone to hurt you. I think that's why you're always . . . doing what you do."

I raise an eyebrow and set my teeth on edge. "And what is it that I do exactly, Matt? Fuck men that aren't you?"

Matthew shakes his head. He looks like he might cry. I think if that happens, I will climb out of the car and walk the rest of the way home.

"Because that's what this is really about, isn't it?" I go on, my voice rising. "This bullshit psychoanalysis? You just can't handle that I don't want to be with you and so you think the only explanation is that I must be damaged?"

"Forget it," Matthew says, starting the engine. "Forget I said anything." A faint breeze blows in off the sea. Matthew reaches for my hand again. I let him hold it, limp in my lap. I can't stand him in this moment; the weak desperation that radiates off his body makes me ill. "I'm sorry," he says. "You just scared me today. You have no idea how much that scared me."

"Just take me home, Matt," I say. He gives my hand a squeeze, and then lets go. He nods once, quickly, and then again, as if affirming some silent decision.

Matthew drops me off at the main entrance to the hotel and I enter through the lobby. No one is at reception, and the security guard is away from his station too. I check the main office, but it too is empty. I head to the bar, where most of the staff have gathered around one of the tables. Over the loudspeakers, instead of the usual reggae and calypso, a local AM radio station airs. My parents are there too, but they don't seem to be telling any of the staff to get back to work. My mother looks up when I arrive, her face shifting into a dozen different expressions before settling on a frown.

"Where have you been?" she asks, stepping towards me.

"I was with Matthew," I say, hoping she won't notice that I'm not in school uniform.

"We've been worried," she says. "We thought you were with . . . we thought you might have been there. Why are you all sandy?"

My father shushes us both and turns up the volume. It's a call-in show, and the host is on the line with someone who claims to live near to the demolition site. The caller is describing the implosion, the sound it made. Then the host interrupts. They have the project manager on the line, who will be able to provide more information about the accident.

At the sound of Odie's voice, I lock eyes with my mother, who nods, anticipating my question. I open my mouth to speak but she signals for me to be quiet.

"We're working with the local corps of engineers as well as the police to determine what happened," Odie says. "At this time, it's too early to draw conclusions. We are, of course, deeply saddened by this tragedy and express our condolences to the families of the deceased."

"Given the police involvement, are we to assume the deaths are being treated as suspicious?" asks the host.

"There's no reason to suspect that this was anything more than a tragic accident." Odie's voice sounds familiar but distorted through the radio. I bring my hand to the speaker, and it vibrates gently against my fingertips. The show goes to commercial.

"Alright everyone," my father says. "Back to work."

"Daddy, what happened?" I ask.

My father removes his glasses, wiping them with the collar of his shirt. "Something went wrong with the demolition. People died."

"How many people?"

"They haven't confirmed. At least two boys from the village. They think they might have snuck in to watch."

My mother shakes her head. "I said from the get-go that whole thing sounded so dangerous." This is the first time I've heard her say this, but I don't comment. I turn to head back to the lobby. I need to know what happened. To find out what went wrong, who is to blame. I will catch the bus to Odie's house and I will wait there until he comes home. But my mother calls after me. "Where it is you think you're going?"

"Just for a walk," I say.

My mother sucks her teeth. "You're going inside to take a shower. And then you're going to do your homework and help me with dinner."

I look to my dad for support, my eyes pleading. But he shakes his head. "Listen to your mother, Calypso."

"Can we call Uncle Z?" I ask, desperate. "Ask him for more information?"

"He will be busy right now," my father says.

"Their poor mothers," my mother says, speaking mostly to herself. "Why wouldn't they check that the property was empty, first?"

I collapse onto one of the bar stools, my legs finally giving out.

"People will be vex," my father says, his voice grave. "The residents were already unhappy about being displaced by the construction. This could get very ugly."

"But it's not Odie's fault," I say. "They can't blame him because some children scaled a fence." I close my eyes and press the heels of my palms into the sockets.

My mother widens her eyes at me. "You don't even know that man," she says, in her churchy voice. The one I hate the most.

"Whatever," I say, turning to leave.

"You're staying here tonight," my father says. I turn back to look at him. His face is unreadable. Even after what happened at the party, my parents never explicitly addressed my relationship with Odie. I don't know how much they know. I suspect they think I have a schoolgirl crush. Do they know that most nights, when I say I'm studying with friends, I'm with him? I almost always make it home early enough so as not to arouse suspicion. "People will be angry," my father says. "The streets won't be safe."

I nod, and then go up on my tiptoes to kiss his cheek. He takes my hand for a moment, and I think he might say something else. But he lets it go and busies himself behind the bar once more.

In the cottage, I try calling Odie at home, but no one picks up. I collapse onto the bed, not bothering to shower. My skin is caked in sand and salt. When I close my eyes, all I can see is billowing smoke, brick crumbling into clouds of dust. I picture the two boys. I imagine them still alive, trapped beneath all that rubble. I know the hotel had been empty for years before the explosion, but in my mind's eye, the boys are buried beneath fine furnishings, soft bedding, beach towels. I wonder if the boys had ever slept in a hotel. I wonder if they would have been allowed on the premises of Odie's new resort.

When I fall asleep, I dream of a breakfast buffet, fruit and pastries piled almost to the ceiling, waiters in tuxedos serving tourists who dine in surf shorts and bikinis. I walk beside the long, laden table, my plate empty, unable to decide what to eat first. It all looks too good to be true, the fruit waxy and plastic. I hear a small voice. Someone is hiding beneath the table. It's a boy. I lift the edge of the cloth and crawl in to join him. His eyes are wide and he's laughing, so I laugh too.

"How did you get in here?" I ask him.

But he only giggles in reply, his little chest puffed out like a proud pigeon. He brings a finger to his lips. "Shh," he says.

"You have to go home," I say. "It's not safe here. These people, they will eat you up. Don't you know that? They will eat you alive."

🍐 *CHAPTER TWELVE*

CONSTRUCTION ON THE NEW HOTEL HAS BEEN SHUT down pending an investigation. The two boys who died were ten and twelve, brothers. They lived in one of the houses in the village that had been displaced by the construction, and so they knew the neighbourhood, were easily able to sneak into the site.

They were just curious, their mother says to the news cameras when they show up at her front door early the next morning. She is a big woman, and when she wails, it seems like she is emitting a tidal wave from her body. The reporters all step back, as if bracing for impact. Her hair is in rollers, and when I watch her on the morning news, I wonder what it will be like when she takes them out, knowing that when her hair was pressed and set the day before, her children were alive.

It's been three days since the accident, and it's all anyone can talk about at school. Today I eat my lunch alone at one of the picnic tables outside the canteen while my classmates gossip nearby. LeDonna, whose mother is Permanent Secretary for one of the ministers, claims that the government plans to shut down the project entirely. Matthew watches me from a nearby table. He looks like a dog on a leash, his body wound up tight, his jaw clenched. He keeps cracking his knuckles as if he's ready for a fight. I don't know who exactly he's angry at, me, or Odie, or the whole damn world. Every time someone brings up the death of the boys, he shakes his head violently like he's trying to get water out of his ears and says, "Someone needs to do something about it."

Nadine joins me at my table. Her hair is pulled back into one puff today, the fly-aways held back by a thick headband. She doesn't say anything, only pulls out her lunch and lays it out on the table between us like a picnic, several spreads and dips in small jars.

She offers one to me, its contents an unfamiliar greyish goop. "Baba ghanoush?"

I shake my head and Nadine shrugs. I wonder what she really thinks of me, how much of the gossip she hears, or pays attention too. We sit in silence together through lunch. Nadine never brings up the demolition or the boys' death. When the bell rings to signal the end of lunch, she places a hand on my forearm and squeezes lightly, the touch so brief I almost miss it.

That evening, I help my mother make dinner. My father is in the living room, sprawled on the couch, listening to *Down to Brass Tacks*, the call-in radio show. The deaths at the hotel dominate the news. People call in from all over the island, neighbours, people who knew the family, but strangers too, calling to give their condolences, to vent, to cry. In the kitchen, I can't make out the words, but I can feel the anger in the rhythms of the voices. I try to tune it out but it's as if they're speaking right

to me, their lips against my ears. The air in the kitchen is hot
and still, the stench of the hotel dumpsters mingling with the
steam from the pot of rice my mother is boiling. I feel like I
could take a hundred showers and never be clean.

My parents go to bed late, and so it's almost one a.m. when I
sneak through the living room and out onto the hotel grounds.
I let myself into the reception office. The computer terminals
hum softly in the dark, their power lights flashing. The hotel
lobby is lit up bright, and Malcolm, one of our security guards,
gives me a small wave from his perch. I wave back. He's used to
seeing me here at night. I sometimes come to do my homework
or use the Internet when everyone else has gone home.

Now, I pick up the phone and dial out. I call Odie on his
landline, just like I have every night since the demolition, but
again he doesn't pick up. The phone rings ten times, and then
goes to voicemail. In the lobby, the occasional guest passes by,
and I make sure not to turn any lights on in case they come
and ask for something. I sit in the dark for a few more minutes, spinning the chair in slow circles. Then I call again,
planning to leave a message, but this time Odie picks up after
a few rings.

"Hi," I say.

"Hi you," he says, exhaling.

"I heard what happened," I say, "on the news."

"It's been a rough couple of days," Odie says, his voice small,
"very rough. I miss you." This is the kind of thing I'm always
hoping he'll say to me and I always thought I'd feel victorious
when he did, like I'd finally won the game we've been playing this
whole time. But I feel nothing. I press my cheek into the phone,
try to imagine the feel of Odie's cheek against mine, but when I
close my eyes all I see is rubble and smoke. Ruin and death.

"Come get me," I say.

Odie breathes quietly in response. "I'll be there in twenty minutes."

We drive along the coast in silence for a while, until the road curves inland and the hotels disappear, replaced by government offices, rum shops, and public housing. We cruise along Bay Street and into Bridgetown. The city is quiet on weeknights, and we pass through it without seeing another car. Odie doesn't head back to the coast road, but instead takes us through the tangle of arterial roads just outside the capital, the part of the island most tourists never see, where all the houses crowd in on each other like too many teeth. New Orleans, Deacons Farm, Grazettes. He navigates the small streets easily and I want to ask him what he's been doing on the nights he's not with me that could possibly bring him to this part of the island. But I'm scared to know the answer.

"Can you tell me what happened," I ask, instead, "with the explosion? What went wrong?"

Odie doesn't respond. He smokes his cigarette in long drags, not looking at me. I reach across the gear stick and poke his knee.

"I don't want to talk about it, Cali," he says. "I came and got you because I want to get my mind off all that."

Shame blossoms in the pit of my stomach, curdling into anger. I reach for the pack of cigarettes and take one for myself. I smoke in silence, willing myself to let it go. Not to provoke him. But every time I blink, I picture myself back in the sea, watching a piece of my home collapse into rubble. I can't stop thinking about the boys, their mother, the sound of her cries like someone had lit her on fire from the inside, like she was burning to death but no one could see it.

"I'm not a fucking distraction," I say finally, my words disappearing out the window with my cigarette smoke.

Odie doesn't take his eyes off the road when he replies. "That's exactly what you are."

"Pull over," I say, "I can't stand another second in this car with you." I don't really mean it so I'm jarred when Odie immediately wrenches the car to a stop. We're on a quiet street, the houses all dark, their curtains drawn like shuttered eyelids.

I hesitate. I'm too far from home to walk and there are no buses at this time. I don't even know exactly where we are. Odie's face is placid beside me, but I can see the grim line of his mouth, the way his hands twitch on the steering wheel.

"You don't give a fuck about any of it. Do you?" I say, my voice shrill and desperate. I hate how I sound but I can't stop. "You don't give a fuck about me. About this island. About those boys. They were just collateral damage, right? The cost of doing business? You're sick. You're a murderer. You—"

Odie's hands are around my throat before I can get another word out. He exhales, his breath mingled with smoke, and raises a finger to my face. I freeze, growing perfectly still like a small prey animal trying to make itself invisible on a wide-open plain. My heart pounds beneath my rib cage. This close I can smell the rum on his breath, almost taste the sickly sweet stench of it on my tongue. I hate him, I realize in this moment. I hate him and I hate myself for wanting to be with him still, despite it all. Odie's grip tightens and my vision blurs. I don't fight it because I know that's what he wants. For me to thrash beneath him like a pinned animal, scratch his face, make him bleed.

Odie leans in closer. "You fucking bitch," he says, his hand still wrapped around my throat. "You don't know shit about me. You don't know anything. You're a child. You think that because you strut about that hotel and fuck any white man who looks at you twice you know something about the way the world works but you don't. Who are you to judge me? I know all about the people you come from. Z has told me all the family secrets."

He lets me go then, and I collapse, lungs burning and eyes watering, onto the seat. I take a few shuddering breaths, none of which seem to reach my lungs. I wonder if this is what drowning feels like. "Z," I manage finally, "is a liar and a drunk."

Odie laughs. "Oh yes, he's a drunk, a sloppy one. The kind of drunk who likes to get weepy and talk about his father. About how he was haunted by all the things he'd done. Your precious Cronus, the legend, was a murderer. And Z is still cleaning up the mess he left behind."

"You don't know what you're talking about," I say. My heart pounds against my rib cage and I can still feel where Odie's hands were against my throat a moment ago, a phantom presence.

Odie speaks again, his voice dripping with contempt. "Cronus murdered his own father. Your grandfather Iapetus saw the whole thing and it drove him insane. He ran away from home. Drank himself half to death. Knocked up some girl and then left her to fend for herself. She was so desperate she gave your father up in exchange for a few hundred dollars. Those are the people you come from. And that's what you are. A lunatic and a whore."

Nothing he's saying is making sense. But I can't keep track of my thoughts. I try to remember what I wanted to tell him tonight, but my brain is empty, but for one word. *Murder, murder, murder*. It bounces around my skull like loose change. Odie is the murderer. Those boys. He killed those boys. He just tried to kill me. Why is he saying these horrible things about my family? I don't know what to believe. My stomach roils. Oh no, I think, not here, not now. I swallow back the vomit and press my hands into my belly, willing it to settle.

Odie is calm now. He puts his face in his hands and leans against the steering wheel. He takes a few long breaths like this, and when he looks back at me, the fire is gone from his eyes. He reaches across the gearshift to take my hand. I flinch, but let him.

"I'm sorry, Cali," he says. "I shouldn't have told you all that. Today was just so fucked." He brushes his thumb across my cheek, wiping away a tear I didn't know had fallen. And then he sits back in his own seat and starts the car.

I think he will take me home—it's almost dawn at this point—but instead we drive to his place. "Stay here tonight," Odie says.

"But it's almost morning," I say. I feel like I've entered some kind of warped reality. Like the current has shifted suddenly and I'm too tired to swim against it, so I let it sweep me away.

Odie smiles, a benevolent deity. "That's okay. We can make an exception tonight. I don't want to be alone."

Run, I think. Just get out of the car and go home. But instead I follow Odie inside. He pulls me to him, stripping me down to my underwear right there in the hallway. I brace my hand against the wall as Odie enters me. There just beneath my left palm is the blood stain from the last time Odie had me up against this same wall, when I cut my cheek. I scratch at the dried blood with my fingernail, but it won't come off.

Afterwards, in bed, Odie lights cigarette after cigarette, the butts piling up in a mug on the bedside table. I'm scared to fall asleep. I'm gripped by an irrational fear that if I do, I won't wake up. But my body is depleted and soon I can't fight it anymore. I fall quickly into a deep sleep like stepping off the edge of a sandbank and into the dark blue sea.

I dream I am sweeping the bar at the hotel. A strong wind blows sand in from the beach, and every time I look down the floor is buried beneath another layer. Soon the sand reaches my ankles. I sweep and sweep but there's nowhere for the sand to go. Odie is there, drawing lines in the sand, intricate maps that disappear in the breeze as soon as he completes them. I reach out to him but he swats my hand away.

Then Odie is gone and it's my father who draws in the sand. His back is to me, and when I touch his shoulder, he doesn't turn. I fall to my knees behind him, banging on his back with my fists, but he still doesn't turn. "Look at me," I'm screaming. I jump onto his back, wrapping my arms and legs around him. And then we're in the ocean, and I'm still clinging to his back, the waves crashing around us. I taste the salt, it burns my tongue, my throat. "Hold on," my father says. "Don't let go."

I wake to Odie shaking me, screaming my name. The room is full of smoke, thick and black, and I can hardly make out Odie's face above me. "The house is on fire," Odie says, "get up, quick."

"Was it the cigarettes?" I ask, stupidly, still half asleep. But the butts sit squashed in the mug beside me. The smoke is growing thicker.

"We have to go, Calypso, move!" Odie says, pulling me from the bed. The windows are barred, the only way out is through the house. But that's where the smoke is coming from, seeping under the door. Odie taps the door handle and pulls his hand back quickly, scalded. I pull on my underwear and one of Odie's T-shirts. The rest of my clothes and my shoes are strewn about the hallway, where Odie stripped them from my body just hours ago. Odie finds a pair of sweatpants and tosses them to me.

"Shoes," Odie says, pointing me to his closet. I pull on his workboots and lace them up as tight as I can, but still my feet slosh around inside them. Odie strips the bed, carrying the sheets into the ensuite. He throws them into the tub and fills it with cold water, then he takes the sodden sheets and wraps one around my shoulders and the other around his own. "Hold this against your face," he says, thrusting a wet pillowcase into my hands. "We're going to have to run very fast, okay?"

I can only nod. We stand at the bedroom door, Odie with a soaked towel wrapped around his hand like a boxer's glove. He looks at me once and wrenches the door open. Then there is nothing but fire.

Never have I felt anything like it, a great wall of heat that forces me, stumbling and coughing, back onto the bed. Odie turns away from it. He's screaming my name, but I can't hear him over the roar of the fire. This is hell, I think, I've died and gone to hell. Odie grasps me by the arm and pulls me into the belly of it. I can't breathe. I can't see. I cover my face with the pillowcase and let Odie lead me blindly through the flames.

The walls are crumbling. Everything is burning. The curtains, the furniture. The cracking wood sounds like the snapping jaws of an angry animal. The fire is above us, all around us. I feel it burning away the bottoms of my feet, eating me from the ground up. I can see nothing but black smoke, and red, bright, burning red. We emerge into the night air, out onto the driveway. I want to collapse there, but Odie keeps pulling me out onto the street, through the gate, and across to his neighbour's lawn, onto a patch of grass. He finally lets me go, and I fall onto the damp earth. I feel every blade of grass like a scalpel to my skin. I heave into the ground, but there is no air, no breath left anywhere in the world.

I roll onto my back. Above me, the sky is starless, the moon a bright and yellow crescent. Odie stands in the middle of the street, his hands on his hips, watching his house burn down. I suppose it isn't really his house. This is what I'm thinking as I watch him watching the fire. What does this all mean to him, really? A rented home, a borrowed life. A man emerges from a neighbouring house and approaches him. Then a woman, a child in hand, a cordless phone tucked under her ear. I watch this happen from where I lie, marooned on my patch of grass.

Time passes in flashes of colour. Green grass, brown skin, blue lights, the watery lilac of dawn. I slip in and out of sleep. When at last I'm able to stand I see the house is smouldering, thin plumes of black smoke still seeping out of it like shadows. Other than the black outlines of the windows and door, from the outside the house looks much the same as it always did. This feels impossible to me. Insidious, like slicing into a piece of shiny fruit and finding it rotten in the middle.

I check my own skin for evidence, but find I too am unmarked. I bring my hands to my face, my head. When I pull them away, my fingertips are covered with my own charred hair. I must have missed the fire being put out, because the firemen mill around now, not seeming to do much. A crowd has gathered on the street. They stare at the smoking house as if expecting it to burst into flames again, the way you might watch a staticky TV set, expecting at any minute for it to once more entertain. Odie has disappeared. No one talks to or even looks at me. It occurs to me that they might not realize I was in the burning house at all. I might just appear to be another nosy neighbour, there to witness someone else's tragedy.

I approach a woman who stands nearby. She is wearing black tights and a large green T-Shirt with the words *Fun Run 1995* emblazoned across the front. "What happened?" I ask her. It hurts to speak, and my voice crackles like a bit of crumpled paper.

"Wuh I aino," she says, glancing at me. "I was out for my morning walk and I see the smoke and come cross to see what going on. Them saying someone might have set the place on fire." She leans in, her eyes wide. "You know who live in there, right? It's one of them men from the new hotel. The one who was on the news when them two little boys dead."

She is joined by another onlooker, a man. They seem to know each other. "I knew something like this was to happen," the man says. "Leave room for God's wrath. 'It is mine to avenge, I will repay,' says the Lord."

The woman bobs her head. "That's right," she says. "You live bout here?" she asks me.

I don't reply. My throat still burns. I cough, the sound like breaking glass. The woman looks at me in earnest then, maybe registering my singed appearance. "Wait, you was in there?"

At that, the other neighbour turns to look at me. "She was in the fire," the first woman says to the man, her voice carrying through the crowd. "She was inside the white man's house when it catch fire."

"No," I say, moving away. I push through the other onlookers, fighting my way down the street, away from the burned-out skeleton house, away from Odie, away from the sun that rises in the east, dawn light growing violently bright.

I reach the playing field at the end of the street and bend down to untie Odie's boots, leaving them on the grass and continuing barefoot. I think if I can just keep walking, I will eventually reach the ocean. There I will bathe, wash the night away,

and be saved. I walk across the field and into the neighbouring village. It's still early, and the streets are mostly empty, only
a few commuters watch me warily from bus stops. Eyes turn
away from me as I pass, like I'm something it hurts to look at,
like roadkill, or the too-bright sun.

There is a thrilling kind of freedom in this. I shed pieces of
myself as I walk, bits I leave behind me, scattered like bread-
crumbs. But no one is following my trail, no one tries to find
me. These are parts of myself I can feel, even in this moment,
are lost forever. I know this feeling, I've felt it before. Once,
when we moved into the hotel. Again, years later, with the delegate. A great loss. A new understanding.

I reach the hotel, but don't go to the beach as planned.
Instead I go in search of my mother. I find her in the office,
sitting in front of a stack of papers, her glasses pushed up onto
her hair. She looks so old, so grey.

"Mum," I say, and she turns to me, as though she has been
expecting me, shoulders tensed up for a fight. But then she sees
me, really sees me, and her hand comes to her mouth.

"My child, what happened to you," she says, rising from her
chair.

"I have to go to the hospital," I say. "I have to make sure the
baby is okay. He's all that matters."

My mother stands before me now. She brings a hand to my
hair, the charred tips, then to my cheek, and finally to rest on
my stomach, which bulges slightly beneath Odie's shirt.

CHAPTER THIRTEEN

BABY'S GROWING IN ME LIKE A PRAYER. I CAN FEEL him, heavy as a sack of flour in a famine. I spend all day in bed in one of the hotel rooms, the a/c blasting. Odie brings me KFC and pizza and Chinese food. All this baby wants is grease. The room is littered with soiled wrappers. The air is dry and reeks like stale ice in the back of a freezer. I've made a nest of sheets and pillows and I lie curled up in the middle of them.

After the fire, Odie moved back into the hotel. Then, when I was put on bedrest, I moved into this room with him and the world outside ceased to exist. Now it's just me and the baby and Odie, on a lifeboat out to sea. It's been a difficult pregnancy. Though, I don't have anything to compare it to. Maybe this is normal, maybe this is just what women do. I vomit several times a day, even now, at close to thirty weeks. The room spins every time I roll over or try to sit up. Even shifting my weight slightly is enough to trigger my vertigo.

My belly hangs low and hard, a sign I'm carrying a boy, says my mother. I don't need her folk wisdom to tell me this, I know I'm having a boy. I've known from the beginning. I know so much about him already, his hopes and fears, his worst habits, his secrets. I know he will be a swimmer, a traverser of seas. The only time my motion sickness eases is when I'm in the bath.

My belly is so big now it's impossible to submerge, but still the buoyancy helps. I fill the tub to overflowing and then add Epsom salts. In the bath, baby sleeps and the world rights itself for a little while. I can't get out of the bath without help so sometimes I spend hours in there, topping up the water whenever it gets cold. When Odie gets home, he wraps me in towels and heaves me up, the water cascading out of the tub, drenching his clothes.

At night, Odie sleeps with his body wrapped around mine. I like to imagine that I am something soft and small, like a sea creature, and he is the hard shell of a home that I carry with me. Some nights, he's quiet, normal. We lie in silence together, him staring at the ceiling, me with my hands pressed into my eyelids like a child playing hide and seek, willing the room to stop its spinning. Other nights he paces, talking to himself in low murmurs. Sometimes he locks himself in the bathroom, not coming out until I bang the door down, demanding to use the toilet. When, finally, he opens the door, I find him sitting with his knees bent to his chest, head against the wall. I coax him into bed, curl up beside him, pressing myself into his crotch until he hardens. He'll enter me desperately then, as if there are answers to be found somewhere inside me, and when he comes his whole body shakes with the effort of it.

The hotel project has been abandoned. The site is a mound of a ruin and rubble, and all the foreigners have gone home, except for Odie. The development company is being sued by the government, as well as by its foreign investors. For the first few weeks after the project shut down, Odie still dressed each day as if for work. But now I'm not sure what he's doing for money. His skin is rum-yellowed, gut bursting through his suits. I'm aware he's losing his mind, being driven mad by drink, and sun, and the sticky island heat, the air always wet and heavy, loud with insects that buzz through the night. But I find I don't much care. There's something comforting in his slow unravelling, like he's finally meeting me in the middle. I no longer dream of leaving together, I feel certain it will never happen. All I can hope for now is that he will stay here and take care of me and the baby. That we will be enough for him.

"Set me free," he slurs on those nights when he comes home stinking of some other woman, crawling into bed beside me, his cheeks slicked with tears. He begs me to let him go. To release him from the spell he thinks I have cast over him.

And on those nights, I cry too, pull him to me, baby cradled between us, and reply, "I can't. Please don't leave me." And every morning there he is.

Today, my nausea is particularly bad. I haven't left the bed once, not even to pee, and my bladder throbs, an aching pleasure against my cervix. Rain beats a steady rhythm against the window. We're in the middle of a tropical storm. So much for "October, all over" like we learned in school. It's almost November and they're saying this might be the worst storm of the season. I've hardly seen my parents all day as they're busy tending to worried guests.

There's a knock on the door, and Uncle Z enters without waiting for a response. He comes in a state of busy authority, like how I imagine he enters most rooms—banks, post offices, restaurants—expecting his needs to be met efficiently and without hassle. He is soaked through with rain, his curls plastered against his forehead. He looks like a man possessed.

"It smells like a donkey's ass in here," he says, opening the windows. A gust of wind immediately sends Odie's stacks of paper flying across the room. Through the window I can see the sky is a furious grey. A palm frond whips by. Z appears oblivious to the storm. His face is fixed into a hysterical smile.

He sits at the edge of the bed and takes one of my feet in his hand, giving it a hard squeeze. His hands are cold and wet and rainwater seeps from his clothes into the sheets. I think about reaching for the phone, to call for help. But what would I say? Z owns the hotel and I'm squatting.

"Are you looking for Odie?" I ask. "He'll be back any minute." This is a lie. I have no idea where Odie is. He left hours ago claiming he was going to stock up on supplies for the storm. He's probably off somewhere drinking until he can't stand.

Z shakes his head, still smiling that terrifying smile. "No, no, I came to see my favourite and only niece! How are you feeling? You're glowing!" Without waiting for an answer, he goes on, punctuating his words with a tightening of his fingers along the arch of my foot. "But I would like to speak to you about our mutual friend."

I pull my feet away from his grasp and sit up as high as I can on the pillows. "Odie? What about him?" I try to focus. The nausea has returned with force. The window shutters bang relentlessly and the lights flicker.

Z takes a deep breath. When he speaks, his voice is soft, coaxing. "There's an election coming up," he says, "and the opposition is using the accident at the construction site as ammunition, pointing fingers. The usual mudslinging. The PM has asked, given my personal connection to the situation"—he gestures at my belly—"that I intervene."

"Intervene how?"

"Cali . . ." Z says, "it's time for Odie to go home. There is nothing left for him here. He's risking not only the stability of the island, but his own safety, in remaining."

Typical Z. He lined his pockets when the getting was good, but now that Odie is becoming a liability, he needs to distance himself. Difficult to do with Odie spending every night in Z's hotel, with me.

"What does any of this have to do with me?" The room swims. I can feel anger buzzing in my chest, an itchy rage like I've swallowed a hundred ants.

"It has everything to do with you," Z says, his voice gentle. Anyone else might be fooled by this, but I know I'm being handled. Asked to play my part, to bend as he needs me to, like my father always does. "You're the only reason he's still here."

"I want my son to know his father."

Z stands, rolling his shoulders and popping the tendons in his neck. He paces about the room, fidgeting with the furniture. He looks bloated, as if the anger is leaking out of his skin. I want to tell him to get out, to leave me alone, to let me sleep.

"You don't have any idea, do you?" he asks quietly from across the room. "How much money I lost on that fucking deal?"

"You have plenty of money."

Z freezes at this, and I see the facade crumble. He picks up the alarm clock from the bedside table, weighing it in his hand for a moment before slinging it across the room. It shatters against the far wall. I don't flinch. I stare back at him, insolent. Outside the window, lightning flashes and thunder growls.

Z lets out a low guttural roar and slams his two fists against the wall. I've seen his son Junior do the same thing in the fit of a tantrum. They're all the same, these men. Just get on with it, I want to say to Z. This is life, just get on with it and stop whining, you pathetic man.

I'm sweating through my clothes, the sheets damp beneath my back. I try to move my legs, but they are limp and tingling. Z's mumbling to himself, and I can hardly make out the words. "You foolish child," he says, still talking into the wall. "How could you be so selfish, so goddamn small-minded? Think about your family, our reputation."

"Odie is my family now," I say. I feel quite sure I'll be sick. The room tilts at an impossible angle, and Z stands before me in triplicate. I close my eyes and breathe deep.

Z comes close, sitting down beside me on the bed again. He's hunched over, head in his hands, also breathing heavily. I can only imagine what the two of us must look like—both gasping like washed-up fish.

It's Z who calms first, twisting his body to look at me where I lie, propped up on pillows, my face only a few inches from his face. Still he leans in closer, as if to tell me a secret. His cologne is fruity, like bubble gum. My stomach clenches and I turn away, gasping for air. "Listen to me," he whispers, "I made a promise to my father that I would never let anyone sully our family name, and I've kept that promise, at great personal expense." I have no idea what he's talking about but can't summon the energy to care. Z goes on, "I will not let you bring this family to ruin. You think you know me, but you don't know what I'm capable of. I will sell this place to the highest bidder. And then what will your parents do? Where will they live?"

He sits up, looking away from me. "It's time for this to end.

You can stay until the baby comes, and then I want this room back. We're wasting revenue, having you in here every night. If you want to keep playing house with a married man, fine. But you'll do it on your own dollar. I just hope someone doesn't set your new house on fire."

I think about what Odie said then, about my family, about the secrets we keep. Murderers and drunks and madmen. I don't know this man, my uncle, I realize. I know nothing about him at all. I lean over the edge of the bed and vomit onto the tile. Z jumps up, cursing. The vomit has splashed onto his shoes. He goes to the bathroom to wash them, yelling back at me over the sound of the faucet. I'm a bitch. I'm a whore. I can hardly hear him. I vomit again.

Something is wrong. Baby is rollicking inside me, fighting to get out. "Uncle Z," I say, my voice urgent. "Help me."

He exits the bathroom, wiping at his shoes with a thick wad of toilet paper. He straightens up and throws the sullied paper on the floor, not looking at me. "I'm done helping you," he says, and leaves.

I scream after him but I'm all alone. The room blackens. Rain lashes in through the open window. I feel a flood beneath my legs. I'm drowning, I think. The whole bed is sinking, the room itself is going to float away. I'm lost at sea, an ocean of red.

CHAPTER FOURTEEN

THE DAY AFTER ODIE LEAVES US, IT RAINS. IT'S MARCH, almost a year to the day we met. I'm in the laundry room, elbow-deep in linens, Nautilus asleep in a Moses basket at my feet. My father comes in, carting a load of dirty sheets and towels. Nautilus stirs, fussing. He is barely four months old, and tiny for his age. He came early and spent the first month of his life in hospital. I find it hard to look at him. When I do, all I see is death. Purple skin, a still and silent heart. He was born so premature that for his first week, he was kept alive by machines. He is fragile, nebulous. I fear that any moment he will be taken away from me. My father bends to pick him up, cradling him to his chest. Nautilus quiets.

"You'll throw your knee out," I say. I'm tired. I spent yesterday in a state of stoic busy work, helping Odie pack, seeing him off with dry eyes and a suitcase full of souvenirs: rum cakes, guava cheese, tamarind balls. I promised myself

I wouldn't make a scene, wouldn't leave him with this last-ing image of me: the wailing madwoman, the brown-skinned banshee. I sent him home, back to his frozen land, his loyal wife, his legitimate children, with only the softest of kisses on his cheek.

At the airport, Odie cried, the gruff and silent tears of a martyr, and held on to me for a long time. Just as he pulled away, I slipped a photo into his palm. It was of Nautilus and me on the beach, him naked in the sand, me holding him up for the camera. Odie brought the photo to his lips and kissed it. "Thank you," he said, as if I'd just served him a drink. Then he left, disappearing between the glass doors and into the ter-minal, without looking back. That night I cried until my chest cracked and my throat closed up. I held on to Nautilus and cried into his tissue-paper skin, cried and cried until I was too tired to cry any longer.

"You have someone here to see you," my father says. "Come take a break."

I ignore him, loading more linens into the washer. "We have seventy-five check-ins tomorrow," I say, "I have to get through these. Tell Matthew I'm busy. I'll call him later." Really, my back throbs. The wound on my stomach has not healed well, and it hurts to bend, to lift, to move, to breathe. I relish the pain, it reminds me of what I have lost.

"It's not Matthew. Just come," he says. He leaves the room and I wait a minute, wiping the sweat from my brow before fol-lowing him to the bar. There, sat at one of the tables, is Nadine. I haven't seen her, or anyone from school, since before the night of the fire. I stopped going to school, cocooned first in the hotel with Odie, and then consumed by caring for Nautilus. Once or twice my father has dropped hints about my going back in

September, retaking Sixth Form. But I shut the conversation down. That part of my life is over. It burned up in the fire, like so many other parts of me.

This is the first time I've ever seen Nadine out of school uniform, and she looks as odd as ever, in a long cargo skirt and a colourful anime T-shirt, her dandelion hair hardly contained by a bright pink barrette. She's drinking a Coke from a straw and reading a book.

"I'll take him for a little while," my father says, Nautilus almost invisible in his tree-branch arms. "Let you two catch up."

"He's cute," Nadine says, by way of greeting.

"Yeah," I say. "I think they make them cute so that we don't throw them out of windows."

Nadine laughs. I join her at the table. The bar is busy with tourists sheltering from the rain, and the waitstaff rush to and fro, arms laden with baskets of fries and fish cakes. Business has been good lately, and we're fully booked through the rest of the tourist season. My mother has been on my father's case about asking Uncle Z for a raise. I doubt it will happen. Uncle Z has hardly been around since Nautilus was born.

"How's CAPE prep going?" I ask Nadine. "You sit next month, right?"

"All my SBAs are done so it's just the exams left now," she says. "We'll see."

"You'll do great. You'll be an island scholar for sure. Have you applied for any universities yet?"

She shrugs, but I can tell she's pleased. "Mona, for medical school."

I'm surprised that she's going to Jamaica. I thought she was the type to choose a more far-flung destination to study. "That's great," I say. "I'm happy for you."

"What about you?" she asks. "Are you going to repeat the year?"

I shake my head. A cool breeze blows in from the sea, carrying the rain with it, and our napkins flutter on the table, and then fly away. A calypso song is playing on the speakers, "Fool's Paradise" by John King. The tourists sway on their seats, tapping out the rhythm with their feet. I wonder if any of them are even paying any attention to the lyrics. Calypso: for locals it's been known as the poor man's newspaper, but for tourists it's just the soundtrack to their vacation, as innocuous as the sound of lapping waves. I feel disgust and anger like the embers of a dying flame flaring to life within me. I ignore it. This is my life now, serving these people. Rachel Pringle, after all.

"You were always smarter than me," Nadine says. "I know everyone thought we were neck and neck, but that's bullshit. We all knew you would get the top marks."

I laugh, gesturing around the bar. "Yet here we are."

Nadine reaches for a bag at her feet, holding it out to me. It's filled with notebooks and papers. "I cleared out your desk for you."

I accept the bag, not looking inside. "Thanks," I say.

"I included some mock exams in there. In case you change your mind about CAPE. I really think you should sit them. I could help you study. Or babysit Nautilus for you, if you want. Before I go to Jamaica."

"Why are you being so nice to me?" I ask. It comes out like an accusation, but Nadine doesn't flinch.

"Why not?"

It's such a simple response it stuns me for a minute. "I don't know," I say, "I guess I'm just used to people not liking me. I thought it was the default. The girls at school. I mean, you get it."

Nadine shrugs. "They were just scared of you. You didn't care what anyone thought and that freaked them out."

"I did care. I cared a lot, actually."

Nadine takes a sip of her Coke and leans in. "Yeah," she says, in a conspiratorial whisper, "so did I."

We're quiet for a moment, and then Nadine laughs, Coke spraying out of her nose and across the tabletop. I join in, laughing so hard I'm crying. Laughing so hard it hurts, a pleasurable pain in my chest, my heart pounding, loud and present.

After Nadine leaves I head down to the beach in search of my father and Nautilus. Not finding them, I sit in one of the lounge chairs, watching the sea. The beach is empty in the rain. The surface of the water dances with drops. But under the shelter of the beach umbrella, I'm dry and cozy. I reach for the bag Nadine brought and pull out the books. There, among the assigned texts, is the book Mrs. Cossey gave me. A collection of poems by Audre Lorde. I flip it open, planning only to skim the first page, but before I know it, I'm almost a quarter of the way through. I feel something building within me. It's a feeling similar to the one I had in the bar earlier, but different. A flame, but not one I fear will devour me from the inside out. More like a candle in the dark. I keep reading, becoming absorbed in the book, and only stop when my father approaches, calling my name.

I rise and join him at the shore. The rain is falling heavier now, soaking us through. Nautilus coos against my father's chest. He loves the rain, loves all water, like I knew he would. I lean over and breathe in the top of his head, that smell like freshly baked bread, yeasty and alive.

"That was nice of your friend to bring your books," my father says.

I nod and my father grows quiet. We stand together, the

waves lapping at our toes. I can sense he wants to say something else. Probably something about school. "What?" I ask. "I can hear you thinking."

My father smiles, but it's a sad smile that doesn't reach his eyes. "You didn't deserve the things he did to you," he says, finally, eyes on the horizon.

I hesitate, caught off guard. "It wasn't Odie's fault," I say, carefully. "I was deluding myself into thinking I could keep him here."

My father shakes his head. "Not him." His voice is soft and slow. "The other man. The scientist."

For a moment I'm confused, until it dawns on me. The delegate. He knows. "That wasn't what you think," I say, embarrassed. "I chased after him."

"You were a child," my father snaps. Nautilus begins to fuss in his arms. The rain comes heavier, thunder rolling in. "I should have shot him dead. Taken him out on the boat and buried him under the sea. But Z . . ." He pauses, scratching his beard. "We needed the booking. And Z said it would cause nothing but trouble. But I shouldn't have listened to him. I should have stood up for you."

I see now how old he is, my father, how worn. I take his hand in mine and squeeze it. I want to tell him that there is nothing he could have done to save me. I want to tell him that I wouldn't change any of it, even if I could.

I think about what Odie told me, about Cronus. For months now I've been turning his words over and over in my mind. *Z's still cleaning up the mess he left behind.* I wonder what he meant by that. Maybe I'm better off not knowing. Late at night when I wake to pull Nautilus onto my breast, his tiny body flush against mine, I wonder about the family I have brought him into. I still don't know if anything Odie said was true. He could have been making it all up to hurt me. But it was too specifically horrific to be a lie. So many times, like now, I've thought of telling my father, but the words always die in my throat. Cronus is the only father Atlas ever knew. The memory of him, his legacy, is all my father has left. I can't take that away from him. He's lost so much already.

"Too early for rain," I say, instead.

"We'll be okay," my father replies, releasing my hand.

My mother treks onto the beach, sheltering her head with a towel, and joins us. "What are you two doing in the rain? Atlas, take that baby inside before he catches a cold."

My father sighs, winks at me, and turns back to the hotel. My mother remains. "You coming?" he asks her.

"In a minute," my mother says. She turns to face the sea. We watch it together, and I'm reminded of that time at the Met, when we stood before the painting. Finally, she asks, "Has your father ever told you about that time when you were a baby, when I left?"

I glance at her, not understanding. "You left Dad?"

"I left both of you. You were only a few weeks old. I snuck out in the middle of the night and didn't come back for three days."

I hear her words but still struggle to make sense of them, to reconcile them with the mother I've known my whole life. Sensible, reliable, devout.

Sensing this, she laughs, a small, sad sound. "I know," she says. "Hard to believe. But it's true. I almost didn't come back."

"Where did you go?"

"Church." I roll my eyes. She laughs again, adding, "It was the only place I could think of where Atlas wouldn't come looking for me. Father let me sleep in the little room they keep for visiting priests. It was a tiny room, so small that if I lay in the middle of the cot and stretched my hands out, I could touch either side."

"What did you do?"

"Cried mostly. Prayed. Asked God for forgiveness for leaving, and strength to go back."

"Why did you?"

"What, leave?"

"No," I say. "Come back."

She looks out at the sea, her slender hands still holding the towel above her head. I notice that her fingernails are painted a faint peach, so pale they look almost bare. I can't recall if she always paints her nails, if this is just the first time I'm noticing it.

"Because I missed you. And your father. And because I had awful dreams while I was away from you. Dreams of drowning and death. I woke up with the worst headaches. I was unable to eat. My body wouldn't let me stay away. I wanted to be with my family, I needed to be. But I was bitter, for a long time. I felt like I had to make a choice. That the only way I could be a good mother to you, a good wife to your father, would be to kill all the other parts of myself. And so that's what I did. Not right away, but slowly, so slowly I didn't even realize it was happening."

She reaches for my hand and I let her take it. I don't know what to say. I feel my insides shifting, like puzzle pieces fitting together.

"I know I've been hard on you," my mother goes on. "I think I envied you. Your spirit. Your determination. And I think I was always trying to bring you down to earth because I didn't want you to feel the disappointment I felt when my life didn't turn out the way I planned. I wanted you to be ready. But you would never do what I did. Never let anything stand in the way of your dreams."

I shake my head. "That's all over now. Odie's gone."

My mother sucks her teeth, something she rarely does, and I laugh, more out of shock at the gesture than anything else. "That man," she says, the words spitting out of her mouth like watermelon seeds, "that man was never the answer. He is not your story."

"But the baby . . ."

"Nautilus will be fine. I'm here. Your father is here. He will be loved. The best thing you can do for him is live, live a whole life." She punctuates each word with a squeeze of my hand, so hard it almost hurts.

The rain is really lashing now. My mother laughs and drops the towel she was using as shelter. The rain soaks through her bandana, ruining her hair, which I know she ironed straight just the day before. She doesn't seem to mind though, tilting her head to the sky, mouth open. Then she looks at me, eyes twinkling. "Fancy a swim?"

I laugh. "But what about the sea ants?"

"Oh," she says, "a little sting won't kill us. Come on." She edges closer to the sea, the water up to her knees, her work skirt fanning around her like the tentacles of a man-o'-war. I follow her into the shallows. It's warmer than it is in the rain. I wade out, the waves swirling my dress around my thighs, then I dive in, pulling long strokes beneath the surface. I stay down for as long as I can, until, lungs bursting, I come up for air.

Part Three:
NAUTILUS (2018)

CHAPTER FIFTEEN

THE SEA IS FLATTER THAN THE SKY, NOT A BREAK IN sight. I straddle my board, my back to the shore, eyes on the horizon, searching for any sign of a swell. The sun burns my back, even through the rash guard. A plane flies by overhead, probably full of tourists. A few might even be checking into the hotel later today. It's the last week of July, and I'm on summer holiday, so I ought to be there, helping out with turnover, but I fled this morning when Daniel texted about rumours of a decent left break on the west coast. But once we made it down here and saw how glassy it was, the boys parked out on the beach instead. I'm the only one still in the water. I lie back and stare up at the hot white sky. I don't want to go in, to spend another afternoon nursing warm beers, talking about the same dumb shit we always talk about. And I definitely don't want to go home and face another lecture from my grandfather about my "failure to contribute."

I flip over and paddle in. The boys are already laughing as I approach, my board tucked under my arm. "Always the last one out, red man!" says one of the older guys, a veteran surfer everyone calls Chicken, for reasons that have never been explained to me. Most of these guys are old-school surfers. They've been getting chewed up and spat back out at Soup Bowl long before I was born. I'm too green to hang with them, really, but they put up with me because they know who my great-uncle is, know that if something happens to the light-skin boy from the hotel it will be their asses on the line.

"I caught a few good sets," I say.

"First one in, last one out," Chicken says again, slapping me on the back.

I shrug, though I'm pleased. I don't want them to think I'm weak. I'd much rather they think I'm fanatical.

I collapse onto the sand. "Where's D?" I ask, and the men all laugh.

"Where you think?" one says, gesturing down the beach.

It takes me a minute to spot him. He's perched on the edge of a beach chair, chatting up a couple of tourists. He's giving one of them a massage, the aloe dripping in fat globs down her back. Daniel burrows his thumbs into the flesh beside the knobs of her spine, and even from here, I can see the effect it has on her, her mouth hanging open like a contented dog.

Daniel's fingers are long and thick-knuckled, and when he cracks them, which he does often, the sound both thrills and nauseates me. Sometimes Daniel will sneak up behind me and crack his knuckles against my ear, the sound burrowing down and settling somewhere in my gut. I watch him touch the tourist for a minute more, unable to tear my eyes away. I take a swig of my beer, forcing the warm liquid down.

The beach isn't busy, yet beach chairs still crowd every square inch of sand, most of them empty. We sit under a manchineel tree, on a craggy patch of sand between two resorts, a little square of unclaimed territory. The manchineel fruit litter the sand around us, rotting in the sun. They look like small green apples, and sometimes tourists will eat them, not realizing they are poisonous. At our hotel, we put up signs warning the guests not to touch the fruit, but sometimes they do anyway, as if they don't really believe anything bad could happen to them in such a beautiful place.

Daniel has rejoined us, a ten-dollar note braided through his fingers. He sits beside me, his legs extended. Daniel's legs are long and bowed, the dark brown skin shiny and nearly hairless, the soles of his feet the same bright white as the sand. I wonder, not for the first time, what would happen if I took hold of his big toe in my fist and pulled until the joint cracked. If it would make the same sickening sound his fingers make. I think about sliding my thumb down the centre of his arch, pressing my nail into the tough, cracked skin at the heel. I wonder if he would flinch or laugh or like it. This is how horny and useless I am. Dreaming about feet and ankles and calves and thighs. I can't bring myself to picture the warm and sandy mess of curls and hardness beneath his shorts. This would be too much, the thought of it would undo me. So instead, I think about his toes, and I sip my beer, half listening to the talk of the other men.

They're talking about women, or rather, parts of women. They talk about their breasts, their asses, their mouths. Their irrational demands and their incomprehensible behaviour. The things they say during sex, or arguments, filthy fragments never quite adding up to anything resembling a whole. I listen to their puzzling and resist the urge to chime in, often finding the solutions to their female woes glaringly obvious but afraid my logic will betray something about me, as if my ability to understand women makes me less of a man.

I was raised by a woman who cannot tolerate being misunderstood. "Are you listening?" my mother often says, the question demanding a response. What she's really asking is, "Do you see me? Do you really see me?" When I was a child, before she left me at the cottage with my grandparents and moved into her own apartment, she would sometimes shake me awake in the middle of the night, needing to share something that happened to her or an idea she was working on, even though I was too young to understand whatever it was she was talking about. Maybe that was the point, I was a captive audience. Even then I understood my mother wasn't someone who could be broken into smaller, more manageable parts.

The men's talk turns to the tourist, the woman Daniel was working. They want to know how much she's worth, what Daniel can get from her, if she has friends with her. They all make a little money this way, seducing the tourists, becoming their guides, showing them "the real Barbados." Daniel laughs along but doesn't divulge any details. From where he sits, I can't tell if he's looking at me. The sun creeps over our shoulders, dipping down towards the horizon. I'm on my third beer and I'd like to go home and take a nap in one of the vacant hotel rooms. I can usually sneak in for an hour or so before my grandmother catches me and throws me out. Though our cottage is on hotel grounds, it doesn't have a/c, and sleeping in one of those cool hotel rooms feels like diving into another life. I feel restless, a familiar heat that builds around my neck and ears. The men won't shut up about Daniel and his tourist.

The sand is hot and itchy against my skin. Technically beaches in Barbados are public, but the hotels claim all the sand above the high-water mark, spreading out their beach chairs so there's nowhere left to sit. This is normal, our hotel does it too. But today the sight of those empty chairs enrages me. Why do we have to sit on the ground when there are so many empty chairs? Daniel's tourist has rolled onto her back and is taking selfies with her phone, squinting her eyes against the setting sun. I glance back at Daniel and catch his eye. He frowns slightly, and then looks away. I saunter over to the nearest empty lounge chair and flop down.

"Look at this fool," says one of the men, "can't take him nowhere, hear?" The others laugh. It feels good.

I'm always doing stuff like this, picking fights, starting shit. I want the men to see me as fearless. In primary school I had trouble making friends and got picked on a lot. Back then everyone called everyone else a buller, words tossed around like paper planes. But when they said it to me, it felt like they meant it. It didn't help that I was mixed. And that everyone knew my father was a foreigner, some white man who got my mother pregnant and fled.

Eventually, though, I figured out no one wants to pick a fight with a madman. I started cussing the teachers, smoking cigarettes in the bathroom. Whenever I was sent to the principal for a flogging, I went with a grin on my face, showing off my welts to the class afterward. By Third Form I'd been suspended twice. During the summer, I let my hair grow long and matted and I walk around barefoot most of the time, even in town. Better to be thought of as a prickle than a buller. No one fucks with me anymore. I'm seventeen, still small for my age, but it's been a long time since I've had my ass kicked. These days I ride around the school grounds on my skateboard, my shirt untucked, a joint in my pocket. The teachers have more or less given up on me, but my grades are decent enough that I haven't been expelled yet.

My grandfather says I'm wasting my potential, that I need to figure out what I want to do with my life. To make something of myself. I've always hated that expression. How am I supposed to make something of myself when most days I feel less like a person than a walking piece of exposed wire. I don't know how to tell him that I'm just trying to survive, from one day to the next.

Only my uncle Z gets it. Whenever I get in trouble, he's the one who talks my grandparents into going easy on me. He tells me he was like me when he was my age, partying too much, skipping class, picking fights. "Your grandparents played by the rules," my uncle told me once, "and look where it got them. People like you and me, we don't live by other people's expectations. Where others see a no-entry sign, we see an invitation. And that's a good thing."

Uncle Z tells me I should come and work for him, after I graduate. He says university is a waste of time. He says he can teach me how to have real power, make real money. I don't really know what it is my uncle does for a living, but I do know that he would never let anyone tell him where he can and can't sit.

A few of the other guys have joined me on the chairs, hamming it up, pretending to flag down the waitstaff for drinks. The security guard watches us from his perch in the shade on the other side of the beach, by the hotel bar. I feel a kind of euphoria, the giddiness of knowing something, anything, is going to happen. Something to break up the monotony of this day, my life.

"Whappen, D?" I say to Daniel, who remains on the sand. I pat the empty space on the chair beside me, my eyebrows raised, suggestive. The move is bold and reckless, and Daniel ignores me, playing with the sand, letting it fall through his loose fist.

"Wunna about to get we throw right off this beach," he says, glancing back towards his tourist.

I turn away from him, my teeth clenched. "Pussy," I say, loud enough for him to hear me. He only shakes his head.

The security guard ambles over, big and slow on the soft sand in his polished Oxfords. His uniform resembles a police officer's, pale blue button-down and thick navy slacks. He seems winded from the walk over. "Alright fellas, you know you can't sit here," he says, his voice high and wheezing. "Move it."

I stare up at him, feeling that nagging heat return to my face. I suck my teeth, a long and wet sound. "Look, Stabby," I say, eliciting another laugh from the boys, "why you don't waddle back over where you came from and leff we alone? Nobody ain't checking for we. Half the chairs on the beach empty anyhow."

"That's not the point. These chairs are hotel property and you are trespassing." He rolls his tongue around the word like he's sucking the last bit of sweet from a hard candy. He gestures often with his hands when he speaks. He reminds me of my grandfather. I picture my grandfather in the sun, on a beach identical to this one, gathering old towels and bringing drinks for the guests. I wonder how far from the beach this man lives.

How many buses he catches every day to get to work. But the angry flame beneath my skin won't die.

"How we could be trespassing on a public beach?" I suck my teeth again. "Fuck you, old man."

He bristles at that, shuffling his weight between his two legs like a pigeon on a telephone wire. I rise from my chair now to get in his face. I get like this sometimes, angry and cruel. I don't know why. The guard is about a foot taller than me, but he's outnumbered. The sweat beads on his upper lip. I can't see his eyes behind his dark sunglasses, but I know he's afraid. Shame burns my chest, but I swallow it back like bile.

"You see these stripes?" he says, voice shaky, pointing to the three diagonal white stripes on the epaulettes of his uniform. "These give me the authority to remove any undesirables from the premises." He enunciates every syllable with care, like each one means something to him. Maybe they do.

Behind him, the sea glitters. A few tourists look up from their books, half listening. The boys gather their boards and set off down the beach without me. Only Daniel remains. The guard lets out a long breath and steps back, reaching for his radio.

"Lord help me, hear? I ain't know what is happening to the youth of today but I not standing for it." He struts a few paces away from me and speaks something inaudible into the radio. I watch him, still seething. Then I feel Daniel's hand, rough and dry on my shoulder.

"Get your board," he says, "we're rolling." He turns to head up the beach, not looking back. He knows I'll follow.

We toss our boards into the bed of Daniel's truck, then climb inside. I'm shaky, anger still humming beneath my skin, my whole body hot and trembling like an idling car. Daniel puts the truck in gear but hesitates, looking over at me, his mouth twisted to the side.

"What?" I ask, not looking at him.

Daniel laughs. "You've got issues, you know that, man?" He places a hand on my shoulder and gives me a rough, brotherly jostle.

We drive for a few minutes along the coast, heading south towards my hotel. I check my phone, where I have several missed calls from the hotel reception. Those will be my grandfather, surely. Calling to yell at me for skipping out on work again.

For as long as I can remember I've felt like a problem my grandfather was trying to solve. No matter how hard I worked, he never seemed satisfied. He would force me to stay up at night, memorizing times tables until I could hardly keep my eyes open. Or set me to weed the bougainvillea, not letting me rest for hours, even when the thorns pricked my skin and I cried. When I was younger, my grandfather's toughness motivated me, his eternal dissatisfaction with everything I did a puzzle I was determined to solve. But I've long since given up trying to impress him. I don't think there's anything I can do to change the way he sees me. I will always be the thing that ruined his daughter's life.

I don't want to go home yet. My body tenses with dread at the thought of facing him again, another day, another fight. Now that it's just Daniel and me, riding around in his truck, the music turned up as loud as it can go, there's nowhere else I'd rather be. There's a new kind of energy pulsing through me, triumphant, like I have skirted the edge of some great abyss. This is a feeling I crave constantly, the high of near disaster.

"You're always chasing trouble and don't know what to do when you find it," my grandfather likes to say.

"My belly is hitting my back," Daniel says, pulling into the Holetown gas station. "You want anything?" he asks, climbing out.

"Get me a hot dog," I say, reaching for my wallet.

He waves my hand away. "I got you, man." He heads towards the shop, greeting the gas station attendants on the way. The women call out to him, big smiles on their faces. Women always look at Daniel as if they want to feed him. A group of men are unloading a stack of wooden pallets from a parked truck. Daniel jogs over, joining in the effort. Then he heads inside, holding the door open for a group of tourists, their arms laden with bottled water. All of this before I've managed to light my cigarette. I watch him, feeling like a cat chasing a shadow.

The gas station, located at a busy intersection in the heart of the west coast, is bustling with locals and tourists. Minibuses cruise down the main road, blaring reggae music, the conductors hanging out the doors, looking for customers. The nearby supermarket crawls with traffic, cars seeming to pour in and out of the lot in no discernible order. The summer heat lies heavy across the island like a wet blanket, the sky feels close enough to touch.

The tourists, sweating in their sarongs and surf shorts, navigate this chaos, stepping out onto the street, only to jump back, having looked the wrong way before crossing. I study the tourists, searching their flushed faces, their eyes squinting beneath wide-brimmed hats. What I'm looking for, I don't know. Kinship, maybe, something familiar. I often wonder, when I look at tourists, what it would be like to be one of them. To come from a place where I could feel okay being . . . whatever it is I am. But they are foreign to me, the tourists. They move in a languid haze, sun drunk. Such a contrast to the Bajans who haul their shopping into their cars with grim focus, strapping their children into back seats, lining up at the gas station to fill their tanks. They are stoic at the bus stop in their jeans and sneakers, their business suits, their uniforms, just trying to get home for the day.

Daniel re-emerges from the store, jogging over to the car juggling two hot dogs in one hand and a couple bottles of Guinness in the other. He places the hot dogs on the seat and uncaps the beer bottles with the car key, a trick I taught him. We eat the hot dogs and sip the stout. "Feeling better?" Daniel asks. I throw my empty hot dog wrapper at him and he starts the truck, laughing. We pull out of the gas station, continuing south. I turn to the window, watch the wall of condos and hotels blur by, a monolith of white stone and red tile roofs. Traffic slows behind a minibus.

I gesture to the window. "Who do you think lives in these?" I ask, tapping the glass with my knuckle.

Daniel shrugs. "Probably nobody. Investors. I don't know."

"My grandfather says that when he was young, you could drive the coast road from Speightstown to the port and see the ocean the whole way. Now it's just this shit."

We're stopped beside an imposing limestone wall. In front of it, the street is busy with pedestrians. The nearest public beach access is another mile or so down the coast, but between here and there is a wall of no-access zones, villas like this one. "The beach belong to we," sang the Mighty Gabby, but how can you own something you can't reach?

"I wonder what it's like in there," I say, and this time Daniel turns his head, following my gaze.

"We should find out," he says, grinning. "You could probably stroll straight in there and not even raise an eyebrow."

I suck my teeth but don't argue. It's true, I have access to
places Daniel doesn't. I'm blue-eyed and light-skinned, and
even with my summer dreads I can pass for a tourist. "Alright,"
I say, "let's test that theory."

Daniel glances over at me. He's driving with both hands on
the wheel, ten and two. His surf shorts have risen up, baring
his upper thighs, which are a few shades lighter than the rest
of him. He has a speckling of sand on his upper lip, just below
his right nostril. I have one foot propped up on the dash, in
an effort to look casual. I'm minutely aware of my body, of
the positioning of it. Without saying anything, Daniel flips on
his turn signal, and checking both his mirrors, pulls off onto
the hard shoulder. He turns off the engine and gets out of the
car. I follow. We wait for a break in traffic and then cross to
stand in front of the villa. Up close, the guard wall is even
taller than I realized. There's no way we can scale it without
anyone noticing.

"It'll be easier from the beach side," Daniel says. I want to
ask him if he's ever done anything like this before, but don't
want him to think I'm scared. We continue along the sidewalk until we come to a beach access, a narrow pedestrian path
between two hotels, linking the main road to the shore. We
emerge onto the beach, finding it mostly deserted. It's late, the
sun slung low on the horizon, the sky lit pink. The water here
is rocky and rough. A fisherman stands in the shallows a few
hundred yards away, net in hand. A couple of tourists stroll
by, stooping often to collect sea glass. We backtrack down the
beach until we find the villa. It's protected by the same imposing wall on this side, but here, there is a narrow wrought-iron

gate with a keypad entry. Through the gate we can see the garden, lush and dense.

Daniel hangs on to the gate with both hands, giving it a shake. "Hello!" he calls out, "anybody home?"

I yank at his T-shirt and he steps back. "What the fuck are you doing?" I ask.

"I'm seeing if there's a guard. If someone comes we'll just make something up." But no one does. The wind carries with it the salt of the sea, mingled with garden—frangipani, mango, tamarind. The garden seems to whisper at us from within. Curiosity and fear compete for space in my chest. "You ready?" Daniel asks, and without waiting for an answer, heaves himself up and over the gate, his body dropping lithely to the other side. I look around and then follow, less gracefully, landing badly on my right ankle. I curse, hopping in pain. Daniel shushes me and, following a path of evenly spaced stone slabs, strides steadily into the quivering green.

We creep around the property, tense and silent, until it becomes clear there is no one else here. Daniel peers in through the locked windows, to the interior, where the furniture is covered in white sheets. The pool is littered with leaves. "Looks like no one's been here for a while," he says.

"Such a waste," I say, "you could house five families in here."

Daniel looks at me over his shoulder, an eyebrow cocked. "Is that what you guys do at the hotel with your empty rooms? House the homeless?"

"That's different," I say, though I'm not sure how.

Daniel calls my name. He's standing on the pool's diving board. "You watching?" he asks. He does a double flip, careening through the air and landing with a triumphant splash. He disappears for what feels like a long time, and when he finally re-emerges, he's gasping for breath. "Did you see that shite?" he says. "That had to be almost a minute I held my breath." He removes his T-shirt and throws it in a sopping pile at my feet, before diving back under.

Daniel's every movement is joyous, the way he stands on his hands, his feet sticking out of the surface of the water, swaying to and fro like weathervanes. He's always the one who climbs the highest, sprints the furthest, surfs the waves everyone else is scared to. The anger I'd been feeling before, at the beach, has morphed into nerves. I'm always getting myself into situations like this, climbing too high into the branches of a tree on the playground, only to be trapped there by fear, paralyzed by my own recklessness. But Daniel splashes and swims, unbothered. I sit down, dangling my feet over the edge into the pool. He swims over, coming to stand in front of me, his hands braced on either side of my knees.

"So what do you think?" he asks. "Should we move in? Take over the place? Start a squatters' paradise?"

I kick some water in his face in response. He grabs my foot by the ankle. His grip is tight, almost painful. I try to wriggle out of it, but he holds firm, yanking me towards him until I fall, sliding off the deck and into the water. I bob there for a minute, trying to find my footing, but Daniel doesn't hesitate. He lunges for me, pressing both hands onto my collarbones, holding me under. I don't panic. I can hold my breath for a long time and it isn't the first time we've played this game. Instead I still, not resisting, and soon he lets me go.

When I surface, we're inches apart, only our heads above water. I spit a long spout that lands in Daniel's eye. He curses, reaching out to grab me by the back of my neck. This time I fight back, grabbing his neck, our bodies mirrored. We tussle like this for a while, our arms taut, neither of us relenting. We're playing, but not really. I'm giving it my all and I know Daniel is too, neither of us willing to accept defeat. Daniel loosens his grip, and for a second, I think I have him, but then he reaches for my hair instead, wrenching one of my dreads. I scream, less out of pain than shock. I've never liked people touching my hair. Daniel releases me, and I swim away from him, wading over to the shallow end to sulk.

"So you pulling hair now," I say, panting slightly. "Like a little bitch."

Daniel grins, swimming over to me. "A bitch that kicked your ass," he says. He moves through the water slowly, only his eyes visible, like a crocodile stalking its prey.

"Stop," I say. "I'm done."

"No, you ain't," Daniel says, inches from me again. "You're done when I say you're done." Then he pounces, launching his body into mine like a torpedo. We both go under. The water is only a few feet deep at this end of the pool, and my back scrapes along the rough cement at the bottom. When we come up for air, Daniel's arms are still wrapped around my torso. I thrash against him like a fish in a net, but his arms are crossed firm around my body. I feel something warm on my shoulder, soft, followed by a bright searing pain.

He bit me.

I stop fighting, relaxing into his arms, which remain locked around my chest. Daniel brings his lips to my shoulder again, and this time it's all wetness and warmth. He kisses my neck, takes my earlobe in his mouth and holds it gently between his teeth. I don't move. I've pictured this moment so many times before, frantic dreams from which I always awake feeling sick and sorry for myself. I don't want it to stop, to do anything that might startle him away. His erection presses into the small of my back. I moan, the sound automatic, escaping from my body like air from a punctured tire.

Daniel loosens his grip on my chest, his hand flat against my stomach now, moving steadily down between my legs. I don't know what I expected another hand on my penis to feel like, but the sensation is so acute it's almost painful. When I look down, the sight of our bodies together beneath the rippling surface of the pool, his skin against mine, is almost more intense than his touch. I come instantly, spasming against him, a sob gasping from my throat. Daniel breathes heavy against my neck. He's still hard, and I feel the promise and threat of that hardness against my spine. He's still holding my penis, which withers quickly in his hand. We stay like this for a minute and then I turn to face him, pinning him awkwardly beneath me. I stare at his face as if it's an instruction manual, but he only stares back, looking as helpless as I feel. I try to kiss him, but he turns away, my lips grazing his chin.

"Do you want me to . . ." I gesture down at his lap. Daniel shrugs, climbing up out of the water and onto the deck. I follow and lie down beside him, on my side, my head resting in one hand, the other on his chest. This pose doesn't feel right, too feminine. So instead I lie on my back, looking up at the sky, now the dark purple of twilight, and reach blindly for his shorts. I fumble with the Velcro and reach for him before I can overthink it. The weight of him is familiar, and not, and I feel as though I'm trying to write my own name with my left hand instead of my right. But Daniel doesn't seem to mind my awkwardness. He moans.

I can't look at him, so I keep my eyes on the sky, on the bats that swoop low overhead. The air is full of night sounds. Whistling frogs, their constant high chirping. In the distance a dog barks incessantly, the low growl of a larger animal. Waves lap on the nearby shore. Daniel bucks against my fist, then stills.

We lie panting. I pull my hand from Daniel's shorts, wiping it dry on my own. Tomorrow, I think, my head will be filled with questions. I can sense them already, on the periphery of my consciousness like flies buzzing against a windowpane. But for now, I feel the kind of stillness I only ever experience on the water, waiting for a wave, the quiet hum of anticipation drowning out all other thought.

"Don't," Daniel says, still not opening his eyes.

"Don't what?" I ask, nervous.

Daniel rolls onto his side, looking at me finally. I can hardly see his face in the darkness, his eyes like oil slicks or those shimmering mirages the sun makes on the asphalt sometimes. "Don't go into Nautilus mode. Zero to sixty. I can hear your brain revving already."

I laugh, too loudly, giddy with relief as the tension eases from my body. "I'm cool, man. Don't worry about me. I'm just here calculating how much this is going to cost me. What's your going rate these days?"

Daniel punches me on the shoulder, not gently, and I fall back onto the pool deck, still laughing. Daniel jumps to his feet, catlike, and stretches his arms up above his shoulders. I follow the planes of his stomach down to the waistline of his shorts, the Velcro still loose. I try to conjure the memory of what he felt like in my hand, but already it's fading. No, I think, it can't be like this. We can't just go back to what it was before.

As if reading my mind, Daniel reaches a hand down to where I lie, helping me to my feet. Once I'm standing, he doesn't let it go. We stand there for a minute, close enough to feel each other's breath on our cheeks, only the tips of our fingers touching. "Lewe go," he says. "If I miss dinner again, my mother will skin my ass."

I grin. "Caw blen," I say. "I don't ever want to get on Janice's bad side."

"You're already on her bad side."

"Why!? What did I do?"

"She thinks you lack broughtupsy."

"Is it because she saw me at Cost U Less barefoot that one time?"

Daniel pulls me closer. "She thinks you're a bad influence."

I'm about to retort when he kisses me, the softest of gestures, a breath of air and a faint pressure on my lips. It's over before I have even registered it happened, then Daniel is stepping away from me, tugging on my hand, looking back at me over his shoulder, a dumb grin lighting up his face.

We reach the gate, and I scale it first. I'm almost over the top when I hear it, footsteps heading towards us, moving fast.

"Shit," Daniel says. "Go, go go!"

I try to climb again but I slip, sliding back to the ground just as the swoop of flashlights descends on us. A pair of hands has me by the shoulders, yanking me off the gate and onto the ground.

I struggle, but the man is bigger than me and stronger. He wrenches my arms behind my back and pushes me face-first into the grass. My shoulder pops out of the socket, the sound like a Coke can being opened. I scream into the dirt, the whole world gone bile yellow.

The man kneels on my back, his hands still around my wrists, and leans in close, his breath hot against my ear. "Don't fucking move," he says, and then releases me.

I roll over onto my back, unable to see, unable to stand, to speak. I look around for Daniel, but I can't find him. Maybe he got away. This thought rises to the frothy surface of my brain, above the pain. The man who wrestled me to the ground stands above me, speaking into his walkie-talkie. He glances down at me, clearly deciding I'm not a threat, and then sets off into the shadows. After a minute I'm able to sit up. My arm dangles sickeningly at my side. The man returns, this time with his partner, and Daniel. The two men have him by either arm, and it takes both of them to wrestle him to the ground beside me. Once he's on his knees, one of the men binds his wrists with a cable tie. The men each keep a hand on Daniel's shoulders, though he isn't struggling anymore. He hangs his head to his chest, a line of bloody saliva dangling from his lip.

Almost as an afterthought, one of the men turns to me. "You don't want to restrain this one?" he asks.

"Nah," says the other, "that one ain't going nowhere." They're not wearing uniforms, but it seems obvious now that they are police officers. They hold themselves with the kind of righteous authority of men who've been given permission to be mean. They both wear dark denim and black T-shirts, with batons and radios clipped to their belts. One is taller than the other, but other than that, they are almost identical in the darkness of the yard: close-cropped hair, broad shoulders, large bellies pouring over their belts.

"Just let us go, man," Daniel says. "We weren't stealing nothing." The taller policeman gives him a rough shove on the shoulder but doesn't say anything in response. We stay like this for what feels like a long time. The policemen never take their hands off Daniel's shoulders. They talk quietly amongst themselves. I'm crying, and I hate that I'm crying but I can't stop. Daniel won't look at me. The policemen swat at mosquitoes, dab their faces with handkerchiefs. A radio crackles with static.

"They're here," says one of them. Then, to Daniel and me, "On your feet, fellas." I try to stand but the pain in my shoulder makes me dizzy, and I end up back on my knees.

"Get the fuck up," says one of the officers. I sway slightly and vomit onto his boots. The officer leaps back, cursing. Then, without hesitation, backhands me across the face. I've been punched before, piled on by schoolboys, but compared to this, those fists were like soft rain on my skin. The pain engulfs me like a mistimed wave, full in the face, robbing me of breath. I go under. Daniel bucks against the hands that hold him. I can hear him as if from far away, hurling curses at the men. I hold on to the distant sound of his voice the way a driver in a spinning car clings to the steering wheel. But Daniel cannot save me now. We are powerless. We are only boys. And this is my final thought before everything goes dark. We're just boys. And maybe I say it out loud, but either way, no one is listening.

CHAPTER SIXTEEN

I'VE NEARLY DROWNED BEFORE. ONCE, WHEN I WAS A baby, in the bathtub. My mother says she left me for just a minute, and when she returned I was face down, my nose against the drain, as though I was trying to swim away through the pipes. This is how she put it. My grandmother likes to say that my mother suffers from too much imagining. "If a chicken escapes from the yard all I want to know is who left the gate unlocked," my grandmother once said, "but your mother wonders where it is headed, and what it will do when it gets there." But even my grandmother agrees there was something strange about that day in the tub, when I was a baby. Something not quite right about how easily I flipped over, as though I was determined to get my head under water. She brings it up sometimes, whenever I get myself into trouble. "There you go again," she says, "finding a way to drown in an inch of water."

When I was about six years old, I nearly drowned again. This time I was in the shallow bay in front of the hotel. I was playing with an American tourist, competing to see which of us could hold our breath the longest. I was winning. Each time I emerged from the surface of the water, the other boy threw his arms up in defeat, the gesture of a much older man. "You see this guy?" the boy would say, as if to some invisible audience. "I can't believe this guy!" Then he would swing his arms around my shoulder and say something like, "You're going places, kid." And I would submerge, again and again, as if chasing some prize at the other end.

But then something went wrong, and I lost my footing in the sand. A shift in the current pulled me out beyond where I could stand and, exhausted from our contest, I struggled to tread water. Each time my head emerged from the water, I looked around, desperate for someone to save me, but the boy was gone. Finally, one of the watersports guys from the hotel noticed and swam out to rescue me, hauling me, sputtering and terrified, onto the sand, while the tourists looked on. The American boy sat on a nearby lounger with a towel draped over his shoulders, eating an ice cream cone.

The next morning my mother woke me before dawn and carried me, still half asleep, down to the shore, wading into the sea in her nightgown. The security lights from the hotel swept the beach, the sand grey and undulating, swarming with crabs. Z had hired a company years earlier to sink cement blocks a few hundred yards offshore to form an artificial reef around the hotel, called a breakwater. This created a shallow, sheltered bay in front of the hotel. The water here is always flat and clear and warm, calm enough that you can wade in up to your waist and sip your rum punch without spilling a drop. But just on the other side of the breakwater, the Atlantic booms. Its waves crash against the rock barrier and send plumes of spray into the cove, creating tiny whirlpools of white foam. The sea floor on the far side of the cove is a rocky field of corals, thick with sea urchins, their thorny bodies piercing upwards from the shadowy depths like a warning. Few guests venture beyond the breakwater, but that morning, my mother kept going, carrying me out into the open ocean.

The water rose quickly, around my knees, my stomach. When it reached my chin, I began to cry, climbing higher on my mother's chest, yanking at her hair. I couldn't see her face in the dark, but I reached for it, my nails scratching at her chin in panic. She kept walking until she herself couldn't stand, and then she swam, holding me out before her like an offering. At that hour the sea was all thundering black, the crashing waves yawning like great white mouths out of the dark horizon. More than once, a wave would engulf us both, sending me coughing and crying into her arms, begging to go in to shore. But my mother insisted we stay until I could float on my own. "It's not enough to learn how to swim," she said, "you have to learn how not to drown."

Now, when I come to in the police station, I think I must be drowning again. My feet are wet, and when I look down, I'm horrified to discover I'm sitting in a puddle of my own urine. The stench of it is overwhelming, mingled with my own sweat and the chlorine from the pool, which has left my skin dry and ashy. I can't breathe right, the air bubbling in my chest, never quite reaching my lungs. Pain hums through me like white noise. The room is dark. One of my wrists is bound to the back of the chair with a cable tie. I cradle the other hand in my lap. When I try to move that arm, the pain makes my eyes roll back in my head, so I don't try to move it again.

I yell out, my voice weak and scratchy. No one comes. I call out again and again, but I'm not sure anyone can even hear me. The police station is quiet, but outside, the street is busy with life. Through the window I can hear the passing melody of a minibus blowing its horn. Laughter. Someone yelling out to someone else, asking them to wait or to stay, I can't tell which. I have no idea what time it is. Midnight, maybe. I figure I must be in Holetown police station, that would be the closest to where we were arrested. I have never wanted so badly to go home.

I begin to cry, silent, blubbering tears, and I hope none of the officers come in the room now. I don't want to be seen like this, sobbing in a puddle of my own piss. But of course, this is when the door finally opens, and the two men who arrested Daniel and me enter. One of the men flicks on a light, revealing a room far less sinister than what I had been imagining in the darkness. On the wall hangs a portrait of the prime minister, next to a Banks Beer calendar, opened to the wrong month, Miss April astride a neon-green motorcycle. A yellowing devil's ivy dangles from a basket in the corner.

One officer approaches, stooping to snip the cable tie with a pair of small scissors. He recoils slightly. "You piss youself?" he asks, his voice accusatory. I don't respond. He sucks his teeth and pulls up a chair next to me. His partner remains standing by the door, a file folder tucked under his arm.

"Why don't you go ahead and tell us what it is wunna was doing on the property this evening?" It is the shorter officer who speaks, the one nearest to me. Neither takes notes.

"We just wanted to see inside," I say. "We weren't trying to cause any trouble."

The shorter officer shakes his head. "Regardless of intent,

breaking and entering is a crime." He lets this hang between us for a minute, and then, as if making conversation, says, "You ever been inside of Dodds?" He doesn't wait for me to answer, he already knows I've never seen the inside of a prison. He lets out a whistle. "Dodds is a real rough place, boy. You know 'bout boogaloos?"

I shake my head. The officers make eye contact with each other and laugh.

"Let me tell you about boogaloos," the short ones says, cracking his knuckles. "In prison, the mandem does cut into their penises, using whatever them can find. Rusty nail. Broken glass." He reaches for my good arm, and holds it upright between us, his grip firm. With his other hand, he scratches lightly at the skin of my forearm with his fingernails, which are long and yellowed. He leaves thin, white dashes against my dry skin. I do not squirm, but I know that I am about to cry again. I look away. The officer cups my chin and gently turns my face back to his.

"No, no," he says. "Pay attention. This is important. The men slice their penises. And then they take some marbles, or pieces of broken dominoes. Like this." He reaches into his pocket, pulling out a small bead. I wonder where he got it from, when exactly it was he thought to pocket it, how long he'd been planning this performance. He runs the bead along the skin of my forearm, from wrist to elbow, pressing lightly. "And they insert the objects into the shaft, just below the skin, like so." He presses a bead into the soft folds of flesh at the crux of my elbow. I'm crying openly now, the tears dripping freely off my chin and into my lap.

He leans in, so close I can feel his breath against my wet cheeks. "You're so soft," he says, still trailing the bead lightly along my skin, "soft boys like you don't last long in a place like that." He means prison, but I think, maybe, he means something more than that. He means I'm trying to live a life I'm not made for, and I'm fooling no one. And as soon as he says it, I know it's true. It's what I've always suspected.

"There is also," says the other officer by the door, speaking for the first time, "the matter of the nature of your arrest." I flick my eyes up at him, wiping the tears roughly with the sleeve of my T-shirt. "Now I'm an open-minded type of man," he goes on. "I don't like to interfere in any one's business."

"What two people do in the privacy of their home . . ." says the other.

"Is their business," finishes the first. "So long as they don't bring that shite 'round me." The two officers laugh at this. "But," he says, "to be carrying on so in public, that's a different matter." The two of them stare at me, but I keep quiet, waiting them out.

"A high brown boy like you, from a good family, caught with his hand 'round some next man's dick . . ." He spits the final word at me and I flinch. The officer smiles. "These kinds of salacious details are exactly the kind of thing that sells newspapers."

"Please," I say, before I can stop myself. I don't want to beg but I'm desperate. Daniel and me, our pictures blurry and grey in the morning paper. I can't stomach the thought. "What do you need me to do?"

The officer approaches from the door, removing a single leaf of paper from the file folder and extending it towards me. "This is our report of the events that occurred this evening. Sign it, and there's no reason *The Nation* nor *The Advocate* need ever know you were here."

I scan the document. It basically recaps everything that happened, except it makes no mention of my injured arm. I sign it and am released within minutes. I step out onto the street, feeling not fully awake. My aching arm is the only evidence that I didn't dream the whole thing. Across the road is the same gas station Daniel and I were in just a few hours before. A couple of tourists meander by, making their way towards the bars of Second Street. They steer well clear of me where I stand swaying on the sidewalk, my arm cradled to my chest. I must look like a paro. A minibus rumbles towards me and I flag it down.

The lights are on in my grandparents' cottage when I get home. My grandfather is sitting at the kitchen table, surrounded by paperwork. He doesn't look up at first. "I will not even comment on the hour," he says. "There's stew beef on the stove still."

"Granddad," I say, from the door. And he does look up then.

"Oh," he says. And in his face, I see first confusion, and then recognition. He looks as though he's been waiting for this moment to come since the day I was born.

₿ CHAPTER SEVENTEEN

IN MY FAMILY, THERE ARE MANY DIFFERENT VERSIONS of what happened after my father left. In my mother's, she overcame the odds to raise me alone, all while finishing her studies and going on to have a successful career as a poet, performance artist, and local celebrity. This is the version she tells the students at the poetry workshop she teaches at UWI, the version repeated in the newspaper profiles and interviews.

The truth is more complicated. My mother did re-enroll in secondary school and completed her CAPE exams when I was about three years old. She excelled, earned a scholarship, and was accepted into the singing program at a prestigious conservatory in Berlin. This is where the details get murky. She studied in Berlin for almost a year, and then she dropped out of the program and travelled around Europe for a while, until her visa expired, and she had to come home.

I was too young to remember much about this time. All I knew was that suddenly there was a strange woman in the house, her presence making everything brighter, like someone had boosted the saturation on my days. She played music constantly, strange German techno that she danced to late at night, her heavy footfalls making the floorboards rattle. She never seemed to sleep and would ply me with sugar so that I would stay up with her. My memories of those days are all blue tongues and glitter and sticky fingers. Midnight dance parties and pillow forts and forgotten cupcakes left to burn in the oven. I thought she was magical.

And then she was gone again. But this time, not to another country. She was still living with us, still sharing a bed with me every night, but it was as if she had evaporated. She hardly left the room most days, and when she did, it was only to shuffle into the kitchen and back. The house was silent then, the TV always on mute, my grandparents hushing me constantly, saying, "Your mother needs to rest." I began to think of my mother as one of those hibernating animals I learned about in school, hunkering down for a long sleep.

She did emerge, re-energized, with a new plan. She enrolled at UWI and finished her degree, this time a BFA in creative arts, specializing in theatre. She spent her days on campus and performed her original songs at the hotel in the evenings. My grandparents have a video recording of her onstage at the hotel from that time, slouched over on a stool, looking down at the microphone, her long braids almost completely shielding her face from view. She never smiled or danced around or tried to engage the audience in any way. But still she was mesmerizing onstage, her performances like witnessing some private, sacred act, like a call to prayer. Her shows were enormously popular, even drawing guests from nearby hotels.

In addition to singing at the hotel, she also staged a monthly experimental theatre production with her school friends, a mix of spoken word and interpretative dance and protest art. She even made international news for one performance when she coated herself head to toe in sugar and spent twenty-four hours camped out in front of the statue of Lord Nelson, a colonial admiral, demanding it be torn down.

She quickly became a well-known and polarizing figure on the island, the subject of admiration, mockery, and bemused affection. The local eccentric artist. And the more attention she got, the more she began to inhabit this character, until she became indistinguishable from it. If she walked barefoot down Swan Street or sunbathed topless at Accra Beach or trawled the bars of The Gap, singing drunken karaoke until the dawn hours, no one thought anything of it. Her life became one long performance.

I was in primary school during these years, skittish and small, feeling all the time like my heart was a pile of marbles scattering across the floor. I was anxious, prone to crying at the smallest provocation. I had nightmares so intense they made me vomit and so my grandmother kept an empty bucket by my bedside each night.

I idolized my mother, craving her attention the way a lizard longs for a patch of sunlight to curl up in. I kept a copy of every newspaper that mentioned her, begging my grandparents to let me stay up and watch her hotel performances. When she moved out of our cottage and into her own apartment on the west coast, I pleaded with my grandparents to let me move in with her, convinced that they were the ones standing in the way. It took a long time for me to figure out that it was my mother who wanted to live alone. My childhood was defined by the ebbs and flows of my mother's moods. Her long absences, and sudden, manic returns.

Like once when I was ten and she took me out of school in the middle of the day to go on a hike. She claimed there was no education better than the one she could provide.

"One day soon," she explained, as we walked deep into the forested hills of St. Joseph, "the world as we know it is going to end. All the luxuries on which we rely will be gone. This island, and the people in it, are going to have to learn to rewild themselves."

I nodded along, not understanding, excited to be alone with her, to have her to myself for an adventure. There were no trails, no paths. We had to bushwhack our way through cow itch and ivy, mud up to our knees. My mother marched ahead of me, a cigarette dangling from her lips, wielding a cutlass she'd borrowed from one of the groundsmen at the hotel. After an hour, I was hungry, tired, crying to go home. But my mother pressed on with gleeful determination, mumbling about the end of the world.

After another few hours, it became clear that we were lost. As the sun crept higher in the sky, the afternoon heat choking the air around us, her mood grew darker. Soon, she stopped speaking to me entirely. I cried and cried, reached out for her hands but she shook me off, as if I were one of the bugs. Eventually, we emerged onto a gravel road. We walked along that for a while, until my mother was able to flag down a passing car.

When the driver pulled up alongside us, she smiled and leaned against his window. It was like she became a different person—flirtatious, charming. The performer. The man gave us a ride back to our car and we went home. That night, it was my grandmother who washed the dirt away, dabbed calamine lotion on my bites, held me as I cried myself to sleep.

I'm seventeen now, the age my mother was when she had me, and I've long since given up expecting her to be a normal mother. Our relationship is more like that of aunt and nephew. I run into her sometimes, when I'm out with my friends, and she makes a big show of buying a round of drinks. All my friends worship her, especially the girls. When I try to convince them she's mad, they don't believe me. "She's an artist," says my friend Toya, her voice hushed with awe. "You're so lucky. Your mother is so cool."

But growing up it was my grandmother who cooked my meals and made my school uniforms and my grandfather who taught me to read and write and repair a bike tire. And tonight, it's my grandmother who sets my dislocated shoulder and wraps it in a sling. And when I fall asleep on the couch, it's my grandfather who picks me up and carries me like a baby in his arms, laying me down in my own bed. I cling to his collar, suddenly terrified at the thought of being left alone. My grandfather peels my fingers away one by one and sits beside me on the bed until I fall asleep, his heavy hand a comforting weight on my chest.

The next morning, he wakes me up at dawn, entering my room without knocking and switching off the fan. I have slept for a little under two hours.

"Come," he says, standing above me. "Your grandmother needs help in the garden." Gone is the tenderness of last night, and in its place is my grandfather's usual stoic disposition. I sit up, too tired to argue, too tired to question my grandfather's reasoning in forcing me out of bed at this hour, after the night I've had. I assume this is the beginning of a long penance. His arms are crossed. He's young for a grandfather and fit for his age. Tall enough he has to duck under most doorways. He used to carry me on one shoulder when I was young, his frame so wide I could sit comfortably in the curve of his clavicle and not even hold on for balance. He looks at me now over the tops of his glasses, as though he expects me to refuse.

"Alright," I say, "I need to get dressed." He doesn't move, and we stare at each other for a minute. I wonder if he is wait-ing for me to say something about last night, to apologize, to explain. And I know I should. This is far from the first time I've fucked up, but last night was bad. I've crossed an unspo-ken line, I've endangered the family name, the worst of sins for a Bajan. But still I can't bring myself to apologize. I've always been like this. Stubborn. Ready to double down in a fight.

When I was seven, I had to get my tonsils out. From then on, every time I got in trouble—like the time I was playing cricket on the beach and smacked the ball for six, straight into the face of one of the hotel guests, breaking his nose, or the time my grandfather had to come pick me up from the super-market because the general manager had caught me stealing rock cakes, or the first time I totalled my grandfather's car— my grandmother blamed the surgery. "You were such a good boy, until they took your tonsils away." It was a joke, of course, but I think there's a small part of me that believed it. I've always suspected there is a piece of me missing, that self-preserving instinct that stops people from walking themselves to the cliff edge and jumping off.

I find my grandmother out back, on the small patch of land that separates our cottage from the hotel grounds. This land was once overgrown and weedy, but my grandmother began to tend to it right around the time I was born. "I wanted you to grow up surrounded by living things," she said.

I kneel beside her now in the dirt. She is dressed in a long, floral smock with a wide-brimmed hat. Like my grandfather, my grandmother is young, but she dresses like how I think she imagines a grandmother is supposed to dress. Even at this hour the sun is punishing on the back of my neck, and my left hand shakes as I pull weeds, my right arm still immobile in its sling. After about ten minutes I'm soaked through with sweat. I haven't eaten anything since the hot dog with Daniel, and bile sloshes in my stomach, burning my throat.

"Granny," I say finally, "is this punishment?" I try to keep the hurt out of my voice. I know I will suffer consequences for last night. But I expected this kind of sentencing through toil and labour to come from my grandfather, not her.

She sits back on her knees, fixing her skirt in a prim gesture. She looks at me, tilting her head far back so that she can make eye contact beneath the generous brim of her hat. "No, baby," she says. "I just wanted to spend the morning together."

"In that case, can we hang out tomorrow instead? I really need to sleep."

She hesitates, then removes her gloves, taking my hand in hers. "I know that things haven't always been easy for you. Your mother . . ." She looks down at our hands for a moment, then sighs. "We did our best to give you the life you deserve. We all did, me, your mother, your grandfather."

I scoff at this and she squeezes my hand in protest. "No really, even him, especially him," she goes on. "He has always looked out for you, always tried to protect you."

"He hates me."

My grandmother shakes her head, her expression pained. "All your grandfather has ever wanted, ever since I've known him, which is a very long time, is a life of his own. He grew up without a father, just like you. But he didn't know his mother either. Can you imagine what that feels like? Belonging to no one?

"When your mother and father started their relationship," my grandmother goes on, "we didn't intervene. Your mother was headstrong and precocious, and we were so busy, so tired. We looked the other way. We made excuses. We told ourselves that it was just a fling, that she was almost eighteen and that it was her life to live. We didn't see how bad it had gotten, how deep Odie had sunk his teeth into her, how lost she was, how alone. She needed us, and we weren't there. I don't think your grandfather has ever forgiven himself for that. He finally had a family of his own, something that belonged to him at last . . . and he failed to protect her. He let the wolves in. Do you understand?"

I nod, feeling the comfort of a familiar ache. "That's why he's so hard on me. Because I remind him of my father, right? Of the man that hurt Mum."

"No," my grandmother says, firmly. She puts a finger under my chin so that I'm forced to look at her. This close, I can see the wrinkles that have formed around her eyes, her skin weather-beaten, pulled tight around her cheekbones like polished mahogany. "No," she says again. "Last night, that was your grandfather's worst nightmare. Mine too. That we failed again. That we nearly lost our most precious thing, again. We can't let that happen. You are too important to us."

"I'm sorry, Gran. I didn't mean to scare you. But I'm okay. See?" I smile, gesturing down the length of myself. "I'm not lost. I'm right here."

My grandmother laughs, but her eyes are closed, tears pooling up along the length of her lower lashes. I've never seen my grandmother cry before. I feel a panic brewing in my chest. There's something she's not telling me. The sun continues its relentless ascent. Our hands are still entwined in the dirt between us. My grandmother opens her eyes, the tears escaping down her cheeks. She's about to speak when my grandfather's voice calls out to us from the house. My grandmother takes a long breath, and then rises to her feet, dusting off her skirt. I stand too, and we head for the house. At the door, my grandmother stops, turning to me, her voice low and urgent. "You always have a home here," she says. "Always."

She takes my hand again and we enter the cottage like this, my grandmother in front, me trailing slightly behind.

When we enter the living room, I stop short. There waiting are my grandfather, my mother, and my great-uncle Z. My mother is still in costume, glitter smudged on her cheeks, her eyelids painted a bright purple, drooping under the weight of her fake eyelashes. It's Crop Over season, the busiest time of the year for her. She performs almost every night at different cultural events across the island. Now, she sits like a teenager on the sofa, her legs tucked under her, chewing on her thumbnail.

My grandfather sits beside her, and Z in what is usually my grandfather's chair, the large wingback, his feet crossed on the matching footstool. The TV is on to the cricket, the West Indies are at bat. Z sips from a small glass of rum, the ice almost melted.

I'm still standing in the entryway, unsure where to sit. My whole family never convenes in our cottage like this. I suppose this is my sentencing hearing, where I find out just how grounded I am.

My mother won't look at me. She seems a little twitchy. She's probably had less sleep than I have. It's my grandfather who breaks the silence first, clearing his throat and reaching for the remote to switch off the TV. But Z holds up a hand to stop him. "I want to see the end of the over," he says. So we wait, all of us watching the game now. The ball glances off the bats-man's glove and straight into the hands of the wicket-keeper. He's out for thirteen runs. Z sucks his teeth and waves his hand again, signalling that my grandfather can switch the TV off, then he turns to me. "So," he says, his tone all business, "I've spoken to the station sergeant who has assured me that there will be no record of your arrest."

"What about Daniel?" I ask. "Did they say anything about him?"

Z doesn't answer for a moment, looking at me over his stee-pled fingers. "I did not inquire after your friend."

I nod. D is probably fine, at home sleeping it off like I wish I was. I'll send him a text as soon as I can get away from my fam-ily. I hope this doesn't take long. "I signed something," I say, "I don't know what it was."

"Nautilus," my grandmother says, "why didn't you call us first?"

"It's fine," Z says. "It was just a witness statement. The offi-cers showed it to me. I think they were worried they would get in trouble, for roughing you up." He gestures to my arm in its sling. Of course, once the officers ran my ID and figured out who my uncle was, they just wanted me out of that station as soon as possible. "You did the right thing, Nautilus," Z says, "not taking the fall for that boy's mistakes."

Somewhere in the cloudy depths of my brain, it all clicks

into place. The statement. I only skimmed it. Had it mentioned what would happen to Daniel? "But he didn't do anything wrong," I say. "The whole thing was my idea."

"Enough," my grandfather says, speaking for the first time. "It's done now."

I just want to get away from all of them. Even my grand-mother, normally an ally, sits across from me now, her face like a closed door. I want to crawl back into bed and sleep until this ache in my skull subsides, and then I want to go and see D. Maybe there's a chance he will speak to me. Maybe there's a chance we can go back to where things were, to that moment when his face was inches from mine in the pool, glistening wet in the moonlight. "Fine," I say. "Can I go now?"

"Nautilus," my grandfather says. "Sit."

"Uncle Z," I say, "thank you for your help. For going down to the station and all that. But if we're all good I just really need to sleep."

"Boy, I said sit," my grandfather says, this time leaning for-ward on the sofa as if to rise. Z turns towards him and waves his hand in a calming gesture. My mother shivers on the couch like a wilted leaf, still not looking at me. I pull up a chair at the dining room table and sit.

"I've spoken to Junior," Z says, "and he says it shouldn't be any issue getting you enrolled at the high school near his place in time for September. But it's best if you go now, to sort out the paperwork."

Junior is Z's son, technically my third cousin though he insists I call him Uncle. He lives with his wife and young child in Canada. "Toronto?" I say, not understanding. "Why would I go to Toronto?"

"It's for the best, Nautilus," my grandmother says. "It will be easier there, for someone like you." Her hand flutters to her lip as she says it, her eyes wet and wide and pleading.

I feel the heat again, building at the base of my spine, spreading upwards. "What the fuck is that supposed to mean?"

My grandfather is on his feet and in my face in a flash, my shirt in his fist, hauling me to my feet. I don't flinch. I stare into the black of his eyes and dare him to hit me. He raises a finger to my face. "Watch yourself," he says, and releases me.

I shake him off and stumble away from them. "I'm not going to fucking Canada." I say it loudly, my voice rising and breaking, betraying the panic I feel.

"Cuss in this house one more time, boy."

"Atlas," Z says, "let him be."

The room spins. "Mum?" I say, turning to her. She's blurry through my tears, frozen on the sofa, staring blindly at some spot in mid-distance. I go over and squat in front of her, taking her hands in mine. "Mum, look at me, please. I'm sorry. Don't do this, Mum, please." But she looks straight through me. There she goes again, disappearing into herself. Anger flares once more. I let her hands fall. "This is what you've wanted all along, nuh? To get rid of me." Finally, she reacts, a whimper, like the sound of steam escaping a kettle. Z is silent, staring at the darkened screen of the television. He looks like he wishes he could continue watching the cricket.

"How dare you," my grandfather says, his voice quiet. "For years I've let you run wild. I tried my best with you, God knows I did. Tried to stop you from becoming . . ."

I rise, turning to face him. "Becoming what? Say it."

"Your father left you and your mother with nothing," my grandfather says, his voice quiet now, all the fight gone.

"His own son and he couldn't even spare a dime to help bring you up. But he was good for one thing." He reaches into his back pocket and pulls out my passport. My Canadian passport.

Daniel had whistled when I showed it to him, years ago. My Canadian passport meant I didn't have to stand up in long lines in the afternoon sun at the US embassy for a visa. It meant that one day, if I wanted to, I could leave the island. I could go anywhere on a Canadian passport, no visa required. Daniel and I had a list of all the places we wanted to surf. Big Sur. Oahu. Nazaré. But it wasn't supposed to be today. Not like this.

I turn to my uncle, my last resort. He always said that he saw something of himself in me, of the same passion that fuelled him when he was my age, the same wildness. If I can convince him to let me stay, the rest of my family will follow. They always go along with Z. "Uncle Z," I say, "if I stay, I can come work with you next year, like we talked about. This was just a stupid mistake. You remember what it was like when you were my age. Ignoring the no-entry signs. Just like you said, right?"

Z looks at me like I'm a fly that landed on his arm and that's when it sinks in. Whatever kinship I thought existed between us died the moment my uncle found out about Daniel. I'm not the endearingly rebellious nephew anymore. I'm something else entirely.

"The flight is booked, Nautilus," my uncle says. "Go and get some rest. And then start packing. You leave in two days."

The next night I go out with my friends to The Gap, my grandmother having convinced my grandfather I at least deserved to say goodbye. I stick to the fringes of the dance floor, my head down, my locks framing my face. The DJ plays mostly moody rap and reggae and I'm in my own head a lot, thinking about leaving. My friends splurge on a bottle and I drink it in big swigs, Toya's phone in my face. In her Instagram story I look pale and bony, my finger pointing to the camera as if to say, "I see you." It's a night like many I've had before, except my friends keep throwing their arms around my shoulders, planting soft kisses on my cheeks, a million small goodbyes. By dawn, only Toya and I are left and we walk down to the beach to watch the sunrise together.

Toya and I used to "deal" back in Third Form, when we were about thirteen. This meant that we held hands at house parties and sometimes she would let me feel her up behind the pavilion at school, enjoying the notoriety it earned us more than the actual touching. Mostly I would go to her house and play *Call of Duty* while her mother swept the hallway outside her bedroom over and over again, finding new excuses to stick her head in and check on us. Now we're just friends. Toya and I have never talked about my secret, but she knows, in as much as anyone can know something about you when you hardly know it yourself. Tonight, as the night sky gives way to the weak blue of sunrise, she holds my hand. "Maybe it won't be so bad," she says. "I've heard Toronto's cool."

I shrug. "It won't be the same. I won't know anyone. You won't be there."

Toya smiles, eyes on the sea. "Or D," she says.

"Have you heard from him?" I ask, trying to keep the desperation out of my voice.

Toya shakes her head. "Nah, but I heard they let him go. I heard his father picked him up from the police station this morning."

"Shit," I say. D's father works for the Water Authority. I imagine him then, in his uniform, streaked with grease and dirt, walking into the police station to pick up his son. I wonder how much they told him.

When I get home, tipsy on the champagne Toya bought, I call Daniel again and again, his phone always going straight to voicemail. I listen to the recording but hang up each time without leaving a message. I listen until his voice becomes something completely detached from his body, no more a part of him than the hollow echo of a conch shell belongs to the ocean.

The next day I try to sneak out to see him, but Z comes early to drive me to the airport, and there isn't time. It's only when I'm on the plane, and about to switch to airplane mode on my phone, that D finally messages me back.

He sends a YouTube link, with no explanation. I click on it, praying it will load before the plane takes off. It's a surfing video, a wipeout compilation. A three-minute loop of bodies tumbling down walls of blue, disappearing into foam. I watch it again and again, looking for clues, and finding none. I watch it ten times, until the flight attendant comes by and makes me put my phone away. The plane takes off, and I press my nose to the glass, searching for our hotel on the shoreline. I think I see it, hardly distinguishable from the other hotels along the coast, but then we pass above the clouds and the island disappears from view.

CHAPTER EIGHTEEN

I'VE BEEN IN THE SHOWER FOR LESS THAN A MINUTE when the banging starts. I ignore it, turning the hot water to full blast and burying my head in the spray. It's only October, but I'm cold all the time. My uncle Junior says to get used to it because he won't be switching the heat on until it reaches below freezing. The banging on the bathroom door is incessant now. I turn the cold water off first and stand under the scalding stream until my skin can't stand it, and then I get out. When I open the door, Junior is leaning both hands against the door frame, nostrils flared like a bull about to charge. I step aside, and he barrels in, slamming the door behind him. "Good morning, Uncle!" I yell to the closed door, but he doesn't respond.

Junior and his wife don't actually live in Toronto, but in the suburb of Scarborough. Their apartment is on the third floor of a four-storey building at the corner of Morningside and Ellesmere. When I arrived two months ago, he refused to pick me up from the airport, insisting that it would be best for me to get used to the transit system right away. I lugged my two cases onto the airport express bus, rode the subway the length of the green line to Kennedy, and then caught another bus further east, a journey of almost two hours. I bypassed downtown entirely, saw no skyscrapers, or highways, or any of the sights I expected when arriving to a big city. Instead, the final bus of my journey deposited me at nondescript street corner, a gas station on one side, the glass facade of a local college on the other. I trekked up a small hill to the address provided, the ugly brown building one of several in a complex of other brown buildings, just as ugly.

The apartment itself is sparse and haphazardly furnished. Some items, like the large white sofa, seem modern and expensive, while others are falling apart. The ceiling is water-logged, and the carpet peels up at the corners of the room, smelling faintly of some animal's urine. There's an elevator but it's faster to take the stairs, which reek of weed and some dish that smells like a mix of pumpkin and fish. Sometimes groups of hooded boys sit on the stairs, one above the other as though posing for a family photo. They tried to deal to me at first, but they soon realized that I was too broke to be a decent customer, and now they don't speak to me at all.

"Your uncle has done very well for himself," Z had said, as we stood in the departure terminal at Grantley Adams Airport. He had insisted on driving me himself. Maybe he was worried my grandparents or my mother would give in at the last minute and let me stay. "You'll try to make yourself useful," Z went on. "He's busy with work and won't have time to babysit you."

The exact nature of Junior's "work" is as yet unclear. He is usually the last to wake up, often still sleeping when I leave in the mornings. On the days he is up early, like this morning, he rushes around the apartment in his boxers, yelling at his wife about the creases in his slacks and his inability to find a pair of socks that match. He always has a Bluetooth device attached to his ear and is often late for some meeting he claims to not have time for. His time, according to him, is in very high demand. More often than not, he returns from these meetings blind drunk and spends the afternoon asleep on the couch, his arms folded across his gut, content and drooling.

There are always boxes arriving to the apartment, where they remain unopened for weeks in tall stacks in the living room. Junior counts the boxes each morning, staring at me as he does so, and always seems slightly disappointed to find nothing missing. I'm almost certain he's involved in something illegal, but I've never been able to confirm my suspicions.

His wife, Freda, is a slight Haitian woman who has yet to speak more than a few words to me at a time. She slumps around the apartment in the same stained nightdress, and never seems fully awake. She's still breastfeeding their infant son, Didier, who spends half his days at her chest and the other half screaming from a bassinet in their bedroom. During my first few weeks in the house, I offered to help Freda with the baby while she made breakfast or folded one of her interminable loads of laundry. But with each offer she only held the baby more tightly, and shook her head, her eyes big, fearful, and a little glazed over.

I felt very sorry for Freda in those early weeks, until one night I woke to the sound of her and Junior arguing, and when I peeked out into the living room to investigate, saw Junior cowering in the corner like a child, his hands over his ears, snot and tears streaming down his face. He was naked from the waist down, his penis a shrunken shadow beneath his T-shirt. Freda stood over him, her face lit up like someone had finally found her On switch. Her nightgown glowed white in the dim light of the moon, her hair spiking around her head like a crown. "You nasty little man," she said, digging the toe of her fuzzy slipper into her husband's chest, knocking him to the floor.

I watched, unable to look away, as Junior took hold of her foot and caressed it, planting kisses along her calf. Freda yanked her foot away and spat on him, a fat glob that landed with impressive aim between his eyes. Junior only cried harder, reaching for the hem of her dress. With her free hand, she snatched it up and away from his reach, as though she were wading through some filthy bog and wished not to be contaminated. I closed the door to my room, burrowing my face in my pillow to stifle my laughter.

My room is actually a pantry, a narrow space without a window just off the kitchen into which Junior has wedged a thin piece of foam. This "mattress" takes up all the floor space, and so I have to stand on it to access the shelves, which I use as a closet. Junior made a big deal of the room when I arrived, claiming that he could have rented it out to "any of those rich Chinese undergrads" for six hundred a month. Freda had to move her canned goods out of the space to make room for me, and they remain stacked just outside the door, as though she is waiting for the opportunity to put them back. I'm sure my uncle Z is compensating Junior for putting me up, but still Junior takes careful inventory of everything I eat, making comments about the rising cost of dairy if I don't finish every last drop of milk in my cereal.

Technically, school started a month ago, and as far as Junior and the rest of my family are concerned, that's where I spend my days. But when the first day of school rolled around back in September it occurred to me that I simply didn't have to go. In the constant battle with my grandfather, school had always been the one thing we could agree on. I would always show up, and I would do the work. I would graduate, and probably do well enough to continue on to Sixth Form or community college. If I could pull this off, so the unspoken agreement went, he could handle the dreadlocks, the smoking, the shirking on chores, the fights. He could even handle the other thing, the one we didn't talk about, the great rift around which we danced every day. School was the compromise. But now my family hadn't held up their end of the deal, they'd sent me here, to this frozen hell of a city, to live with Junior, possibly the worst person I've ever met.

So every morning I pack a backpack with a water bottle, a blanket, and a couple of granola bars from the stash I've been hiding in my room, pilfered from Junior's cupboards when he and Freda weren't looking. Then I head out, pick a random direction, and start walking. This is how I spend my days, traversing the city by foot. The only thing that helps with the homesickness is to keep walking, keep moving around the city like a shark through shallow reef. Sometimes I hop on the bus to Kennedy station and go downtown. But mostly I stick to the lakeshore. I find its expansiveness calming. I've only ever been able to breathe properly when I'm looking out at the horizon across a large body of water.

This morning I head out before Junior gets done in the bathroom. In the stairwell, the air is dank, smelling of weed and dirt and something else, a smell that reminds me of Daniel, of his car on a hot day when he's been sweating behind the wheel. The memory sears like I've been stung by a man-o'-war. I pick up my pace, taking the stairs two at a time.

As always, a couple of boys huddle at the door to the building, smoking and looking out into the alley. They glare at me as I approach, and I stare back, my face blank. This is an expression I've perfected over the years. I've learned that to look away is to show weakness, but to mirror their expressions is a challenge. I communicate with my eyes: not a threat, but not someone to fuck with either. The boys lift their chins and step by to let me pass, but not fully, and I still have to make myself small to fit between them.

I'm almost through the door when one of them grabs my arm, not roughly, but firm enough that to shake him off, I'd need to make a scene. I glance down at his hand on my arm, and then back at him. He lets go, bringing his hands up to his side in a gesture of peace, grinning.

His teeth are bright white and a little crooked. He's young I realize, younger than me even, with a skinny face and big brown eyes. A bit of snot has crusted along the rim of his right nostril. His age makes me more afraid, not less. He must be about twelve, thirteen. I remember that age. I was wound even tighter then than I am now. This kid's body is warm beneath his coat, and he's shaking slightly, the way boys his age do, their bodies always humming with repressed energy. His friend is older and bigger, and not smiling. The bigger guy shifts so that his whole frame is blocking the doorway. The three of us stand on the threshold in a tight circle. I take a step back into the foyer.

"Where you from, bro?" the kid asks. "I never seen you around before." His accent is what I've come to understand as distinctly Scarborough, the tight, nasal vowels of Canadian peppered with something else, a borrowed Jamaican that took a detour through East Africa.

I shrug, adjusting the straps on my backpack, and decide to play this out. "The islands," I say, not bothering to get more specific.

"Say word," the kid says, "my mans here is from Jamaica. You ever been there?"

"Yeah, a few times," I say, addressing the big guy in the doorway. "I've got fam in Mandeville." But the guy only shrugs, his expression blank.

"I wish I was in Jamaica right now, yo. Can't stand this cold no more," says the first kid, his expression suddenly pensive.

"I should go," I say, "I've got class." I take a step forward, but the big guy doesn't shift from the doorway.

The kid grabs my arm again. "Don't be rude, bro, we're just talking to you."

"Yeah and I'm saying I've got to go." I shake his arm off and step up towards the big guy, so we're only a half a foot apart. He doesn't blink, his expression vacant. He reminds me of a grazing animal, like a cow in a pasture.

The kid goes nuts, pacing the way a small dog runs circles around your feet, nipping at your ankles. When he speaks, his voice is high and excited. "That's disrespectful, man. We're just talking to you, like, you're cheesing right now, fam. You can't be talking to people that way. Like, that's just disrespectful."

I step back. "Aight, man, sorry. I'm just late, you know?"

The kid stops pacing suddenly, his mood shifting again. I feel disoriented, like I've lost all control of the situation. "I feel you, man," he says, nodding solemnly. "My pops always says a real man shows up on time. He's an imam, you know. Real serious guy. But still, you can't be disrespecting mans like that." He's pacing again.

I start considering my options. Back up the stairs and into the apartment? But then what? I lock myself inside and never leave? My only option is to play this out. The kid stops pacing and takes a step towards me, calm now. He throws an arm around my shoulder and I try not to flinch. "You're new to the city, man, but you'll see. It's a good thing we met, I can teach you. If I was some other mandem, bro, you'd be dead right now." He lifts the hem of his jacket slightly to reveal the butt of a small black gun.

"Musa!" A voice sounds from the stairwell behind us. The kid jumps, dropping his jacket and stepping away from me. A man comes down the stairs and I realize, despite his booming voice, he's barely a man at all. He looks about my age, and he's also wearing a backpack. He shares some features in common with the kid, the long skinny face, their skin the same shade of clay tile. When he reaches us, he ignores the kid entirely, addressing the big guy in the doorway. "What's he still doing here? His bus left fifteen minutes ago."

The big guy shrugs, which seems to be his primary form of communication. This shrug seems to say, "What am I supposed to do about it."

The new guy turns his attention to the kid. "Where's your bag?"

The kid gestures vaguely up the stairs. His demeanour is sulky now, shoulders hunched, eyes down.

"Go get it," the guy says, and the kid groans in response. The new arrival narrows his eyes and the kid heads for the stairs, taking them slowly, heavy-footed. The guy watches him leave, and shaking his head, turns to me. "I apologize for my cousin," he says, "he's a little hyperactive." I almost laugh at this understatement, but I haven't gotten a read on this new guy yet and I'm still on edge from the glimpse of the gun in the kid's waistband.

"There's medication for that," I say, meaning it as a joke.

But his expression is sober. "Pills are for white people who can't control their children," he says, and the words are strange coming out of his mouth, like he's parroting someone older.

I want to say it doesn't seem like Musa is under control either but decide not to push my luck. Musa reappears then, a backpack dangling off one shoulder, not appearing to have anything in it. The new guy, his cousin, cups him playfully by the back of the head. Musa shakes him off, looking at me, chin still raised in challenge.

His cousin pulls a wallet out of his back pocket, unfolds a twenty-dollar bill, and passes it to the big guy. "Give him a ride for me," he says, and then turning to look at Musa, adds, "right to the entrance. And wait around for a bit to make sure he goes in."

Musa rolls his eyes in response, the gesture making him look even younger. The big guy shifts from the entrance and shuffles out onto the street. Musa follows, but stops to look back at me, flashing that grin again. "See you around, island man!"

I watch him swagger to the big guy's car, his hood pulled high and his pants low, and I feel a mixture of pity and relief, and something else, a recognition that gnaws. I think about telling his cousin about the gun but decide against it. None of my business. Instead, I give him a nod, thank him for his help, and turn for the door.

"Hold up," he says. "I apologize for Musa. He's living with us right now. Things are . . . difficult for him at home. But he won't bother you again. You have my word."

"Don't worry about it." I wait a beat, and then, curious, ask, "The big guy, he works for you?"

He tilts his head and squints at me, sizing me up. "In a way. He won't bother you either."

"I can handle myself," I say, automatically.

"I'm sure you can. I can sense that about you." He smiles, and I'm not sure if he's making fun of me or being sincere. "I'm Mazin," he adds, extending a thin-boned hand.

"Nautilus," I say, and his eyes light up.

"Great name," he says. "I love names. They're important, don't you think? Mine means rain clouds. What does your name mean?"

I shrug, but Mazin is unfazed. He promises me he will find out. "It must be water related, the etymology. My mother named me Mazin because she was pregnant during a drought. Where we are from, droughts, they are very deadly. Many people starve. But the minute I was born, the rains began to fall. She says she knew I would be a saviour. Someone to bring the rain when it is needed most."

"That's a lot of pressure," I say.

Mazin laughs. "I am my father's eldest son. Pressure is inevitable. Do you live here with your family?"

"No," I say, not wanting to claim Junior as any part of me. "My family is back home."

"So you are alone here?" He sounds sad, but not pitying.

"Yes, but I don't mind it."

We're quiet for a moment, and then, knowing instinctually that he will like this detail, I say, "I was born during a hurricane." This is true. My mother delivered me at the hotel. My grandmother has told me the story many times. Palm fronds flew through the sky and landed like bombs on the roof. There

THE ISLAND OF FORGETTING

was no electricity or running water. They called for an ambulance but it didn't come in time, all the roads were flooded. So my grandmother put my mother in the tub and filled it from the bottled water. Then everything went quiet. When I let out my first cry, it pierced the stillness. I had waited for the eye of the hurricane to pass right above us before I made my entrance.

"You see?" Mazin says, excited. "I told you names are important. Brothers in the storm." He says the last part with a laugh, and I decide then that I like him. I feel seen, for the first time since I left Barbados. He gestures to the door. To the trash-strewn parking lot, and the street beyond. "I don't want to keep you from class. Do you go to UTSC?"

"No," I say, debating how far to stretch the truth. "I don't plan to be in Toronto for long. I'm still figuring things out right now."

Mazin frowns at this. He's dressed his age, in fitted jeans, Nikes, and a cargo jacket, but even so he looks like a dad, the way he rolls onto the balls of his feet when he speaks, his head bowed in concentration. He reminds me of my grandfather. "I was figuring things out once, too," he says, "unsure what direction to take. I felt like I was at a crossroads, standing at the corner of a busy intersection. The cars were flying by, people were shoving past me. It felt like everyone but me knew where they were going, what they wanted. Have you ever felt that way, Nautilus?"

"I think everyone has, at one time or another," I say.

Mazin nods, pleased with this response. "So, I stood there on the edge, watching the world go by, for a very long time. But eventually I had to choose a path, even though I wasn't sure it was the right one. Because it's only once you start walking that you realize each path leads to another intersection, each one bigger than the last, the choices branching off in multiple directions now. And then you choose again and again, and soon, you don't feel stuck anymore."

"Musa says your uncle is an imam," I say, smiling.

Mazin laughs. "Yes," he says, "and giving sermons is a family affliction. I apologize."

"No, that's okay," I say, meaning it. "It's good advice."

We stand together at the door in silence, surveying the empty parking lot. I think of Daniel, of standing shoulder to shoulder with him on the beach, watching the sea, reading the tides, the swell. The big guy's car pulls back into the lot, but he remains in the driver's seat, the engine idling. Mazin raises his chin towards him, a silent question, and the big guy nods.

"Nautilus," he says, turning to offer me his hand again, "it was nice meeting you." I shake it, understanding that I'm being dismissed, but I don't leave. Mazin looks at me, as if anticipating my question.

"Musa, and this other guy, they deal for you, right?" I ask.

Mazin doesn't react, except to frown slightly.

"I only ask," I say, stammering, "because I'm looking for a job too."

I wasn't planning to say this, but it feels true once it's out. I would only need a few hundred dollars for a one-way ticket back to Barbados. Then maybe a few grand to set myself up once I get there, maybe find a small place to rent. If I could just get back to the island, I could make everything right with Daniel. Everything could go back to the way it was.

Mazin still doesn't respond. His eyes are a deep brown, almost black, and unreadable. He stares right at me, not blinking, and I resist the urge to look away. I picture myself at the corner Mazin spoke of, the busy intersection with the people streaming by, my feet balanced on the curb.

Finally, Mazin blinks. He smiles and slaps me on the shoulder. "I'll see you around, Nautilus," he says, and jogs out to the car. His backpack bounces as he runs, the words BLACK EXCELLENCE emblazoned in whiteout across the front pocket. I watch him, feeling deflated, until he reaches the car. Then, with the passenger door open and his body half in, he calls my name. "Tomorrow. Same time, same place," he says, with a small salute. And then they are gone, the car pulling slowly out of the lot.

❦ *CHAPTER NINETEEN*

At night, I lie awake in my room and see ghosts. They are the same tormentors of my childhood. The bacoo and the steel donkey and the heartman. Characters lifted from those stories my grandmother told to scare me into behaving. For a lullaby, she sang an old calypso about a bacoo named Conrad that lived in the belly of a woman named Doris, driving her mad from the inside out. "One more word from you and I'm going to fetch Conrad," she'd say, and I'd immediately quiet down.

My grandmother was baptized Anglican, like most Bajans, but converted to Catholicism shortly after my mother was born because, as she explained to me once, she fell in love with Mary. "What a classy dame," my grandmother would say often, looking up at the Blessed Virgin in stained glass above the high altar of St. Patrick's Cathedral. I suspect what she loves most is the solemnity of it all, the hymns, the eucharist, the rites and rituals. The blood and sacrifice. She's a superstitious woman, just as

likely to draw from bush wisdom and the Bible in equal measure. Her devils take many forms: bacoos, duppies, soucouy-
ants. "At the end of the day," my grandmother says, "there's
good and there's evil. The rest is just semantics."

My grandfather and my mother never go to church anymore, but when I was a boy, I used to accompany my grandmother. I liked spending time with her, away from the hotel.
But even then, sitting and squirming in the pew, I knew I didn't
belong. Whenever the priest asked us to remember our sins,
thoughts rose unbidden in my mind like memories of a life not
yet lived, all those sins already sprouting within me. And so
when my grandmother spoke of good and evil, of all the devils
that were watching me, waiting to pounce, I knew it was only
a matter of time until they came for me. I never let on how
scared those stories made me, how even well past the age when
I should have known better, I would lie awake at night, waiting
for the ghosts to appear.

When I was still a boy, still with some softness left in me,
though getting harder and harder each day, pain soldering my
skin like armour, my grandmother asked me to help her clean
out the office at the hotel. As we were sorting the old files, I
came across an envelope in my grandfather's desk. In it was a
faded photograph of two boys. One was about the age that I
was then, the other a bit older. I showed it to my grandmother.
"That is Cronus. Uncle Z's father," she said, pointing to the
older boy who stood stiff and proud in a khaki school uniform.
I could see the resemblance, not in their features, but in the way
Cronus stared at the camera, as if willing it to tell him something he didn't already know. Z has the same stare.

"And the other boy?" I asked. My grandmother hesitated,

only for a moment, but long enough to let me know I was about to hear something new. There was so much I didn't know then. So much I didn't understand. Like why did my mother sometimes hold me in her arms at night, her hot tears drenching my pajamas, and tell me I was the only reason she had for getting out of bed in the morning? Only at other times to look at me as though she wasn't quite sure who I was, or where I'd come from, her eyes dead and glassy? Why did she leave for days at a time? Who was my father, and why wasn't I enough to make him stay?

"That's your great-grandfather," my grandmother said, finally. "That's Iapetus. Your grandfather never met him. He . . . had a difficult time of things. He died young."

Over the years, I was able to put together a fractured portrait of Iapetus's life, built of tiny fragments my grandmother shared, piecemeal, as though she were rationing the truth, making it stretch as far as she could. What I learned was that my great-grandfather was like me. A fuck-up. An outcast. And that he had disappeared, simply walked away from the life he was born into, and chose something different, a harder, dirtier life, but a freer one.

My mother chose the same. Through her I learned that madness is a curse, but also a superpower. It's as though, the more attention my mother got, the more of a spectacle she became, the freer she was. I wanted to be free. Free from the bullies who tormented me in school. Free from my own weakness, all that hope that lived in the soft centre of my being. Hope my mother would love me properly. Hope my father would come back. And so, I learned to play the part of the madman too. I learned how to flatten out my expression so my eyes reflected nothing, like cloudy skies. I would climb the highest tamarind tree and jump out, just to see what the fall was like. I picked fights I knew I couldn't win, until other boys got bored of fighting me. What's the fun in hurting someone who's chasing pain like it's the only thing that will save him?

And now I wonder if the madness has come for me at last, just as it did my mother and my great-grandfather. The duppies watch me from the shelves of the pantry, where they sit, swinging their thin legs back and forth like children on a playground. They grin at me, licking their fingertips. Except now they aren't characters from stories, but real people, with real faces. There's the police officer, the one with the long nails. He drums them into the shelves, the sound like rain on a galvanized roof. There's Daniel, his face bloodied and bruised, his shorts still undone. He stares at me, sullen and dead-eyed.

But then, a shift in the shadows. Freda turns on the kitchen light, a thin beam lights up the floor of the pantry, and the duppies disappear. The fear recedes, leaving me washed up, like some creature spat out from the sea floor in the wake of a storm. I didn't put up a fight when my family sent me away. I was caught off guard, still reeling from the arrest, but my head is clear now. I will work for Mazin and save up enough money to go back. Not back to the cottage, I'm done living on Z's charity. I'll get my own place, somewhere in the countryside, somewhere in those fields and hills beyond recall. Somewhere I can shed the armour I've been hiding under all these years. Maybe, just maybe, Daniel will join me there. I can't control the madness that runs in my bloodline. Maybe it will come for me, maybe it won't. But freedom, that's mine for the making.

In the mornings, I wake early and I'm out the door before Junior stirs. Working for Mazin, my days aren't much different than they were before. Like before, I leave Junior's apartment each day, as if I were headed to school. Only now I meet Mazin in the lobby of our building and he hands me a backpack and a cellphone. The cellphone is only to be used for work, and is returned to Mazin each night, along with the backpack, when I meet him again in the lobby to hand over the cash, minus my cut, and any remaining product.

Before I started dealing for Mazin, I could name three types of drugs: weed, coke, and molly. But in my first week working for him, I sold more Adderall than anything else, most popular among university students. Mazin's supply varies, but he has regular weed customers, people who for whatever reason prefer to avoid the government supply. He sells shrooms, when he can get them, though he says they're more popular in the summertime. Ketamine, LSD, cocaine, MDMA. No meth and no opiates, Mazin explained, because the customers are too difficult to deal with.

I don't know where Mazin sources his product, and I don't care to ask. The less I know, the better. I just take the backpack and the phone and head out. Like before, I spend my days wandering around the city by foot and transit, but now the cellphone determines my destination. Sometimes, Mazin has already set up appointments, which I confirm via text the morning of. But mostly I just respond to the messages as they come in, the work taking me from UTSC, where I meet stressed-out undergrads in their dorms, their eyes red-rimmed, their teeth on edge, to Forest Hill, where white kids in sweatpants and hoodies meet me at the ends of their massive driveways, glancing over their shoulders and generally acting exactly like you'd imagine people buying drugs to act.

As I roam around the city, I imagine inserting myself into

the lives of the people I meet. In the gay village, I sell to yup-
pie couples who are always inviting me in. I catch glimpses of
their apartments over their shoulders, windows into another
life, but I never go inside. I don't know why. Something about
the men—clean-shaven and strong-jawed, leaning confidently
against their door frames in expensive jeans. Could I be myself
with men like that? Sometimes I think the real me is over
that threshold. But other times I think the real me is still in
Barbados, with the local boys, drinking lukewarm beer under
a manchineel tree.

Mazin worries I won't make the appointments without a
car, but I'm never late. I like travelling the city this way, through
its veins and capillaries, getting to know it from the inside out.
After the first month, Mazin is impressed. I'm reliable, he says.
I wonder how anyone could be bad at a job this easy but apparently Mazin struggles to find good help. The big guy, whose
name I now know is Curtis, is always messing up, getting into
arguments with customers, missing appointments. Mazin's big
on punctuality. "This is what keeps my customers loyal," he
says, "consistency." Mazin is a business major at Centennial
College and is always throwing around terms he picks up in
class. The drug dealing, he says, is a "short-term way to ensure
positive cash flow for my future interests."

Two months in, I've met most of the regulars at least once.
I have my favourites, like Mrs. Mukherjee, a Trinidadian
woman in her eighties who lives alone in a three-bedroom
house off Lawrence Avenue. She makes the best roti I've ever
tasted and her living room reminds me of home, with its dated
mahogany furniture, crystal figurines, and lace curtains. She
buys a gram of weed a week. The government online store,
she explained to me, is too confusing. She tried going to a

dispensary once but hated the experience. "It was like going to one of those fancy computer stores," she said, "horrid music. Everyone grinning and holding iPads and going on about this strain and that strain. I couldn't understand a word." After my third delivery to her, I suggest she make a larger purchase so that she doesn't have to text me as often, but she seems wounded by the notion that I don't want to visit her, and so I never bring it up again. I guess she likes the company, all alone in that big house.

Not all customers are that friendly, and there are those I'm wary of, like the sketchy guy who lives in a glass high-rise near Scarborough Town Centre who goes by "Mr. Anderson." He often answers the door in nothing but boxers and is always trying to pay with crypto. But mostly, they're harmless. It helps that I work in the daytime, Monday to Friday, while Curtis handles the evening and weekend deliveries, the house parties and the club scene. Still, Mazin warns me to be careful. Never reveal where you live, or any personal details, he tells me. When he was first starting out, he let slip to a customer that he attends Centennial. The guy started showing up to campus, asking for him. One night, when he was leaving the library at closing, the guy jumped him, looking for coke. I asked Mazin how he got the guy to leave him alone. Mazin smiled and slapped my shoulder in that fatherly way he is fond of. "There is no problem without a solution, my friend," he said, and, thinking of the gun his twelve-year-old cousin keeps in his waistband, I decided not to press for details.

It's Friday evening, and I've got my final appointment of the day. It's a customer I've never met before, saved in the phone under the name Angelo. He requested a bulk order of LSD. I asked Mazin about him this morning when we met in the lobby as usual. "Strange man," Mazin said. "I don't think he leaves his apartment very often." Angelo lives by Sherbourne station, in one of those old white high-rises, each indistinguishable from the next, except for Angelo's, which is marked by a giant mural along the side of the building, a phoenix, its body painted in bright blues and pinks, its head an explosion of yellow at the building's highest point. The buzzer isn't working, but the main door is being propped open by a stack of phone books, so I head straight in and up to the twenty-fourth floor.

Angelo answers the door and a shock of wet heat escapes his apartment and into the hall. He looks nothing like what I expected. He is young, in his early twenties maybe, with a close-shaven head. In each earlobe he wears thick black earrings, the kind of wooden ones that stretch the piercing out. Around his neck, he's wearing a string of brown beads that at first I mistake for a rosary.

His skin is almost the same shade as mine but faded to a wan yellow. He is small, but muscular, the thick tendons in his neck giving way to a sharp jaw, high cheekbones. His eyes are deep brown slashes, as if carved as an afterthought into an otherwise intricate face. He is so beautiful, I stand momentarily paralyzed in front of him. I am flooded with desire, so suddenly, as though a storm cloud opened up above our heads and drenched me in it. Angelo sees it, and I see him seeing it and I look down and away, embarrassed at how easily I betray myself.

"You're not who I was expecting," he says, his voice low and quiet.

"Sorry?" I say. Then, understanding, "Oh, you mean Curtis? No, I'm new. I'm Nautilus." I extend my hand and Angelo looks at it without taking it.

"Tell Mazin he has to let me know before he sends strangers," Angelo says, and then he closes the door, leaving me alone in the cold hallway. I hear the sound of a deadbolt sliding into place. I blink at the closed door, feeling suddenly parched.

I call Mazin but he doesn't answer. Unsure what else to do, I slide to the ground to wait it out. I don't want to leave, only to have Mazin call and sort it out, and then have to come back downtown later. But, if I'm being honest with myself, I really just want to see Angelo again. I wait another fifteen minutes and then send Mazin a text, explaining. He answers right away. He's in class, he says, but will be done soon. I spread my legs out across the grimy carpet of the hallway. No one is coming or going. Through the closed doors of the neighbouring apartments, I can hear what sounds like a video game being played, a baby crying, something sizzling in a pan. Living sounds. They lull me to sleep and soon I am dozing against the wall. In my half-sleep, I dream of a jungle.

It's a dream I've been having almost every night since I left Barbados. I'm walking through the thick damp green, the leaves pressing into my skin like hands, pushing me forward. I can see someone ahead of me through the foliage, just a flash of a white T-shirt, brown skin. But I can't reach him. The jungle engulfs me, holding me in an embrace of roots and branches. It feels like when I was very small and my grandfather would pull me into a bear hug, my tiny chest pressing against his cavernous one. He held me, and I felt every one of my bones resist, my tiny heart struggling against the pressure of it. There is something miraculous about giving yourself up to another completely in this way, in those moments when you accept the crushing weight of your own smallness, in the face of something infinite. When

I was a child, my grandfather seemed infinite to me. I wonder if this is how birds feel when we trap them in our cupped hands. Terrified, but so very alive. This is the same thrill I get surfing, when I'm tumbled in a big wave, the ocean tossing me about like a plaything.

This time, in my dream, when the jungle recedes, I find myself not in the garden of the villa but in a small apartment. I still can't find Daniel, but I'm not alone. Angelo is there. He's surrounded by green, but it doesn't crush him the way it did me. The leaves slither around him, vines crawling along the floor, up the walls. But he seems to be the one in control, like Moses parting a great sea.

I wake to Angelo staring down at me. He's watching me, and for a moment, I'm convinced he can see what I was dreaming of. Then I shake myself fully awake and get to my feet. I remind myself that I'm here to work. "We good?" I ask, extending my hand. This time Angelo takes it. His hand is soft and a little damp. I see a flash of green and shudder. Angelo doesn't let go. He lets out a soft sigh. "I suppose you better come inside," he says. Then he turns, my hand still in his, and leads me into his apartment. Immediately I begin to sweat.

And what is this feeling when the door closes behind us, and without a word, Angelo unbuttons my coat? This is madness, what I'm doing, with this strange man in his jungle apartment. I undo the ties of his bathrobe and push it to the floor. Somewhere the duppies are howling, ready for a feast. Somewhere, my grandmother weeps. But I know, too, what my great-grandfather Iapetus must have known: there is no freedom in the familiar. Only comfort, and slow death.

Up close, I can see the skin around Angelo's lips is white and flaking. Sweat beads on the bridge of his nose and when he kisses me, he tastes like salt. We are almost to our boxers by the time we make it to the living room. I turn my back to him, my hands braced on the back of the couch, while Angelo runs a messy line down the length of my spine with his tongue. I struggle to remain standing, my body all liquid. He bites into the flesh at the small of my back, just above the elastic of my boxers, and then he spins me to face him.

From where I stand above him, I can see a small tuft of hair he must have missed when shaving his head, sprouting up from the crown like crabgrass through pavement. He doesn't ask any questions, he doesn't speak at all, until the moment right before he takes me in his mouth, his fingers curled through mine, our bodies slippery as eels. "Yes," he says. And it's a question, and not a question. I nod. Yes, I think, yes and yes and yes.

Afterwards, I lie awake in Angelo's bed and stare up at the ceiling where a devil's ivy snakes across the rough plaster. For a moment I'm back in the holding cell at the police station where the same plant hung in the corner, and the memory is so visceral I have to silence a cry that arises, unbidden, from some deep and forgotten hole in my chest. Beside me, Angelo stirs but doesn't wake.

I know there's no chance of sleep now, so I get up and potter around Angelo's room, trying to get to know him through his things. By his bed, I examine three tall stacks of books, most of the titles unfamiliar. There are many textbooks, mostly on plant biology, but others on topics ranging from radical queer politics to mechanical engineering. I ignore these, looking instead for the novels, of which there are several, their pages dog-eared as if Angelo is reading all of them at once. My mother reads books this way, moving from one to the other, like someone trying to quench her thirst by diving into the ocean.

A woman's Caribana costume hangs in the closet. I slip on the headpiece, admiring myself in the mirror, the pink feathers and sequins flashing in the moonlight. I left Barbados just a week before Kadooment Day. This was the first year since I can remember that I didn't play mas. I picture my friends decked out in their regalia, dancing down Spring Garden Highway, drunk on rum and sun, all their bare skin pressed together in the band, the music so loud you can almost taste it, the metallic hum of the bass on your tongue. I finger the beads, homesickness like a clenched fist around my heart.

But then I glance over at Angelo where he sleeps with his hands clasped under his chin as if in prayer. I think about what we just did, and the fact that we could do it again right now, and tomorrow, if we wanted to. That night with Daniel, something blossomed in me like a first sapling springing up from starved earth. But now it feels as though the skies have opened up and I'm soil overturned. How can I go back now that I know what I've been missing? I settle back into bed beside Angelo, unclasping one of his hands so that I can wrap his arm around me like a blanket. He wakes for a moment, and then settles into me, his breath on my neck. He's practically a stranger, but when I look down the length of our bodies entwined, it feels as though I have known him forever. Lying here with him in the fragile stillness of the morning, I'm so content I could weep.

I wake mid-morning. Angelo is at his desk in the living room, back in his bathrobe, the cowl pulled over his head. There's something monkish about him and I wonder how often he leaves the apartment.

"I'm heading out," I say. He doesn't pause in his typing.

"The money I owe you is on the coffee table," he says. And

though I know he means the drug money I can't help feeling like I was part of the transaction.

"Can I see you again?" I ask, embarrassed.

Angelo stops working finally and turns in his chair, almost facing me. He runs a hand over his face, a thin layer of stubble having appeared on his cheeks overnight. I want to rub my own cheek against it, like a cat scratching itself on a rough bit of drywall. "I'm not looking for anything serious right now," he says, "but I had a very good time." He speaks slowly, as if carefully measuring each word.

I pull my coat on, and with it, I feel more impermeable, like a child who thinks a thin sheet will protect him from monsters hiding in the closet. "Just message Mazin when you need to pick up again," I say, fishing in my coat pockets for cigarettes. I want to seem busy, distracted. Angelo nods, already turning back to his laptop. I let myself out.

I have several missed calls from Mazin. I've missed our meeting. My first mistake since I started working for him. I try calling him back, but he doesn't answer. When I get home, I go first to the stairwell in search of him, and finding it empty, I head to his apartment instead. I knock once, softly, and when no one comes I rap again, loudly this time. The door is flung open by Musa who looks even younger than usual in a matching pajama set, a bowl of cereal in his right hand and a moustache of milk around his lips.

He wipes his mouth with the back of his free hand and looks me up and down. "You look like shit, bro. You been hiking or something?"

I ignore him, staring over his shoulder into the apartment. "Mazin here?"

Musa rolls his eyes and yells for his cousin, his voice piercing

the Saturday morning hush of the apartment. I wonder if any
adults are home. Mazin appears from a bedroom, looking like
a slightly ruffled version of his usual self in sweatpants and bare
feet. He comes to the door and slaps Musa lightly on the curve
of his head. "Don't yell like that. Your auntie is sleeping." Then
he turns to me, his eyes as unreadable as always.

"Hey man," I say, "I'm sorry I missed our meeting last night."
I reach around for the backpack. "But I have everything . . ."

Mazin puts up a hand. "Not here."

Musa, his mouth full of Cheerios, adds, "Fam, you can't be
doing business like that. Shit's disrespectful."

"Quiet, Musa," Mazin says, and then, to me, "downstairs,
five minutes." He shuts the door.

In the lobby, our usual spot, I prop the side door open with my
foot and smoke two cigarettes back to back. Mazin takes about
fifteen minutes to come down, and when he does, he's dressed in
his usual jeans and sneakers. We stand there for a beat, me looking at the ground, Mazin staring at the top of my head.

"So yeah," I say finally. "Sorry again. Here's everything." I
hand over the backpack. I'm suddenly exhausted and want nothing more than to head upstairs and sleep the rest of the day away.

"What happened? Are you alright?"

I've always found concern more difficult to handle than
anger. I just wish Mazin would give me shit about missing
the appointment, dock my cut, whatever. I can't stand the way
he bows his head towards mine like a worried parent. "Yeah,
I'm fine," I say, my voice icy. "It doesn't matter where I was. I
missed a meeting and it won't happen again. We good?"

Mazin doesn't answer but takes the backpack. I nod and
move past him, heading for the stairs. He stops me with an arm
around my shoulder. I think he's going to give me another one

of his lectures, and I tense up. But instead he says, "I need you to do something for me."

I step back and look at him. I notice now how tired he looks. His eyes are bloodshot and swollen, his cheeks rough with the shadow of a beard. He glances around and then unzips his jacket, removing from the waistband of his jeans a small black handgun. Musa's gun.

I take a step back, my hands up in surrender. "Man . . . I don't think . . . I don't want to hurt anyone."

Mazin shakes his head. "Nothing like that, Nautilus. I just need you to keep it for a little while."

"Keep it? Like on me?"

"Just hide it somewhere safe. I just need it out of my apartment for a while."

"Why? What's going on?"

Mazin lets his jacket fall, bringing his hands to his eyes. He presses his index fingers into the inner corners briefly and takes a long breath. When he speaks his voice has a new edge to it. "You work for me. This is the job. If you don't want to do it, that's fine. I'll find someone else. But if you want to keep working for me, then this is the job."

I could say no. In the two months since I started dealing for Mazin, I've saved more than enough for my ticket home. But I have to admit to myself that it isn't just about the money anymore. I like the job. I like the sense of purpose it gives me each morning. I like being good at something, being relied upon, for once. And there's a small, sad part of me that doesn't want to give up the chance to see Angelo again. I hold my hand out. Mazin places the gun in my open palm. I've never held a gun before, and it feels cold and awkward in my grasp. "Is it loaded?" I ask.

Mazin shakes his head, and I slip the gun into my jacket pocket, not feeling confident enough to put it in my waistband. Mazin takes a step towards me, and for one strange moment, I think he's going to hug me, but instead he reaches up for something in my hair, holding it out for me to see, a single yellowed leaf. We both stare at the leaf for a moment, and then Mazin drops it to the floor between us.

"I'll see you Monday," he says. "Don't be late."

I watch him disappear up the stairs, and I light another cigarette. I could just take the gun down to the lakeshore and throw it into the water, not yet completely frozen over. Or just find a dumpster somewhere. Instead, I finish my cigarette and head upstairs, stopping first to pick up the discarded leaf. Junior is asleep on the couch, in boxers and socks, scratching dreamily at his balls. In my room, I use a T-shirt to wipe the gun clean and then I wrap it up in the same shirt and place it on the highest shelf, just out of sight. It's the same shelf where I keep the cash I've saved working for Mazin. Close to four thousand dollars wrapped into a tight wad and stuffed into one of Freda's old flour containers. Then I lie in bed, twirling the leaf between my thumb and forefinger, until I fall asleep.

CHAPTER TWENTY

CHRISTMAS COMES AND GOES LIKE ANY OTHER DAY, the only upside being that Junior and Freda spend it in Brampton, at the home of one of Freda's distant cousins. I try calling home but can't get through. Christmas is always a busy time at the hotel, as the guests all stay in for lunch. If I were at home, I would have been put to work, probably behind the bar. My grandmother would have snuck me a plate of food from the buffet when my grandfather wasn't looking, and I'd get steadily drunk on the house rum punch as the day progressed. After all the festivities had ended and the guests had gone to bed, I would help my grandmother clean up. She'd put that Joni Mitchell song on, the one about skating away on a river, and get really quiet. Christmas always made my grandmother a little sad. "You know, I've never seen snow, Nautilus," she told me one year. "But you will. And you'll have to tell me what it's like."

Junior left the house bare of food, so in the afternoon I walk down to the gas station for instant ramen. The streets are deserted, no cars in sight. There's plenty of snow, and I think about snapping a picture of it to send to my grandmother, but I change my mind. The snow is brown and dirty, splattered with dog piss. I don't think it's what she had in mind. In the gas station, carols blare from the loudspeakers but no one stands behind the counter, so I leave without paying. Back home, I overcook the ramen and the noodles dissolve on my tongue as I eat.

I have the most horrible feeling, like I am completely alone, not just in the apartment, but in the world. It feels as though something terrible has happened, and everyone has disappeared, leaving me forever. I'm almost relieved when Junior and Freda return late that night, the sound of their bickering like the first song of birds after a storm, a sign of life.

By January I still haven't heard from Angelo, and my pride is fighting a losing battle against the crushing loneliness. It has finally begun to snow in earnest. What I thought was winter before, I realize, was only a prelude to the real thing. Temperatures drop well below freezing and stay there. I find the cold suffocating. What kind of place is this? What kind of people choose to live in a place so cold, it's painful just to walk outside? Every morning I head out to work, and within minutes my face feels as though it's being cleaved off, as though I'm dying, one skin cell at a time. The snow makes my job much more difficult. Just getting to the bus stop takes twice the time it did before, the snowplows not having bothered to venture to this part of Scarborough, the sidewalks slick with ice.

Tonight, I'm at a shisha bar with Mazin, my mood fouler than the weather outside. It doesn't help that he's in one of his lecturing moods, gesticulating with the hookah hose as he speaks. He's asking me about my father, my least favourite topic of conversation.

I was still a baby when my father left us, and I have no memories of him. My mother tried when I was small to tell me about him, but to me these were ghost stories. They only filled me with dread. The photographs of the three of us were like evidence of some horrific crime. My father was not a real man, but a spectre, like one of the duppies from my grandmother's folk tales. Everything about him terrified me, from his pale, burned skin to his blue eyes, freakishly similar to my own. He was the man who carved out my mother's heart, a succubus, a flesh-eating monster, a vampire. He stole something from me that I couldn't even name, some idea of what a mother should be, like my friends' mothers who I met at birthday parties and church picnics, their arms laden with food, rushing to and fro, fussing over their boys. Those women looked like busy miracles to me.

I try to explain this to Mazin but the words don't come out right. When I tell him that my father lives here, in Toronto, Mazin exhales a large, watermelon-scented cloud, his brow furrowed behind it. "That is not right, Nautilus, for a son to be so near to his father, and not visit," he says, "it is disrespectful."

I'm about to respond, but I reach for the shisha instead, taking a long pull. I'm getting sick of Mazin and his sociopathic little cousin telling me what is and isn't respectful. "But he left us," I say, trying to keep my voice level. "He doesn't want anything to do with me."

Mazin sucks his teeth, and I wonder if that's a Somalian thing too, or if he picked it up from living in Scarborough, surrounded by so many Caribbean people. It's impossible to know in this city where one culture ends and the other begins. "This is the attitude of a child," he says. "You are a man now. You must look at things as a man would."

"'When I was a child, I spoke as a child, I understood as a child, I thought as a child; but when I became a man, I put away childish things.'" I say it in one breath, exhaling the words with the smoke. The quote comes to me unbidden, the way these things do, like lullabies sung to us as children. My grandmother, the voice in my head, as always.

Mazin smiles. "Corinthians."

"You know it?'

"Muslim scholars have written extensively on your apostle Paul," he says. "Honour your father. Isn't that something else it says in your book?"

I shake my head and take another pull of shisha. There's no point in arguing with Mazin, about anything. He reminds me of my grandfather, whose answer to any problem is to turn to his bookshelf, pull down a well-worn hardback, sometimes poetry, most often a novel, and push it into the hands of the person seeking advice. "The answers you need are in there," he would say, and usually, he was right.

"You don't understand," I say, unwilling to cede the point. "He broke my mother's heart. Left us with nothing, no money, not even a way to reach him."

"My father did many things I did not understand when I was a boy. But now, I can see the burdens he was carrying, the difficult choices he had to make."

"But he stuck around."

Mazin nods. "Yes."

"So that's different."

"In a way. But your father is not dead. He is a bus ride away. You could have answers, if you cared to ask."

I want to keep arguing, but Mazin has stopped listening. He leans back into the plush sofa, looking across the room. I follow his gaze through the smoke. At a far table, a group of Tamil guys sit huddled, watching us. Mazin raises his chin in their direction. "I have to go," he says, "business."

"Do you need me?" I ask. I'm tense from our conversation, wound up and looking for a fight.

"No," he says, smiling. "It's not that kind of business." He drops a hundred-dollar bill onto the table. "I'll see you tomorrow."

I sit for a few minutes more, smoking the shisha until the last of the tobacco burns acrid in my throat. I pull my phone out, scrolling through my texts. I begin to type one to send to Daniel, but my fingers feel fat and clumsy on the keyboard, the message full of typos. I start over, and then give up. He won't answer me anyway. Instead, for the thousandth time, I watch the video he sent, of the surfers tumbling from the tops of waves, their bodies suspended, spinning, their boards trailing behind them like kites before they land, disappearing into the blue. I've watched it so many times the video has become detached from reality, like a word repeated too many times. I let my phone fall loudly to the glass tabletop, drawing the attention of a group of girls at a nearby table. One catches my eye. I smile, she smiles. I think how easy it would be, how easy it all could be. Then I pick my phone back up, and text Angelo.

Mazin never explicitly told me that I shouldn't copy numbers from the work contacts and save them to my personal phone, but it was implied. Angelo also never explicitly told me that he wanted to hear from me again, outside of deliveries, but when I think of him in his warm apartment, nails thick with dirt, his skin smelling of aloe and thyme and a hundred other plant species, the urge to see him forces every other thought from my head. My message to him is short. I ask if I can come over and I don't offer an explanation. He doesn't respond. I stare at the black screen of my phone and count backwards from one hundred. Then I grab my coat and head outside.

The wind claws like cold hands through the collar of my coat, down my spine. Mazin is always telling me to get a scarf, but I hate the feel of them around my neck. I start walking south, towards the subway. It's been almost a month since the day I met Angelo, when he invited me inside. Now, like then, I feel as though I'm stumbling blindly towards him. Tethered, like when I was a Sea Scout and our troop went night diving for the first time, and we unspooled a guideline through a ship-wreck as we swam so that we could find our way out in the darkness.

Tonight, when he answers the door, he's dressed in worn jeans that hang low on his hips and a sweatshirt. His hair has grown slightly, a fuzzy halo. Even in the hall, I can tell the apartment is as hot as last time, but Angelo shivers, folding his arms around his belly. He seems to take a minute to rec-ognize me.

"Can I come in?" I ask, my hand on the door frame, slightly out of breath, though from what I don't know. Anticipation, maybe. Angelo nods, and walks away, leaving the door open. By the time I remove my coat and boots, Angelo is curled up on the couch, beneath a blanket.

"Are you sick?" I ask, coming to stand above him. He shakes his head, burrowing his face into the brown leather. "Can I get you anything?"

Angelo doesn't respond, so I go to the kitchen. I think I'll make tea but realize this is overly ambitious. The kitchen looks like a living organism. Plants crowd every surface, including most of the floor. In the cupboards mason jars, their contents labelled with masking tape, glow green with mould. I find a teapot, but it too is mouldy. I can't tell whether it is part of an experiment, or just in need of a wash. Eventually I find a mug that looks somewhat clean, and I fill it with tap water. Back in the living room, I place the water on the coffee table and then sit beside Angelo on the couch, placing a hand on his shoulder. He trembles slightly beneath my touch, his body hot, his heart beating too fast, like a newborn animal. He reaches around for my hand and holds it weakly.

"Messed up my mescaline dosage," he says finally, his voice muffled against the couch cushions. I'm so relieved I let out a small laugh. He's just having a bad trip. "Don't laugh," he says, "everything is blue. My plants, they can't survive in all of this blue."

I give his hand a light squeeze. "Your plants will be fine," I say. "I'll look after them."

Angelo rolls over to face me now. Creases line his forehead and he looks small and fragile, like a child just awoken from a bad dream. I feel a sudden rush of tenderness for him. I press my hand to his forehead, and then pinch the bridge of his nose, between his eyebrows, like my grandmother used to do for me when I was unwell.

"Even your eyes are blue," he says. "It's some sort of virus. I have to protect the plants."

"My eyes were always blue," I say, smiling, but Angelo doesn't seem convinced. He sits up, and then tries to stand. I place two steadying hands on his shoulders and guide him into the bedroom, where he lies down, mumbling nonsense into his pillow. I lie beside him and hold him until he quiets, his breathing slow and steady.

Angelo wakes hours later, reaching for me in the dark. And this time we undress each other slowly. I don't know if this will be the last time, if Angelo will send me away again in the morning, and so I try to remember each moment has it happens, to capture them like photographs. Angelo's hand curled around my calf, his fingers spreading up my thigh like a creeping vine on a trellis. The weight of his legs on my shoulders as I lift him slightly from the bed. The way his eyes close as I enter him, a single eyelash escaping and falling to rest on the bridge of his nose.

In the morning, I lie awake beside him and watch the room grow brighter, dreading the moment when I have to leave, to return to Junior's apartment, to the cold pantry, to the before. But this time Angelo wakes with a smile, stretching out beside me, all warm and docile like a well-fed cat. We go out for breakfast, the wind biting at our faces, and Angelo squeezes up beside me as we walk, tucking his arm into mine. I look around at the other pedestrians, but no one even glances our way. Everyone is braced against the wind, hoods up and earbuds in, just trying to get wherever they're going. And what a luxury this is, to be just another pair of bodies moving in the world, nothing special about us at all.

Over breakfast, Angelo tells me that he's had a breakthrough with his Ph.D. dissertation and that he wants to celebrate, so we get drunk on cheap mimosas and stumble back to his apartment to make sloppy love on the living room floor. I can't believe my luck, that I'm not only allowed to want what I want but that I can have it too.

Gone is Angelo's reserved demeanour from last time. Instead he's almost sappy in his affection, his hands on me constantly, cradling my chin, his thumb pressed into my lower lip. We pass the afternoon in a day-drunk haze, and at dusk, Angelo lights a dozen candles and puts an old calypso record on, one of my mother's favourites. So I tell him about her, the good parts. Like how she looks onstage shimmering head to toe in sequins and satin. How she sounds when she performs, the way she can hold a note longer than seems possible, like one of those deep-sea whales that only emerges from the depths every fifteen minutes to breathe.

And Angelo tells me about his parents, who, it turns out, are still together, living a quiet retirement in his childhood home in Markham. This surprises me. I thought Angelo was like me, broken in all the same ways I am. But he had a normal childhood, growing up in the suburbs with his two sisters. His parents are both academics, his mother originally from Trinidad and his father from the Philippines.

He tells me about his research, which is about climate change resilience in the queer community. He tells me about his dream to start an intentional community somewhere in Northern Ontario. "The city isn't where you'll want to be when the shit hits the fan," he says. I should know better but already I find myself picturing our future together, on Angelo's farm, waiting out the end of the world.

"My mother says stuff like that all the time," I say, "but everyone ignores her because she's crazy."

Angelo pauses then, looking at me with a sudden focus. When he speaks his voice is sharp, defensive. "What do you mean by that?"

So I tell him the bad parts too. The moods, the disappear-
ances. The boyfriends who came and went over the years,
always leaving her strung out afterwards, like a smear of paint
spread too thin across a canvas. "I guess I shouldn't say she's
crazy. That's just the only way I know how to describe it. That's
what everyone says at home."

"Is she medicated?" Angelo asks. He sits up and away from
me. Something has shifted, I can feel him pulling away, back
into himself.

"No, no, it's not like that," I reply too quickly. I take in
Angelo's wounded expression and feel a stab of guilt. "I mean.
She's not like . . . sick? You know what I mean. She's just dra-
matic. She likes attention."

"I don't think I do know what you mean," Angelo says
then, rolling away from me and onto his back. I sense I've
made some kind of mistake, that I'm losing my grip on him,
and so I kept talking, trying to gather him back up like a spool
of thread. I tell him about my auntie Nadine, the doctor. She's
the only one who can reach my mother when she gets lost
within herself, the only one who can bring her back. I tell
him about my great-grandfather Iapetus. I try to describe
him without using the words I know will offend Angelo, but
it's like trying to speak a foreign language: I'm missing the
vocabulary.

After that night, I don't hear from him again for almost two
weeks. This time I spend in torment, trolling Grindr for hours
but not messaging anyone. Eventually, though, he calls, and I
go to see him, and everything is right again, until it isn't. After
a few days, Angelo's mood turns, and I sense he wants me to
leave. So I do, another few weeks passing while I wait for him
to call.

And by now, early March, I've grown used to this routine. Eventually Angelo always calls, usually with a strange request, like, "Can you bring me six overripe bananas? The browner the better." Or "I sliced my hand open on a can. Can you come give me stitches? I'll teach you how." And every time I head straight there, opening his front door to a blast of warm, wet heat, the apartment smelling like home.

Sometimes we spend a few days in a row together, Angelo pottering around in his robe and slippers, either working on his thesis or fussing over one of his experiments. His apartment is essentially one large greenhouse, a mess of makeshift irrigation, growing lights, and clear plastic. It's always thirty degrees and humid and I love it there. I keep myself as small and quiet as possible, reading or watching movies on my phone. During our time apart, I think of nothing but him, rehashing every conversation we had, trying to figure out if I said something asinine. Trying to determine if there is something I could do differently next time, so that he will let me stay longer.

In bed, on a particularly frigid night, Angelo asks about home. He wants to know about the earth, the soil, the things that are grown there. I tell him the soil is depleted from too many decades of monocropping sugar cane. I tell him the island is flat and crowded, one of the most densely populated countries in the world, and that hardly anyone lives off the land anymore. The economy runs on foreign investment and tourism. We dug up the mangroves to build hotels, and now the beaches are eroding and the corals are dead. The thing that feeds us is slowly killing us.

But, I tell him, during mango season, the fruits fall by the hundreds. Every year, a glut of mangoes. My grandmother takes them to church by the basketful and comes back with the basket nearly full, no one wants her mangoes, everyone's trying to get rid of theirs. I tell him about the green monkeys, how clever they are and how malicious. The way they will take a single bite out of each and every mango on the tree, so that you go to pick a juicy one only to find a big chunk of flesh missing. I tell him about flying fish, that there is no other fish that tastes like it, the flesh meaty and a little bit sour.

And I tell him about the ocean, what it looks like at sunrise, when the swells are high and the break is good. How it feels to paddle out into the dawn, how you're not fully awake until that first wave, until you feel the salt on the back of your throat. I tell him all of this, but I don't tell him about Daniel, even when, close to midnight, he asks if I've ever been in love before. I can't tell Angelo about Daniel, I can't admit to him what I did, how much of a coward I was that night. How I betrayed my best friend.

We've got the window open, despite the temperature, and Angelo's feet are cold against mine. "No," I say, "I don't think so."

"What would that be like there? Could you be out?"

I feel like I'm in class, being asked a question I should be able to answer easily but can't. I don't know anything about what it's like to be gay in Barbados because I didn't let myself try until that night with Daniel, and then I was gone two days later. I don't want to admit this to Angelo, how inexperienced I am. "I don't know," I say finally. "Like it's technically still illegal, on the books. And the church and conservative people in government don't support it. I mean it's not like Jamaica. People aren't being murdered. But the violence . . . it's still here. The way people talk about us . . . they hate us." I hesitate, realizing my choice of pronoun. Us. I'm part of an us.

"It's funny," I go on, "my mum . . . she always wanted to escape. Her dad too. They dreamt of getting away from the island. But I never felt that way. I love it there. I just wish it loved me back."

Angelo nods. "What about your friends? What do they think?"

"About me? I don't know. We don't talk about it. I think they would be chill, though. Like, they're open-minded people. There was a Pride march last year and a bunch of them went."

"Did you go?"

I contemplate lying but decide against it. I shake my head. "There were photographers. If I'd gone, it would have been a big deal. For me, for my family."

"Would it have ruined your life?" Angelo asks.

I think about this for a minute. Would it? The truth is I don't know. I grew up surrounded by boys—sand-dusted, salty-haired, they passed through the hotel like a dream. They arrived in big groups from England, thundering caravans of lads on a week's holiday. They spent every day by the pool, their skin crisping a terrible pink in the sun, depleting our beer stock in hours. They were so physical with each other, loud and present and boyish, swinging their thick thighs over each other's shoulders to wrestle two on two in the shallow end, pranking each other, pulling their shorts down to reveal asses white as the flesh of a coconut. I watched them, and my mother watched me watching them and she worried. "Never with a guest," she warned. "They drink you up like rum punch 'cus you too sweet but you're not for fucking sale, hear?" So I never spoke to the boys, never gave myself away. At least not until that night with Daniel, when everything changed.

I try to imagine this other life. One where Daniel and I hold hands in town. Or dance in The Gap together. But it's like trying to hold water in cupped palms, the image just won't stick.

"No," I say, finally. "But it would define it."

And this I know to be true. To be gay in Barbados is to be gay first and foremost. That would be how I'd be known, among my family, friends, classmates, people who live in the village around the hotel, the staff, the boys I surf with. I'd be Nautilus, the gay guy. What would it mean to define myself so absolutely in those terms? It would be a declaration. Of what, I don't know. Maybe just a declaration of presence. Like saying, I am here. See me.

The thing is, I've never felt fully alive. I've always felt as if nothing I did really mattered, my mark on life like footprints in the sand. That's why I lived the way I lived. Making stupid decisions, getting into trouble. I don't think I ever really cared what happened to me because I never felt like anything resembling a whole person. I have half a family. Half a heritage. Half a race. There's always been a bigger piece of me missing than the parts I know and understand. To be gay and out would be to fill in one of those missing pieces. But to be more real, to draw yourself onto the page in thicker ink, is only asking for someone to come along and tear the page right out of the book. I don't know how to explain all of this to Angelo, so I don't say anything at all.

Not all nights at Angelo's are like this one. Sometimes, I arrive to find him near-catatonic on the couch. Other times, he gets up in the middle of the night and leaves the apartment, not returning until well into the next day. I never ask him where he goes, and he doesn't tell me. I spend these nights awake in his bed, fear clawing at my throat. I feel like a child again, when my mother used to disappear without warning for days at a time. In my childish way, I thought she had gone to find my father.

I pictured her wading out into the midnight ocean, swimming towards the shimmering light of the moon.

This is the image that still comes to me sometimes in nightmares, my mother, standing at the foot of my bed, her nightgown wet against her skin, seaweed knotted in her hair and her skin bloated like a dead fish. Once, Angelo returned at dawn, and when he crawled back into bed, his body was wet and cold. I woke up screaming. He'd only been caught in the snow, but I was sure he was dead, that he had tried to escape me by swimming away and had drowned. Angelo held me until I fell back asleep, and the next day we didn't speak of it.

Despite all this, I feel an unfamiliar kind of contentment. I feel at home, not in Toronto, but in my own body. The ghosts leave me alone more nights than not, and that itchy burn beneath my skin has faded. I find whole days go by where I don't think of Daniel at all, and no longer does the thought of him twist my gut in shame, guilt, and longing. For the first time in a long time, maybe ever, I've started to have a curiosity about myself, a desire to figure out what it is I like and don't like. Angelo says he will help me with my university applications if I decide to go. I'm only missing a few credits to graduate high school. Maybe this September I will re-enroll.

This is what I think of as a I traverse the city, making deliveries. I've never been able to imagine a life for myself beyond the one I was living. My grandfather always says I don't think about the consequences of my actions, that I have no sense of self-preservation. But it's the opposite. At home, I was like an animal built only for survival, one day bleeding into the next. Now, to allow myself the hope of a future feels like a radical act, scarier than any dumb stunt I pulled as a kid, any fight I got into, any night spent handcuffed to a chair in a police station.

I think about my great-grandfather Iapetus, wandering the island, alone in his madness. I think I understand what it was he was looking for. But unlike him, when I walk down the sidewalk, my coat buttoned all the way up, the scarf I finally gave in and bought wrapped tightly up to my ears, I'm not running from anything anymore, or anyone.

CHAPTER TWENTY-ONE

Even when I'm not at Angelo's, I try to spend as much time out of Junior's apartment as possible. Junior's comings and goings have become even more erratic, his paranoia reaching new heights. A few weeks ago, I woke to a pounding on the door. Freda was home but refused to come out of her bedroom. Junior was nowhere to be found. I opened the door and there stood a stout, middle-aged man in a bright orange puffer jacket. He looked like he could be anyone's father. He stood very close to me, so close I could see the silver fillings in his back teeth and smell the stale, meaty scent of whatever he'd had for breakfast on his breath.

When I told him Junior wasn't home, the man tried to lean his head into the apartment to look around. I angled myself to block the entrance, and for a moment he looked like he might try to barge in, but then thought better of it. "You tell him I was here. You tell him I come looking for him," the man said. And even after I closed the door, he remained in the hallway for a long time, pacing. I watched him through the peephole until he eventually went away.

Things between Junior and Freda also seem to be deteriorating. Their fights have increased in both frequency and intensity. I've taken to sleeping with headphones in, white noise playlists on loop to try to drown them out. While Junior has become more reclusive, Freda has gone the opposite way. She speaks often to me now, or at least at me, long, incoherent diatribes in which she complains about Junior or else reminisces about her childhood in Jacmel, her family there and how much she misses them.

I get back to Junior's one afternoon in early April, snow-dusted, my ears ringing from the cold. Winter has shown no sign of abating, but I find I'm becoming accustomed to it. I take the stairs to the apartment two at a time. I have plans to meet Angelo. We're going to a poetry reading, some event one of his grad school classmates is putting on. This will be the first time Angelo and I go out together, other than just for walks around the neighbourhood or to his local coffee shop. I'm nervous about meeting Angelo's friends, about saying something that betrays how young and stupid I am. But mostly I'm excited to stand next to Angelo in a public place, to put my hand on the small of his back like it's the most normal thing in the world.

When I unlock the door to Junior's apartment, I can't quite put my finger on what is wrong, but something feels off. It's hot, I realize. For the first time since I moved in, the heater is cranked up to max. Gone too are the stacks of boxes that have lined the walls for months. Without them, the apartment is eerily large, like an empty showroom. Freda sits on the couch, folding laundry, Didier on the floor at her feet. She's humming softly to herself. I step towards her, and I notice what else is different. Freda is dressed up, wearing a dated skirt suit in an ugly pale pink.

"Freda?" I say, coming to stand beside her. "Where's all of Junior's stuff? Where's Junior?" Didier fusses on the floor and I squat beside him, rubbing my hand on his tummy until he quiets. He's a cute kid, when he's not screaming. When I look up at Freda, she's watching me with Didier, her eyes more alert than I've ever seen them.

"He likes you," she says, pointing her chin towards Didier. "You want children?"

"I don't know," I say. "Maybe one day. Freda, is everything okay?"

Freda laughs then. An echoing sound like when you blow across the top of a beer bottle. Her pile of laundry is folded, but she picks up the same shirt again and again, shaking it out, creasing it neatly, and adding it back to the pile. Shake, fold, place, repeat. I sit beside her on the couch and take the shirt gently from her hands. "Where's Junior?"

"They took him," she says finally, so softly I almost don't catch the words.

"Who took him? The same man who came the other day?"

She laughs again. "Who? Arnaud? No, Arnaud is a good friend. He tried to warn Junior. But Junior don't listen. Stupid man. You know how we meet?" She doesn't wait for me to answer. "My first day in Canada, wi. I didn't even make it to my aunt's house from the airport. He was my Uber driver. First man I meet, and next thing we marry and I here in this nasty apartment all day. He trick me, you know. He tell me he was a businessman. But he is just a criminal. Now they take him. Stupid man."

"Who took him?" I ask again.

"Police," she says, with a sigh, as if we're discussing a bout of bad weather.

I run to the pantry and climb the shelves until I can see the top. Nothing but dust and cobwebs. The gun is gone, so too is the cash I'd been saving. I jump down onto my mattress, stumbling, panic making my eyes water.

"They took that too," Freda calls out. I go back into the living room. She has Didier in her arms now, and she's speaking into his neck, her voice soft and cooing. "They took everything, didn't they, ti cheri? And Daddy was crying whole time, wasn't he? He was crying and begging them to let him go. But once they found that gun . . ." She lifts Didier up over her head, and he giggles, reaching for her nose. "Uh-oh! Fini. They took him away."

The living room blurs. I lean against a bare wall and try to catch my breath. I collapse onto the floor, my head between my knees, breathing in the damp smell of my jeans. Here I am again, too high up in the tamarind tree, with no one to help me down. I think about going to the police station to turn myself in, to tell them the gun is mine. But then I remember the night of Daniel's and my arrest, the memories sprouting up as if from seeds that have been germinating under my skin. Now they blossom and spread like vines, choking me from the inside out. The dormant pain in my shoulder comes searing back. I can smell my own urine, feel the long nails of the police officer raking against my skin.

Freda watches me with passive interest, like I'm a nature documentary playing in the background. "Ki pwoblèm ou?" she asks finally.

"That money was everything I had. I was saving to go home."

Freda sucks her teeth at that. "You could just ask your rich uncle for money. That's what Junior always do. Calling his daddy begging for allowance like a child. Though lately Z's pockets like them dry up oh! He say he can't afford to keep sending money to Junior. That's why he get involved in all this stupidness and have the police up in our house. God forbid he get a real job. No, always some excuse. Blaming everyone for his problems."

I'm barely listening, thinking about what to do next. I have to find Mazin and tell him the police have his gun. He will know what to do. Freda drones on in the background, complaining about Junior.

"Junior say is your family fault Z don't have no money. Junior say his father always taking care of your family and so have nothing left for us. Letting your grandparents live for free at the hotel all those years. Plus big money he spend each month keeping that old man hidden away. Junior say that old man living in a nice home, wi."

My head snaps up at this. I'm unsure of what I'm hearing. "Freda," I say, "what old man? What are you talking about?"

"Your great-grandfather. Junior tell me not to say nothing but he done telling me what I can and can't do now, mèsi bondye."

My first instinct is to dismiss Freda's words as the ramblings of a jaded housewife, but another, truer part of me trembles under the weight of her revelation. I can't deal with this right now. It's all too much. I file the knowledge away inside myself, swallowing it down where it lodges in my chest like chicken bone. Iapetus is alive. But what good does that do me? My head spins. I have to get out of here.

I rise and head for the door, leaving Freda and Didier

without a word. I close the door behind me, and in the dank, mildewed hallway it occurs to me that everything is falling apart, my new life crumbling around me like the house of sand I always suspected it to be. How did I ever think things could be different?

I find Mazin in the stairwell, head bowed in close conversation with Curtis. He looks up as I approach, his brown eyes narrowed. He looks tired, in a grey sweatshirt and matching pants, his usually meticulously close-cropped hair now growing unkempt at the edges of his scalp. Curtis side-eyes me warily.

"Mazin," I say, extending my hand.

He hesitates and then takes it, dapping me up. "Nautilus," he says. "Glad to see you're okay. The police . . ."

"Yeah man shit's crazy," I say. "Listen, they took the gun. My money. Everything. I wiped it down for prints but—"

Mazin holds up a hand to quiet me. "Outside," he says, looking over my shoulder at the empty stairwell.

We step out into the bracing wind and lumber over the snow to the back of the building, by the dumpsters. There's a small patch of weedy grass where children sometimes play in the summer and a tall wire fence separating our building from the adjacent one. We're away from the main road and the parking lot, and there's no one around. The wind howls, whipping the snow up into blinding clouds, blowing trash across the ground.

I pull my hood up and dig my hands into my pockets. Mazin isn't wearing a coat but seems unfazed, the wind plastering his sweatshirt against his spindly frame. Curtis hangs back, his hood up and a scarf tied around his neck and mouth so that only his eyes are visible.

"So what did you tell them?" Mazin asks finally. His voice is carried away by the wind and I hardly hear him.

"Tell who? What are you talking about?"

"The cops," Mazin says.

"Nothing," I say, too quickly. Mazin raises an eyebrow. "I mean I wasn't there," I add. "I got home and Junior was gone and his wife told me they'd been there. And when I checked, the gun was gone."

Mazin nods and takes a step towards me, putting a hand on my shoulder. "Tell me, your uncle . . . Junior, is it? What does he know about our business?" His hand is still on my shoulder, and he massages my collarbone lightly, emphasizing each word.

"Nothing bro, nothing," I say. "He thinks I'm a student. He's got his own shit going on. Some sort of shady import and export thing. The cops were looking for him. The gun . . . it was just a coincidence. They weren't there for me. For us."

Mazin whistles. "That is good news, my friend."

"Good news?" I look at Mazin through the blowing snow. His mouth is curled into a small placid smile. I shiver, not just from the cold. "Mazin," I say, "my uncle is going to tell them that gun isn't his. He'll tell them that it was my room where they found it. They will come looking for me."

Mazin squeezes my shoulder again. He looks off into mid-distance, his breath clouding between us. His face is pensive, and I think he's about to give me another one of his philosophical speeches. But when he looks back at me his eyes are hard and flat like two plastic buttons sewn onto the face of a doll. "That," he says, "is not my fucking problem."

Anger erupts at the base of my spine, an old, familiar burn. I thought I had buried that part of myself, but the fire lay waiting within me, and it's comforting, that heat. I react on instinct,

knocking Mazin's arm off my shoulder and grabbing the collar
of his sweatshirt, yanking him towards me. His face remains
blank, the only evidence of concern a small, round wrinkle rippling his brow like a stone thrown into the centre of a small
pond.

Curtis materializes beside us, faster than I've ever seen
him move. He grabs my wrist, forcing me to let go of Mazin,
and twists my arm around my back. In the same movement,
he knocks my legs out from under me, pinning me face down
in the snow. He takes me by the hair, lifting me slightly then
slamming my face back into the ground. I can taste the blood
pooling in my mouth. Something sharp pierces my side, digging into the flesh just above my hip bone. Not deep enough to
maim me, but deep enough to hurt.

"You know what this?" Curtis asks, and it occurs to me
in that moment I've never heard him speak before. The knife
presses deeper into me and I scream, the sound muffled by the
snow. Curtis pulls the knife out and holds it at eye level, so I
can see my own blood drip red onto the snow. The message is
clear. After a few moments he puts the knife away and stands
up, allowing me to flip over. Above me, the sky is bright white.

Mazin comes to squat beside me, taking my chin in his
hand. "Nautilus," he says. "Look at me. This is another one
of those crossroads we talked about, remember? This is one of
those times you have to make a choice."

"I thought we were friends," I say. And even I can hear how
stupid this sounds.

Mazin shrugs and raises his hands to his side, palms up.
"There are no friends in the wild. Only allies and enemies. And
now our alliance has come to an end."

"Does this mean we're enemies?"

Mazin smiles. "No," he says, "we're strangers. I don't know you, you don't know me."

He lets go of my chin and pats my cheek in his fatherly way. "You're going to be okay. You're a survivor, like me." With that, he turns to leave, beckoning Curtis to follow.

I stand, clenching the wound at my waist. When I pull my hand away, my fingertips drip red, but I don't think the cut is deep. I sway slightly against the lashing wind. Mazin and Curtis disappear like phantoms in the snow.

I enter the building to find Musa alone in the stairwell. He's playing an old Mavado song aloud from his cellphone. He sits with his hands dangling between his knees, head bopping. He looks up when I come in, eyes wide beneath the fur trim of his coat hood.

"Yo fam what the fuck happened to you?"

I smile, and his eyes widen more at the sight of my bloodied teeth. "I fell off my bike." I pass by him on the stairwell, heading back up towards Junior's apartment.

Musa scrambles to his feet, following close at my heels. "Yeah right, dawg, you got your ass beat for reals. I warned you! This city is cold. You should have phoned me up. I would have had your back. Nobody fucks with Musa, bro. Nobody."

I look back at him. He's standing a few stairs down from me. His coat is about five sizes too big and his eyes are wide and round. I could rat him out. I could go to the police station right now and tell them who the gun really belongs to. I picture Musa then, tied to a chair in an empty room, alone and afraid, like I was once. Like Daniel was. And it's that image, more than Mazin's threats, that cements my decision. I'm not putting another brown boy in jail.

I reach out my fist for him to bump. "Next time, man."

Musa grins and returns to his post, and I continue up the stairs, to Junior's apartment. It's empty, Freda and Didier have gone. In the bathroom I examine my wound. It probably needs stitches, but I don't have time for that. I douse it in rubbing alcohol and bandage it as best I can. Then I wash the blood off my face and look at myself in the mirror. I look exactly how I always wished I did—dangerous. I throw as many of my things as I can fit into a backpack and flee to Angelo's apartment.

Angelo answers the door in his pajamas. "Hey . . ." he says, as if he's not entirely sure who I am. Maybe he isn't. Angelo gets like this sometimes, when he's deep into his work. I don't know if it's the mescaline, or just him, but sometimes I think if I were to stop calling him, to just disappear, he would forget I ever existed.

I push past him into the apartment and collapse onto the couch, my head in my hands. I'm shaking. Angelo goes back to his desk. His face is skeletal in the blue light of the laptop. He looks like he hasn't slept in days.

"Can I stay here for a little while?" I ask. He doesn't turn or respond. "Angelo," I say, louder this time.

He jumps slightly and looks at me, confused, like he'd already forgotten I was there. "Yeah, okay," he says.

"We had plans tonight," I say, "the poetry reading?"

He's already turned back to his screen. If he notices my busted-up face he doesn't comment. "I know," he says. "I'm sorry. I'm . . ."

He doesn't finish the thought. I give up. There's no point trying to talk to him when he's like this. I go to the kitchen in search of food, but of course there's nothing. I find a half-eaten pack of Oreos that I left the last time I came over, and I eat them standing over the sink. I have no idea what to do next. I feel paralyzed, like any decision I make will be the wrong one. I think about Junior being hauled away in handcuffs and I feel sick, the cookies a gummy paste on my tongue.

Whatever happens, I decide, I don't have to deal with it tonight. No one knows about me and Angelo. I can hide out here for a while. A desperate part of my brain thinks I could stay here forever, as if cast away on an island, plucking leaves off Angelo's plants to survive.

I feel small and brittle, like when I was a child and my grandfather caught me doing something I shouldn't. I would never apologize, never back down, even when he threatened me with the belt. My guilt made me hard, and the worse I felt, the harder I became. And this time the guilt envelops me until I feel like I'm cast in stone. Once again, I've ruined everything. How stupid to think I could be anything other than a fuck-up. There is no way I can go back to Barbados now. When Z finds out that I had something to do with his son getting arrested, he will disown me. And in our family, Z is God. My grandparents will never forgive me.

But if I stay in Toronto, what will happen? Junior will tell the police the gun isn't his. How long will it take them to trace it back to me? I shake my head violently, as if trying to exorcise these thoughts from my body. I go to the bathroom and dig around in the cabinets until I find some clean bandages. I rewrap my wound as best I can and then crawl into Angelo's bed, pulling the sheets over my head. I breathe in and out in my little tent of sheets, my sour breath filling the space, until eventually I fall into a restless sleep.

When I wake up a few hours later, Angelo is in the bed beside me. He sleeps as he always does, shirtless, facing the wall, so close that his nose is almost touching the plaster. I watch him for a while, placing a hand on his shoulder blades, feeling his rib cage expand and contract. Angelo's bones always seem impossibly close to the surface of his skin. Whenever I touch him, it feels as though I'm grasping at a skeleton, like he is something closer to a specimen than a real person. He breathes deeply and I bring my ear to rest against his spine. It sounds like the ocean.

I get up and head to the living room. I clear a space on the computer chair, relocating the books there to another stack on the floor, and I sit for a while. The room is thick with the stench of a man living alone. How have I never noticed before how much the apartment reeks? A pair of my dirty underwear, stained white with dried semen, lies on the floor beside the couch, having been left there since my last visit. Soil and dead leaves coat the floor, sticking to my feet. Even the plants, which I once found so comforting, seem to emit a heady, oppressive smell that clings to my skin.

I long for the powdery, perfumed scent of my grand-mother's skin. For the laundered sheets of the hotel, the smell of clothes dried on a washing line. People don't realize the sun has a smell, but it does. I've forgotten what the sun smells like. What the burn of salt from the ocean breeze feels like against my skin. Thoughts of home bring an ache that flowers in my gut as though I've been punched from the inside.

Hours later, Angelo wakes, and I tell him what has hap-pened. He listens in silence, providing neither comment nor comfort. But when I finish, he offers to go out for groceries, which I take as his way of being supportive. When he gets home he cleans and stitches up the wound in my side. He works in silence, his hands shaking slightly. I had hoped he would give me guidance, tell me what to do, but he doesn't. Over the next couple of days, when I try to ask his opinion, he either doesn't respond, or else answers with theory from his research about the policing of queer, black bodies, about the collapse of the nation-state in the wake of late-stage capitalism. "When this is all gone," he says, his voice flighty and nervous, "when this city finally falls, we will be free."

Angelo cannot help me, I see that now. He's not my saviour, he's just a scared and lonely man, hiding in his apartment, preparing for the end of the world by writing essays about it. He's not altogether stable. The more time I spend in the apartment the more I realize how blind I have been to his erratic behaviour. He talks to himself constantly, muttering like a man possessed, except when he's high. Those days he spends marooned on the couch, hardly able to form sentences.

One night while he's sleeping, I power up his laptop and search for his dissertation, but instead I find a three-hundred-page document filled with incomprehensible ramblings. I don't know if he's even enrolled at any institution. He never has any visitors, and I remember now all of the times we've discussed making plans with his friends, and how the plans always seemed to fall through. There's no commune up north, no escape plan, no utopia. Angelo is as lost and alone as I am.

On my fourth day in his apartment, Angelo leaves, and by nightfall he still hasn't returned. I pace in the empty apartment, paranoia nipping at the edges of my thoughts. I wonder if he has gone to the police, gone to turn me in. I don't know why

I suspect this—Angelo is more distrustful of authority than I am—but hunger and fear have taken their toll on me and I'm bent to breaking. The next day, Angelo still doesn't return. I go fishing in his room for clues as to where he might have gone, but I come up empty-handed. Though I know he isn't capable of saving me, there was still a small, pathetic part of me that thought he would at least be here to hold my hand through it. That I meant something to him.

Soon I'm out of food. I'm terrified to go outside, convinced that once I do, the police will be there waiting. Or Mazin and Curtis, come to make sure I'm keeping my mouth shut. But eventually hunger overwhelms me and I walk down the block to the grocery store. There's no one there, no one following me. My rational brain tells me I'm safe, but still I shop as quickly as I can and race back to Angelo's apartment.

When I exit the elevator, a tall man in a cheap, shiny suit is standing outside Angelo's door, knocking. He looks at me and I stare back, trying to figure out if he's a police officer. He sports a Bluetooth device in his ear, and his hair is gelled and gleaming. He's chewing a piece of gum, and every few seconds he blows a little white bubble that smacks against his lips.

"Can I help you?" I ask.

He frowns at me, taking in the shopping bag, the set of keys dangling from my fist. "You live on this floor?" he asks.

"I'm a guest of Angelo's," I say, gesturing to the apartment.

The man raises his eyebrows. "You living here? He's not supposed to have people living here who aren't on the lease."

"No," I say, "I'm just visiting."

"Where is he?"

"Who?"

The man sighs, checking his watch. "Who the fuck do you think I mean? Angelo. Where is he?" I stare back, not answering.

The man exhales, running a hand through his perfectly unruffled hair. "Whatever," he says, "I don't have time for this."

He takes a sheet of paper from his jacket pocket and sticks it to the door with his gum. The words *Eviction Notice* are unmissable in red ink at the top of the page.

He takes a step towards me, his finger in my face. "And you can tell that piece of shit he can fight me all he wants on this. He hasn't paid his rent and he's had his three warnings. This time the tenancy board is backing me up. He's out."

I slap his hand away from my face and brush past him, letting myself into the apartment. I slam the door behind me. The man bangs his fists against it.

"You're squatting in this residence illegally," he yells. "If you're still here tomorrow I'm calling the cops."

He bangs on the door again. I slide to the floor, feeling it shake against my back. The man is still yelling outside, getting more and more worked up. I begin to pray, at first just nonsense words, but soon they form into a familiar psalm. "'Be merciful to me, Lord,'" I whisper, "'for I am in distress; my eyes grow weak with sorrow, my soul and body with grief.'"

I'm crying, scarcely able to form the words. I curl up into a ball on the floor. "'Be merciful to me,'" I pray. "'I am in distress.'"

CHAPTER TWENTY-TWO

I DON'T WAIT FOR ANGELO TO RETURN. I PACK MY backpack with a few non-perishables and leave the rest of the groceries for Angelo in the fridge. I want to write him a note, to say goodbye, but I've never been good at expressing myself on paper and I'm too frantic to think of anything meaningful to write.

I've always lived with shame, even before I could name it. I've been ashamed of my past, ashamed of my mother and her broken heart, ashamed of my light skin and blue eyes that remind me every day of the father I didn't have, ashamed of wanting something I knew I wasn't supposed to want. With Angelo, that shame shrank to the smallest it's ever been, so that some days I could even forget it was there. If he were here, I would explain all that. I would kiss him again, because that was always my favourite part. If he were here, I'd tell him that he made the monsters go away, just for a little while. I'd tell him I hope he finds his paradise one day.

In the end I scribble a quick explanation onto a loose leaf of printer paper. I tell him I don't know where I'm going, but that I won't be back to his apartment because I don't want to put him at risk. I sign it with love. Then I head out and into the hallway where the overhead lights flicker in sickly yellow. I make sure the coast is clear, then I ride the elevator to the third floor and take the stairs the rest of the way, exiting through the back alley by the dumpsters.

It's getting dark, and it's cold. Colder, I think, than it's ever been. Maybe that's just how the cold works: you feel it the most when you know you've got nowhere to go to escape it. I walk aimlessly down Sherbourne Street, until I end up in Allan Gardens. The conservatory is still open for another hour, so I go inside, the warm, damp air so similar to that of Angelo's apartment. I walk among the flowers, trying to remember the names of the ones that look familiar. My grandmother can name every plant on the grounds of our hotel. When I got sick as a child she made me hibiscus tea, soaked bay leaves in rum and had me suck on them for my sore throat. But I never learned these recipes. I think if I ever do make it home, I will.

I stay in the gardens until the guards clear it out for closing, then I head back into the frigid night. I wander around downtown, meandering my way across Dundas Square, over to Queen West. Working for Mazin, I've gotten to know every corner of this city, and as it revealed its hidden selves to me, I'd begun to think of it as home. But now, as it approaches midnight, I realize home is a place where someone wants you. My family didn't want me in Barbados, and Toronto could have been my home, but I fucked that up too. Now I am adrift.

I have about thirty dollars in my wallet and enough food in my backpack to last me the night. But I've been walking for hours and I can't feel my toes. I go into a twenty-four-hour McDonald's and order a small coffee. I sit at a corner table and sip it slowly, sneaking bites of a granola bar every half hour or so. I think someone will come over and kick me out, but no one does.

As the night wears on the crowd ebbs and flows through the place. Other people with nowhere to go, men mostly, their worldly possessions piled up around them. Groups of young people come in, girls in tight dresses under big coats, boys smelling of cheap cologne and weed. I watch them stumble to the counter, laughing, their night only just beginning. What would it take for one of them to end up where I am now? What would it take for me to end up like the other men beside me, the ones who sleep or beg or otherwise just stare blindly out onto the street? The partiers don't look at the homeless. They're omens better off ignored. No one wants to be reminded of how easily the world can forget they exist.

I stay in the McDonald's until daybreak, ordering two more coffees and a small fries, mostly to fend off my shame at squatting. Then I head to the subway when it opens and ride the green line end to end. Even with my bruised face and busted lip, no one pays me much attention. I guess I can still pass for one of them, someone with somewhere to be. By noon I've eaten all my provisions and I'm struggling to stay awake. I give in, curling up into a tight ball. I fall into a restless sleep, waking often to the sound of the subway announcements. At Kipling, by now early afternoon, two police officers board.

They are young, jovial. They laugh quietly, their heads

close together. But they look around often too, eyes sharp. One of them sees me and catches my eye for what feels like a long time. He turns to his partner, who glances over his shoulder at me. I stare at the ground, not breathing, until the officers disembark at Keele. I get off a few stops later. The subway is not a safe place. I have to keep moving.

There is one option that I haven't considered, and as the sun sinks into the west and I face the prospect of another sleepless night in the cold, I finally give in. I pull up a browser on my phone and search his name. Maybe it won't work, maybe he doesn't want to be so easily found. But no, there he is, a LinkedIn page of all things, the first hit. It lists a real estate company as his current place of employment, and when I search the office on Google Maps, it shows up right around the corner.

I tilt my head to the sky, looking at the skyscrapers, and then I laugh out loud. I can see it, the building where my father works. He could be up there right now, looking down from the clouds onto the street below like some lesser deity. Before I can talk myself out of it, I walk the short two blocks to the building and go inside. I locate the name of my father's company in the directory and ride the elevator to the sixteenth floor.

The office is nondescript. A water cooler belches in the corner, generic photography hangs on the wall. A young receptionist sits behind a metal desk, typing away on a laptop, her acrylic nails like artillery fire against the keys. She looks up when I come in, her smile faltering slightly at my appearance. I give my friendliest smile and ask for my father by name.

"Is he expecting you?" she asks, frowning slightly.

"No," I say, laughing. The laugh doesn't seem to ease the receptionist's worries. If anything, she's looking at me with a bit more concern. I try again. "I don't have an appointment. I'm an old friend, from Barbados."

At this the receptionist's eyes light up. "Oh, of course," she gushes, leaning forward onto her elbows. "He always talks about his time there. The sunshine, the beaches, the friendly people."

"Yeah," I say, "the people really are great. If I do say so myself." The receptionist bursts out laughing. She tucks her hair behind her ears, which have blushed pink. I've always been good with girls, one of life's greater ironies. The receptionist rises from the desk and goes in search of my father.

I stand by the window, looking out at the skyline. The building looks onto other buildings, but from certain angles I can see down to the waterfront, the CN tower poking through like a thumbtack upturned. Snow has begun to fall lightly, and lights in the neighbouring offices are flickering on one by one.

At the sound of footsteps, I turn to see my father approaching, the receptionist close behind. He's frailer than I imagined him to be, older looking than my grandfather even. He's dressed in a button-down shirt under a knit sweater with khakis and scuffed brown shoes. His hair is still long, but entirely grey now, and thinning, the ponytail a barely there wisp at his collar. He wears his beard trimmed short and thick-rimmed glasses dangle from a chain around his neck.

Is this it? This is the man who passed through my mother's life like a hurricane, leaving her flattened in his wake? The mythical man who haunted my childhood dreams? I almost laugh at how ridiculous it all is now, the stories we tell ourselves about ourselves. He approaches with his hand extended, his eyes curious but friendly. He doesn't know who I am.

His palm is dry and his grasp firm. My father squints at me. "Deb says you're visiting from Barbados," he says. "Have we met before? My memories from those days are a bit hazy. Too much rum punch!" He laughs, winking at his receptionist, who giggles in reply. I wonder if they're sleeping together. If he's that predictable.

"We met when I was a baby," I say. "You knew my mother."

I see the moment the realization dawns on him. His eyes narrow, his breath falters. He doesn't lose the smile though and recovers quickly. "Of course," he says, "why don't you come into my office and we'll catch up?"

"Can I come too, Dad?" the receptionist asks. "I'd love to hear about Barbados."

I start at this, glancing between them, looking for a resemblance. I see it, in the nose and mouth. Her eyes are brown, her colouring darker, but the similarities are there. I even see a bit of myself in her features, the same ears, the lobes oversized and dangling.

"Maybe give us a few minutes alone first, Deb," Odie says, leading me into his office.

His daughter pouts, but not for long. "Okay," she says, "I'll make some tea and bring it in a bit." She gives me a smile and a small wave as I enter the office, Odie closing the door behind us.

"She seems nice," I say.

Odie sits behind his desk, not looking at me, fidgeting with the items there. A paperweight, a stack of file folders, a framed picture of a pretty woman around his age, two children, Deb and a boy, both with their mother's brown hair and eyes. On the wall behind his desk is a large painting. It's a landscape—a long stretch of beach, a single palm tree, a fishing boat with a lone figure standing beside it. It's generic, could be from any island. This, more than anything so far, is the thing I find the most disappointing about him.

"Nautilus," he says, his tone businesslike, the warmth in his eyes gone. "This is unexpected. I wish you had called first."

"That would have been difficult," I say, "given that I didn't have any way to reach you."

Odie smiles a small, tight-lipped smile. He claps his hands together, changing tack. "No matter," he says, "you're here now. It's good to see you. To what do I owe the pleasure?"

I'm thrown by his change in tone, but I can play this game too. We won't discuss the past, this won't be a catharsis. But maybe I can convince him to help me. "I'm living in Toronto now," I say, "finishing high school here. I'm thinking of applying to Ryerson next year."

He nods, as if all of this is normal, as if we're just two people getting acquainted. Maybe that's what I can do, pretend to be just some kid, as if I'm applying for an internship. This illusion will suit us both.

"International student fees are expensive," he says slowly, his eyebrows raised in question. "You need some help with that?"

"I'm not an international student," I say. "I'm Canadian. You filled out the paperwork. Before you left."

Odie coughs. There's a light knock on the door and Deb enters carrying two mugs. She places them on the desk between us. She lingers for a minute, her hand on the back of my chair.

"Thanks, Deb," Odie says, lifting his chin to the door. "We'll just be a few more minutes."

Deb frowns at this, confused. I wonder how much she suspects. She seems trusting, like someone who has never had the rug pulled out from under her, never had any doubt as to her place in the world, where she comes from, where she belongs.

Deb leaves and Odie and I are quiet for a beat. I speak first. "Listen," I say, "I'm not here to blow up your life. And I'm not looking for a handout. I just . . . I'm in trouble and I need your help."

Odie nods for me to go on. I give him a quick rundown of what's happened, with as few details as possible. I make it sound like something from a bad TV movie. I started hanging out with some kids from the wrong side of the tracks and got in over my head. When I mention the gun, Odie's eyes widen slightly, but he doesn't interrupt.

"It sounds like you're in a tough spot, Nautilus, and I empathize," Odie says, once I'm finished. "But I'm not sure what it is you want me to do about it."

I exhale. "I need you to hire me a lawyer. And come with me to the police station. I'm going to turn myself in and I think I stand a better shot if you're there. I won't just look like some bum, you know?"

"Nautilus," Odie says, "this isn't Barbados. Who you know doesn't matter here. You can't bribe your way out of this. Besides, I'm not connected. I'm just a small-time property developer."

"Who you know matters everywhere," I say, my voice rising slightly. "Please, they'll be more lenient on me if they think I'm a good kid, from a normal family."

"Why don't you just tell them about the other boys. The ones the gun belongs to."

"No," I say. "I don't want anyone else to get hurt because of me. I'm trying to do the right thing."

Odie sits back in his chair. My words hang between us. Odie runs his tongue across his top teeth and breathes out through his nose. Then he sits up, elbows on his desk. When he speaks his voice is tinged with impatience. "I'm sorry," he says, "but I just don't see how I can help."

"I've just told you. We can go right now, it'll only take a couple of hours."

"I can't go to the police station with you, Nautilus. How would I explain that to my daughter? To my wife?" He shakes his head, reaching again to rearrange the items on his desk. I feel as though I'm being dismissed.

"You don't have to tell them anything," I say, hating the desperation in my voice. "Just make something up. Please. You owe me this much."

At this Odie's eyes flicker back to mine. He doesn't respond. We stare at each other for a moment, his eyes narrowed, his lips set in a firm line. I'm shaking, trying not to cry. I don't want him to see that. Odie rises from his desk and walks over to the other side of his office, where a large mahogany cabinet takes up most of the wall. He opens a cupboard, revealing a small safe. His back to me, he keys in a code and fishes out a manila envelope. He looks inside, and then over his shoulder at me, then back in the envelope. As if making a silent decision, he closes the safe and walks over to me, the envelope extended.

"Here," he says, thrusting it in my face. "There's over ten thousand dollars in there. More than enough for a plane ticket home. The police won't chase you all the way to Barbados. Not for something this minor. The rest you can spend on whatever you want. Tuition, maybe, for when this all blows over."

I stare at the envelope, not taking it. "This won't blow over," I say. "If I leave, I can never come back."

Odie doesn't react. The envelope hovers in the air between us, his hand shaking slightly. I take it, the paper crinkling in my grasp.

I don't bother looking inside the envelope. I zip it into my backpack and stand, swinging the bag over my shoulder. Odie sits back down behind his desk. He seems relieved. "Use that money for a ticket home, son," he says. "There's nothing for you here."

I exit through the waiting room without saying bye to Deb. Back outside on the sidewalk, it has grown dark, the night sky milky white with snow. I shift my backpack, feeling the new weight of it. Then I flag down a taxi.

The driver is Guyanese, and we chat about the weather as he merges onto the Gardiner. He hasn't been home in four years, he says. When I ask him what he misses most of all he tells me about the brick house he's building for his family. On every visit, he does a little work on it. One year the foundation, the next time the walls. At this rate, he explains, it won't be completed until his children are grown. "That is what I miss," he says, "all the things I cannot do for my family while I am here, working."

I tell him his family must understand that he's doing it all for them. That he's away because he loves them and wants to give them a better life.

"Ah," he says. "These reasons do not matter to children. They just want you close to them."

I think about my grandfather then, the way my grandmother described him, growing up in that big house, never feeling like he belonged. How different would his life have been had he known his father was alive, living on the same island where nowhere is more than a thirty-minute drive from anywhere else? I think I understand something about my grandfather now. And about myself. Two fatherless sons so hollowed out by our anger and loneliness we became invisible to each other.

When we pull into the departure terminal, the driver asks me where I'm going and I tell him I don't know yet. Home, I think. Or somewhere like it.

CHAPTER TWENTY-THREE

IT'S BEEN TWO DAYS SINCE I'VE BEEN HOME, AND THE dust has only just begun to settle. That first night, I knocked on the cottage door, not sure what I would find inside. It was my grandfather who answered. His massive frame filled the entrance like a boulder at the mouth of a cave, protecting those inside from the wild animals that prowl in the night. Then he stepped forward and wrapped his arms around me, pulling me so tightly into his chest that my feet lifted off the ground and I could feel each of my vertebrae crack.

Uncle Z was furious that I came back, as expected, and told my grandparents that I wasn't allowed to set foot on the property. I offered to leave, to go find my own place, but my grandfather wouldn't hear of it. "You leave Z to me," he said that first night, and then drove over to Z's house to have it out.

I don't know what went down between them, or where things stand now, but Z hasn't been around to the hotel, not once, and my grandfather refuses to answer any questions about it. "This is your home," he says. "I never should have let you doubt that. Z's days of deciding what is best for this family are over."

Now Z's in Toronto, trying to sort out Junior's mess. Freda and Didier have disappeared, probably back to Haiti, though no one knows for sure.

I've hardly seen my mother. I woke early the morning after I got back to find her sitting at the edge of my bed, watching me sleep. I sat up, not fully awake, and reached for her hand. She let me hold it for a while, and we sat in silence until I fell back asleep. When I woke again, she was gone.

Now, on a scorching afternoon, I'm pacing in front of Daniel's door, willing myself to knock. I do, and Daniel's mother, Janice, answers, still dressed for work. She's barefoot, her blouse untucked from her skirt. A spatula dangles at her side. From inside the house I can smell chicken being fried, the grease so pungent it makes my teeth hurt.

"Is he here?" I ask, willing myself to look her in the eye.

Janice is barely five feet tall and terrifying. She keeps staring, jaw locked, eyebrow raised. She lifts the spatula so that it hovers just in front of my nose. She inhales but lets the breath out without saying anything. Her eyes are big and wet and furious. Then she drops the spatula to her side and yells for Daniel over her shoulder.

"Thanks," I say.

"You're not welcome in this house," she says, "you can wait on the lawn."

I nod and walk back down her front steps and out onto the little patch of grass that separates their house from the busy street in front. She disappears inside and shuts the door behind her.

After about fifteen minutes, Daniel still hasn't appeared, so I sit down on the grass to wait. Their property is divided from the sidewalk by a low picket fence, along which Daniel's mother has planted a crocus hedge. The home is a small chattel house, only two bedrooms, but Daniel lives there with his parents, sister, and grandmother. There's no privacy inside, the walls made of thin plaster. Until not long ago, the bathroom was in a separate outhouse in the yard. The house is spotless though, the furniture gleaming with polish, thick, frilly curtains in the windows that his mother removes every few months to wash. Each Christmas, Daniel's mother makes him repaint the whole front entrance.

Another half hour passes and still there's no sign of Daniel. I lie back on the grass and stare up at the clouds. I figure I'll stay until Daniel comes out, or his parents kick me off their land, whichever comes first. I'm almost drifting off to sleep when Daniel arrives, standing above me, backlit by the sun. I sit up onto my elbows. "Hey D," I say.

Daniel has his hands on his hips. I can't see his face, but I can guess at his expression. I think he's going to walk away, leave me there, but instead he joins me on the grass, sitting cross-legged at my side. A car with a broken exhaust goes by, filling the street with smoke. A minibus sounds its horn. Two women pass holding umbrellas to shield themselves from the sun. They laugh at us, and call out to Daniel, who waves back but doesn't reply.

All that seems far away to me. I'm aware of only Daniel, of being near him again, so close I could lay my head on his lap if I wanted to. As if sensing this, Daniel shifts away from me, pulling his knees up to his chest.

"What are you doing here, Naut?" he asks finally.

I should have anticipated that this would be his first question, but still I don't have an answer. I shrug, and immediately regret how casual the gesture seems. Daniel frowns, yanking at the grass around his feet. "I'm sorry," I blurt out. I sit up fully, turning to face him.

Daniel doesn't look at me. "What for?" he asks, speaking into his knees.

"For that night at the police station. I shouldn't have left you there."

He doesn't answer right away. He lifts the neck of his T-shirt and brings it up over his mouth and nose to wipe the sweat, like I've seen him do a thousand times. The gesture is so familiar it hurts to watch, the nostalgia a piercing pain in my chest.

"What would have been the point of staying? So we could both get booked?" he says finally, shaking his head. "You did what you had to do, man."

"But I could have vouched for you," I say, my voice desperate. "I could have told them it was all my idea."

"It's all good," Daniel says. His voice sounds far away, as if he's already retreating from me, already gone. "The homeowners didn't press charges, so I only got charged with public indecency." At this last word, his voice cracks. He coughs and looks away, blinking into the sun. "Judge let me off with community service. I'm still a minor, so they kept it out of the papers."

"But still," I say, my voice high and whining, "your parents finding out like that and everything. It's all my fault."

Daniel looks at me finally. "What do you want, Nautilus? You want me to fight you?"

"I don't know," I say. "I'm sorry."

He rises to his feet and I follow. "I gotta go," he says, "I've got a mock CAPE exam tomorrow."

"Aight," I say. "That's cool." The sound of the traffic comes roaring back to life, as if someone suddenly unmuted the volume. I feel awkward, itchy from where we were lying on the grass. I don't know why I came here. I don't deserve anything from him. "I'll leave you alone," I say. "I shouldn't have come here and upset your mum like that."

Daniel shrugs. He looks over his shoulder at the house. I unzip my backpack and pull out the manila envelope, holding it out for Daniel. He glances down at it, then up at me, before taking it and looking inside. His eyed widen slightly, then he frowns and hands the envelope back to me. "What is this?" he asks.

I step back, my hands in my pockets. "It's for you. It's some money I made while I was in Canada. I want you to have it."

Daniel sucks his teeth, angry. "I don't want your money. I don't need this."

"Give it away, then," I say. "Burn it. Whatever." I take a couple of steps towards the sidewalk. Daniel remains where he is, the envelope still extended towards me. He looks more confused than angry now. He stares down at the envelope for a while, as if trying to solve some sort of puzzle.

"You're a crazy son of a bitch, you know that, Naut?" he says, opening the envelope once more to peek inside before tucking it under his arm.

I laugh. The sun beats down but neither of us moves. I think of Mazin and his many paths forward. I wait, sensing Daniel is about to make a choice.

"Supposed to be good swells this weekend. Down Inch Marlow side," he says. "Unless you forgot how to surf in Canada?"

"Nah," I say, laughing. "I'll be there."

Daniel laughs too. He nods at me. Then he turns and

jogs back inside, taking the stairs two at a time. I watch him go, then I head home on foot, the sidewalk burning through the soles of my sneakers, my skin, pale from winter, pinking in the sun. By the time I reach the hotel, I'm drenched in sweat. I feel like I can't get enough of the heat, like I could bake on the surface of the sun itself and still not feel warmed through.

When I reach the hotel, I stop in at reception to see my grandmother. She's at her computer, her face inches from the screen, squinting behind her glasses. I stand at the door, watching her for a bit. She jumps when she sees me.

"Nautilus!" she says. "You haven't been out in that sun? Go and change before a guest sees you."

I enter the office and bend down to wrap her in a hug from behind. Ever since I got home, I've been like this, hungry for touch. She struggles at first, but soon gives in. She pats at my arm. Eventually I let go.

"Your mother was asking for you," she says.

"Where is she?"

My grandmother rolls her eyes. "Wandering the shore. Looking for seashells. Braiding her hair. Whatever it is artists get up to."

I find her down by the shore, sitting on the sand with her legs extended, her toes just reaching the lapping waves. She wears a thin gold bracelet around her ankle and her toenails are painted blood-red. She looks so young like this, with her face angled to the sun, sand dusting her nose.

I collapse onto the sand beside her, and we watch the sea for a while, the sun low and shimmering, almost set. "In Canada," I say, "I used to listen to wave sounds on my phone to help me sleep. But it never sounded right."

My mother looks at me, her eyes squinted. "Were you happy there?" she asks.

I haven't told my mother, or the rest of my family, about meeting Odie. I haven't told them much about my time in Toronto at all. I admitted the truth to my grandfather, about the gun, and Junior's arrest, but he told me not to mention it to anyone else. "Sometimes," I say now, "I felt like I liked myself more there. But sometimes it was really lonely too."

"Did you meet someone?"

I nod. "Yeah. I think he was even more fucked up than I am though." It feels strange to talk about Toronto now, like trying to recall a dream in the bright light of morning.

My mother laughs at this. "Well, we're all a little fucked up," she says. Then, "I'm sorry I let them send you away. I knew it was wrong. But I worried that if you stayed here, you'd end up like me."

"What's so bad about that?"

She doesn't answer. A large wave pools around our legs, up to our waists, and the sand grows cool now in the setting sun. "I wasn't a good mother to you," she says finally. "I know that." I try to protest but she silences me, her hand on my hand, both slowly sinking into the wet sand.

"When your father left," she goes on, "I let him take a piece of me with him. There was so little of me left, I didn't know how to share it with anyone else. I needed to make something of myself, to build myself into something that he couldn't ruin. That was just my own. That's what my art was. Does that make sense at all?"

I think of Toronto, of days spent wandering the city, trying to build myself into something resembling a whole man. I nod.

"And all you ever seemed to do was fuss and cry," my mother says, nudging me playfully with her elbow. "You were such a difficult baby. I didn't know how to take care of you. So I let my parents do it."

"I had a happy childhood, Mum," I say.

"I wasn't there," she says. "He's the one who left, but I wasn't there either."

I shake my head, but I don't know what to say to convince her this isn't true. She has her own ghosts, and I can't banish them for her.

A little way down the beach, my grandfather is stacking beach chairs, bringing them in for the night. "If either of you feels like helping," he calls out gruffly, "feel free."

My mother catches my eye and laughs. "Can you come with me?" I ask. "I need to tell Granddad something, and I want you to be there."

"What's wrong?" she asks, her eyes big and brown and worried.

I laugh and get to my feet. "Nothing. Everything's okay." I dust the sand off my palm and extend it down to help her up. "You coming?"

She looks up at me for a second, frowning, like she's trying to remember something, like it's right at the tip of her tongue, but she just can't find it. Then she smiles, shaking her head. She takes my hand and lets me haul her to her feet. "Yeah, okay," she says. "Let's go."

EPILOGUE: IAPETUS (2019)

MOST DAYS, I DON'T EXIST. I DON'T EVEN REMEMBER my own name, sometimes. There's no present, no future, only the past, memories like thick clouds that crowd my brain, blinding me. I stumble around in the fog of memory, never sure what's real and what isn't.

But sometimes, this fog clears and the world reveals itself to me. A small room, a single bed. The big window with the view to the cane fields. The sea in the distance, the darker blue barely distinguishable from the sky. The nurse, the nice one with the dimples, who lets me sit outside sometimes so that I can feel the breeze on my skin, smell the fruit trees in bloom.

"Where am I?" I ask her on one of the clear days and she laughs and pats my hand. "You're at home," she says.

"Where is my brother? Where is Cronus?" But the nurse only shakes her head and tells me to swallow my pills, to rest, not to get upset. And if I get upset? If I thrash out or try to run? Then they call for help, for the big men in green who hold me down to the bed until I calm down, until the fight leaves me.

I don't know how long I've been here but I remember the day I arrived. Cronus walked me to the front entrance with a hand on my shoulder, guiding me, just like when we were kids. "It's just for a little while," he told me. "We have to get you better."

And I didn't argue, didn't fight it. Cronus always knows best. And I was just so tired. All those years running and hiding and what did I have to show for it? I was just as haunted as I'd ever been. No matter where I ran to, the ghosts found me. Maybe I needed to try something else. Maybe the only path to freedom lay in the thorny maze of remembering.

I'd shown up at Cronus's house with nothing but the clothes on my back. The housekeeper made me wait in the yard, not believing me when I told her who I was. In the upstairs window two boys stared down at me. One, my nephew Z, so big now. The other I didn't recognize, his friend perhaps. I waved at the boys and they waved back, their eyes wide and curious.

Cronus stepped out to meet me on the sunny lawn. I nearly ran then, when I saw him. Because it wasn't Cronus, it was our father. Our father in his work clothes, his tie loosened around his neck. I stumbled backwards, the scream clawing up my throat. It had been a mistake coming here. They'd found me, the ghosts. They'd come for me. But the man in the suit held me tightly by the shoulders and told me to breathe. And then my father was gone, and there was my brother in his place. A grown man. Almost the age my father was when he died. If my brother was a grown man, then I was too. But I'd lost so much time. So many years spent trying to forget.

I cried into my brother's arms then. Cried like the lost child I was. And Cronus held me, just like he had when we were boys, and told me that everything was going to be okay and that he was going to take care of me. That I could stop running.

And so I ended up here, in the room with the view. With the nice nurses and the mean ones. The days bleeding into each other. Cronus came often to visit me, at first. Promising that soon I would be allowed to come home. As soon as I was whole again. I tried to run away a few times but then I stopped fighting. What was the point? I was where my brother wanted me to be. I was safe but most of all, I was quiet. Even when the night terrors came, even when I screamed about pillows fallen to the floor, about dead fathers and murdering brothers, no one would believe the ramblings of a madman.

Then the visits stopped. Time pressed on, measured only by the wrinkles on the backs of my hands, the grooves and creases in the skin that seemed to multiply before my eyes. There are no mirrors in this place, nothing made of glass or metal. So I hold my hand up before my eyes and examine the aging flesh, trying to remember who I am.

Today is a good day. The kind nurse lets me eat my lunch in the garden, beneath the shade of the shak shak tree. On the nearby road, cane trucks amble slowly by. Harvest season. I breathe in and out. Eat my macaroni pie. Revel in the silence, the voices quiet for a spell.

The nurse approaches from the house, come to bring me back inside.

"You have visitors," she says, smiling, her two gold teeth

glittering in the afternoon sun. It's then that I notice her dimples are gone. A different nurse then. How many nurses have there been?

"Is it my brother?" I ask.

"No," she says, "I don't know them. But they say they are family."

"I don't have any family," I say. Confusion descends like a dark cloud. The familiar fog. I fight against it, trying to plant my feet firmly in the present but it's as though a strong current has seeped in, pulling me down by the ankles, carrying me away.

Inside, I blink into the darkness of the common room, my eyes still spotted from the sun. A group of people stand huddled together, watching me.

"It's a good day, today," I hear the nurse say. "But he tires easily. Try not to overwhelm him."

A man steps forward from the group. Not a man, a giant. I shudder. Is this a new monster? But when the man approaches, his eyes are soft and alight with tears. He reaches one of his massive hands out to me and I shake it, the palm warm and rough.

"Hello," I say, "I'm . . ." But words fail me. Who am I? I had a name once. A home. A brother who tucked me in at night, who stood guard at the end of my bed while I slept, waiting for our father to come home. The brother who made himself big enough that I could hide behind him. The brother who took all the blows so that I wouldn't have to. But where is my brother? And why did he leave me alone in this place?

"I know," the giant is saying. "I know who you are. Do you know who I am?"

"No," I say, "I'm sorry. I don't remember . . ."

But the giant isn't angry. Tears fall freely down his cheeks now and the rest of the group step forward to comfort him. They place hands wherever they can reach, on his back and waist and elbows.

"That's okay," the giant says, taking my hand again. "We can help you. We can help you to remember."

🐦 ACKNOWLEDGEMENTS

Thanks first to my sensitivity readers for sharing their experience and their wisdom. Mia Best, Jonathan Cho, Ark Ramsay, and the others who asked not to be named for their own comfort and safety, thank you. You made this book more thoughtful, nuanced, and true, and for that I am eternally grateful.

Thanks to everyone at CookeMcDermid and HarperCollins Canada, especially my agent, Rachel Letofsky, and my editor, Janice Zawerbny.

This book would not have been possible without the guidance and support of my peers and instructors in the School of Creative Writing at the University of British Columbia. I'd like to especially thank Alix Ohlin for saying yes when I asked her if she thought my ten-page short story could be a novel. Thanks to Kevin Chong for being the first person to call me a writer. Thanks to John Vigna for making me revise even when

I did nothing but complain about how much I hate revising. Thanks to Emily Pohl-Weary and Maggie de Vries for reading the earliest, messiest draft and still believing. Thanks to my cohort for setting the bar.

Thanks to Kiri for asking to read it before anyone else. Thanks to Safiya for getting what I was going for, every time. Thanks to Valerie for always feeling near even when we're far apart. Thanks to Mia for being my oldest friend who is more like a sister and for putting up with me for the last twenty years. Thanks to Molly and Cara for being the best aunties any baby boy could ask for. Thanks to all my friends; there are too many of you to name, and what a blessing that is to be so rich in friendship.

Thanks to all the Sealys, past and present, the smartest, funniest, and loudest clan on the block, for the endless inspiration. Thanks to Whitehall for being my home.

Thanks to my brother for teaching me all the best ways to skip class.

Thanks to my parents for never suggesting I go to law school instead. I'm never afraid to jump because I know I'll always have a soft place to land, and that was the gift you gave to me.

Thanks to Jules for being the why.

And most of all thank you to Ben, for being the how.